≈ ≈ ≈ ≈ ≈ ≈

A cool rain washed over Donovan. His red, hot anger was immediately doused. He realized what he did, and he didn't feel good about it.

"I'm sorry. I shouldn't have said that. You can keep seeing him if—"

"I'm not going to see him again," Kyra stated. She was staring deeply into his eyes. Donovan didn't think she'd blinked at all in the past minute.

Without warning she approached him and wrapped her arms around him. Donovan immediately grabbed her and held tightly. Kyra laid her face against his chest. She said, "Thank you, for everything."

Donovan lowered his head until his nose and mouth brushed the top of her head. He inhaled her wonderful scents. His arms moved slowly across her back as his hands touched and clutched her flesh. Kyra's body was on fire. The best friends hugged plenty of times since she returned, but never like this.

Donovan felt light headed. He didn't realize what was happening until there was a mass of hard muscle between his legs. His manhood pushed against his shorts and then against Kyra.

Embarrassed, Donovan broke away from the embrace. He took a step back. "I'm sorry."

"Sorry for what?" Kyra asked. She didn't look down at what she had felt on her stomach. She wanted to. She wanted to look so badly her heart ached. But she kept her eyes glued on Donovan's. Her expression was daring and alluring and knowing.

"Nothing," Donovan said.

"Then don't apologize. You didn't do anything wrong," Kyra said. She took a few steps back. She felt pressure in her lower belly as she moved. She felt her muscles clench a little lower down. Her legs threatened to give out on her, but Kyra managed to turn and exit the house.

Donovan was mesmerized by the sway of her hips as she moved. For the first time in his entire life he watched Kyra's ass like he wanted it, and he didn't feel one bit guilty about it.

≈ ≈ ≈ ≈ ≈ ≈

THE REALEST EVER

I0589068

THE REALEST EVER

KEITH THOMAS WALKER

KEITHWALKERBOOKS, INC
This is a UMS production

THE REALEST EVER

KEITHWALKERBOOKS

Publishing Company
KeithWalkerBooks, Inc.
P.O. Box 331585
Fort Worth, TX 76163

For information write
KeithWalkerBooks, Inc.
P.O. Box 331585
Fort Worth, TX 76163

ISBN-13 DIGIT: 978-0-9882180-0-0
ISBN-10 DIGIT: 0988218003
Manufactured in the United States of America

First Edition

Visit us at www.keithwalkerbooks.com

This book is dedicated to Cathy Atchison

MORE BOOKS BY
KEITH THOMAS WALKER

Fixin' Tyrone
How to Kill Your Husband
A Good Dude
Riding the Corporate Ladder
The Finley Sisters' Oath of Romance
Blow by Blow
Jewell and the Dapper Dan
Harlot
Plan C (And More KWB Shorts)
Dripping Chocolate

Visit keithwalkerbooks.com for information
about these and upcoming titles from
KeithWalkerBooks

ACKNOWLEDGMENTS

Of course I would like to thank God, first and foremost, for giving me the creativity and drive to pursue my dreams and the understanding that I am nothing without Him. I would like to thank my wife for being my first and most important critic, and I would like to thank my mother for always pushing me to be the best I can be. I would like to thank Janae Hampton for being the best advisor, supporter and little sister a brother could ever have. I would also like to thank (in no particular order) Brandy Rees, Denise Bolds, Sabrina Scott, Dianne Guinn, Kierra Pease, Sharon Blount, BRAB Book Club, Trey Williams and Uncle Steven Thomas, one love. I'd like to thank everyone who purchased and enjoyed one of my books. Everything I do has always been to please you. I know there are folks who mean the world to me that I'm failing to mention. I apologize ahead of time. Rest assured I'm grateful for everything you've done for me!

THE REALEST EVER

CHAPTER ONE
FRIEND REQUEST

Kyra Michelle Reynolds took her son to the juvenile section before she settled into her seat behind one of the 20 computers the library offered visitors. The computer table had cubicle-style walls standing on either side of the monitors that effective blocked Kyra from seeing her neighbor's screen on the right and on the left. But the area was not really private. The computers were in the very center of the library, so anyone walking behind Kyra could see exactly what she was looking up on the World Wide Web.

She thought that would be a deterrent from risqué searches, but the man sitting next to her was on Sports Illustrated's website drooling over pictures from their swimsuit issue. He was totally enthralled. He didn't notice when Kyra took a seat next to him. Her daughter Katavia tried to squirm out of her lap the moment Kyra sat down, but there was no way she was going to let her baby run wild in this place. Kyra barely felt comfortable enough to let her eight year old son peruse the children's literature by himself.

Kyra wasn't very computer savvy, but she found her career builders website fairly easily. She logged-in to her account and was disappointed to see that she didn't have any job offers in her inbox. She created her profile less than a week ago. She didn't expect a miracle, but it would've been nice to see at least one company was interested in her pitiful accomplishments.

Kyra went to her profile and pulled up her resume, wondering if there was anything she hadn't embellished the hell out of yet. She didn't go to college, so there was nothing she could add to the education field. Her high school diploma from Little

Rock was all she had to offer. Kyra looked over her work history and blew out a slow sigh. She wanted to delete her job at McDonalds, but that would leave a two year gap between her gig at Showtime Cleaners and her customer service position at a telemarketing firm. It was bad enough she hadn't worked in nearly a year since her last job at Ricky's Barbecue. And that gap was growing bigger and bigger, every day she remained unemployed.

Kyra backed out of her resume without making any changes. She figured she already had enough going against her. The last thing she needed was some overzealous recruiter to find out she wasn't the manager or even the assistant manager at McDonalds. Kyra had never worked in a leadership position, but she was sure she could do it, if someone gave her a chance.

For the next twenty minutes she scanned a huge list of (*supposedly*) available jobs on the career site. The list got smaller when she weeded out the positions that required experience. It got smaller still when she subtracted the ones that required a college degree. What she was left with was the bottom of the barrel gigs that required manual labor, a mop or a broom and sometimes steel-toed boots.

But these were the jobs Kyra was most accustomed to, so she applied for as many of them as possible. Fibbing was fully acceptable at this point because Kyra was sure that if she made it to an interview, she could talk just about anyone into hiring her. She was attractive, energetic, and she was eager to learn. Plus she was desperate, which was the best qualification of all.

Can you operate a forklift?

Sure!

Have you ever installed awnings?

"Yes, I have," Kyra typed, although she wasn't totally sure what an awning was.

Are you willing to work in extreme cold or hot temperatures?

This one gave her a moment's hesitation, because Kyra didn't like hot environments at all. But as her daughter Katavia (better known as Kat) snuggled against her bosom and resigned herself to sleep, Kyra said "Yes" to the refrigerated warehouse job.

She couldn't think of too many things she wouldn't do to put food in her babies' bellies – especially after the hell she put them through over the past year and a half. Kyra's throat tightened and her eyes moistened at the mere thought of it. She quickly pushed the depressing thoughts from her mind.

She stood to check on her son Quinell. After a quick scan of the library, she spotted him at a table by himself. Quinell was staring at the pages of a large picture book. Kyra wanted to chastise him for not picking a book with more words than pictures, but Quinell was too far away, and she didn't want to shout.

Before she could sit back down, Kyra was surprised to see a young man approach and pull her chair away.

"Excuse me," she told him.

"Oh, you not through?" the boy asked her.

"No," Kyra said. "I still have thirty minutes."

"Oh, my bad." The youngster looked Kyra up and down and decided to try his luck. "You come here a lot?"

Kyra took her chair and returned to the computer. "A little," she said, her eyes on the monitor.

"I'm Quinton," her new friend said.

Kyra turned and looked him in the eyes. He appeared to be nineteen, no older than twenty-one. Kyra was thirty-one, and she had enough on her plate already. She didn't need attention from some boy who probably still lived with his mama.

"That's a nice name," she told him. "I have a son named *Quinell*. He's eight. This is my daughter, Kat. She's two."

Quinton didn't need to hear all of that. He thought Kyra had a nice ass, but she squared the deal with all of that talk about kids. What did she want, for him to buy her some diapers? "She cute," he said and turned and walked away.

Kyra chuckled to herself when he was gone. Suddenly, the chorus of Erykah Badu's *Bag Lady* filled her head. Kyra had baggage for days. She doubted if she'd ever find a man strong enough to bear the load. But she recently fled Arkansas to get away from a man, so they weren't that high of a priority anyway.

Kyra backed out of her career builder site and checked her email. She created the Yahoo account six days ago and was surprised to see three new messages. They were all from another website that was new to her called *Facebook*. One message was a friend request from someone she recognized as a distant cousin.

The second message indicated her oldest brother left a comment on her Facebook page: "Miss you already, girl. Sad to see you go, but I hope you get better."

Kyra's last email notified her that her cousin's fiancé posted a comment on one of the pictures she uploaded: "Damn you fine."

Kyra frowned and clicked the message from her cousin's shifty boyfriend. After logging into Facebook, she saw the picture she posted and the comment Darryl left. Kyra only had three pictures on her profile. She took them all last week at her aunt's house. She was wearing the same outfit in all three photos; a tee shirt and jeans with her hair pulled back in a pony tail.

Two of her pics were close-ups. The one Darryl liked was a long shot from her knees up. Kyra had her daughter in her arms, and she offered the camera a big, beautiful smile. Her shirt wasn't tucked-in, and her jeans weren't tight. Kyra *was* fine, but she didn't think the photo showed off her curves. More likely it was her smooth, brown skin, her large eyes and full lips that caught Darryl's attention. Or maybe it was her 36 C's. Yeah, those babies were an anomaly. Most girls with a good amount of junk in their trunk had two bee stings up top. But Kyra had the best of both worlds.

She deleted Darryl's comment. A moment later Kyra wished she'd sent her cousin a message, telling her to come check her man. Instead she went back to her home page and deleted her brother's post as well. She then went to his profile and sent him a personal message:

"Hey, Duke. I'm doing alright. I miss you too. I had to delete your comment on my page. You said you hope I get better, but I don't want anyone to know I was doing bad. I know I had to leave, but I don't know if things will be any better down here. I can't find a job, and Aunt Ruth is already getting on my nerves. I know it's only been a week, but I get scared sometimes, and lonely. I feel like I don't got nobody here that care about me."

Kyra read her message and thought it sounded too depressing. Generally the truth is always best, but she didn't want Duke to worry about her. She deleted most of her rambling, leaving only the first part.

"Hey, Duke. I'm doing alright. I miss you too."

She sent the message and then looked through her brother's pictures. He had a lot of them. A lot of family and friends, pictures of his children and his wife. A wistful smile spread Kyra's lips as she clicked away, learning more and more about the social networking site. Kyra sent friend requests to a dozen people in her brother's friends list, and then she typed the names of a few of her Arkansas acquaintances and was delighted to see their pictures pop up.

Twenty minutes in, she was amazed by how many people she could find on Facebook. There was a hit for just about every person she could think of. Noticing she was down to her last few minutes on the computer, Kyra switched her focus to Overbrook Meadows connections. Her spirits were immediately dampened.

Home was where the pain was, there was no doubt about that. But Kyra returned to Overbrook Meadows last week looking for a fresh start. It was hard to believe that her life in Arkansas was actually *worse* than her early years in Texas, but somehow it was.

Kyra typed the name of her only *good* memory from childhood and wasn't surprised she got a hit. What did surprise her were the sudden goose bumps that sprouted on her arms and a rapid increase in her body temperature. Kyra took a deep breath, her eyes glued to the computer screen.

Facebook had more than ten possible matches for Donovan Mitchell. Most had profile pics on display, so Kyra was able to rule out half of them because they weren't black. She ruled out another half because their hometowns didn't match. The only Donovan Mitchell listed with Overbrook Meadows as his hometown was at the very top of the list. Unfortunately Kyra couldn't verify this one because his profile pic was the Dallas Cowboys logo rather than a photo of himself.

Kyra's heartbeats became audible as she clicked on the profile. She felt like she was having an anxiety attack, but she wasn't sure why. This was simply a computer. He couldn't see her or even send her a message, if she didn't want him to. Even if he could, Kyra didn't know why she felt unsure of herself. Back when she knew him, Donovan never made her feel anything but loved. Donovan was her best friend fifteen years ago. In fact, they used

13

to refer to each other as brother and sister. And Kyra had never known a better friend or *person* since then.

She tried to look through his pictures, but Donovan's profile was set to *private*. The only pic available was the Cowboy's logo he offered to strangers. Kyra clicked Info and was told that his sex was Male. Beneath that it said, "Donovan only shares some information publically." Kyra began to click on everything associated with the profile, but she was blocked at every turn.

Frustrated and still inexplicably fretful, Kyra hesitated before she clicked the one button that could lead to unlimited access to Donovan's photos. Kyra knew she'd be too embarrassed to answer the first question Donovan would ask her: *What have you been up to?* But she still didn't know if this was the right Donovan. Even if it was, he'd have to ask his hurtful questions over the computer, and he wouldn't see the pain in Kyra's eyes if she decided to write him back.

"I'm sorry, Ma'am, but your time is up."

Kyra looked up at the librarian and nodded. "Okay, I'm getting off."

She clicked the "Add Friend" button quickly, before she could change her mind, and then she logged out of Facebook and left the computer.

The boy who had been waiting on her quickly took her seat. He wasn't flirtatious anymore. He pretended not to see her at all, which was just fine with Kyra. She noticed a lot of men were doing that these days. They saw her face and her body and smiled, and then they saw Quinell and Kat and Kyra's less than trendy clothes, and they looked away.

She went to the children's area and took a seat on one of the way-too-little chairs parked under Quinell's table. He looked up from his book.

"We finna go?"

"No, the bus doesn't come 'til five-twenty," Kyra said.

"Can I check this book out?" Quinell asked.

"I think you need to find a book with more words in it," Kyra suggested.

Kat began to stir in her arms. Kyra shuffled through a large bag she toted and found her sippy-cup. The toddler took the drink graciously, and Quinell got up to find a book his mother would approve of. Kyra checked her watch and rose to her feet, in search of a book to keep her mind occupied for the next thirty minutes.

She couldn't wait for the day when she was no longer dependent on public transportation. But as far as waits go, the library was one of the best places to be.

≈ ≈ ≈ ≈ ≈ ≈

Twenty miles away, on Finley High School's football field, Coach Donovan Lucas Mitchell was wrapping up a light workout with his varsity team, The Mad Stallions. Their season opener wasn't for two weeks, but Donovan already saw serious deficits in his 26 member squad. Most of these problems would not be solved before their first game, and Donovan doubted if he could fix his team before their season ended in November.

You can mold a talented player into an even better athlete, but you can't turn a so-so player into the next Emmett Smith – not in just one season anyway. Donovan's team wasn't *all* bad. But he only had two bonafide stars on offense. Neither of his stars was in the quarterback or running back positions. He had an awesome wide receiver who was in for a bad year because there wasn't enough talent to get him the ball. But such is life.

The date was Thursday, August 14th. The blistering days of June and July were behind them, but the temperatures in north Texas would remain in the mid to high nineties until the end of October. Donovan's team was running a simple back-pedal/shuffle/break drill (without pads), but they had been working out for over an hour, and most of them were drenched with sweat. Donovan brought a whistle to his mouth and blew a short, quick bleat to signal the end of today's practice.

"That's it, fellas. Pack it up!"

Fifty-two grateful eyeballs rolled in his direction, and the young men immediately began to scramble, some heading for the Gatorade table, others grabbing equipment. Most of them stayed where they were, bent over with their hands on their knees, sucking in air like a fish out of water.

"I know y'all not tired," Donovan said as he approached them. "We didn't do nothing today. You don't even have your helmets on."

15

"Yes we did do something," a junior named Kevin Willard gasped. His face was slick with perspiration. His beat up sneakers had seen better days. "It's hot out here, Coach. Why can't we practice in the gym?"

"Go get something to drink," Donovan told him. "Your mama will have a fit if you pass out on this field."

"My mama wanna know when you gon' call her," Kevin said as he headed for the refreshments. "She starting to think you don't like her."

"He *don't* like her," another knucklehead named Calvin said. He was a burly running back who was about to get converted into a fullback if he couldn't lose 15 pounds during the season. "He like Miss Murphy, don't you Coach?"

Miss Murphy was hands-down the best looking teacher at Finley High. She was fair-skinned with a long weave and an awesome wardrobe and one of the best asses known to man. She wasn't an exceptional instructor, but students paid attention when she talked – especially the boys. When Miss Murphy offered after-school tutoring, her classroom was completely full. Even some of Donovan's players tried to weasel out of practice sometimes so they could get some extra learning from Miss Murphy.

"You and Miss Murphy getting married, right, Coach?" another student named Victor asked with a grin.

Donovan shook his head at the kids clamoring around him, but he was smiling, too. In addition to coaching the varsity football team, Donovan taught social studies to juniors and seniors. He was an imposing figure, whether he had chalk or a football in hand. Donovan stood six-foot-four with 231 pounds stacked pleasingly on his frame. In his football days, Donovan played defensive end. It was his job to stuff running plays and sack the quarterback. And he was good at it.

Donovan was a little slimmer now, but still in excellent shape. He was unofficially crowned the most handsome male teacher at the school, and with Miss Murphy being the most attractive single female, the students assumed they would hook up. Some of the faculty felt that way, too.

"Miss Murphy is my *co-worker*," Donovan told the squad for what felt like the hundredth time. "That's all she'll ever be to me."

During his social studies class and for most of their time on the football field, Donovan would never allow such friendliness with his students. But after school and after practice he maintained a mentoring relationship with all of his boys. They would come to Donovan when they were bullied or if their mother forgot to give them lunch money. They would talk to Donovan about problems they had at home or trouble on the streets. The school's principal often joked that Donovan should get an extra paycheck for being a part-time counselor.

Of course that was never going to happen.

A slight vibration in his front pocket notified Donovan of a new email. He retrieved his cellphone and stopped cold when he read the message. His jaw became unhinged as he stared at it, not believing he read it right. Donovan's massive chest heaved with a quick intake of air. He stuffed his phone in his shorts' pocket and had to fight off an overwhelming urge to sprint to his office in the back of the gym.

"Calvin! Hurry up and get those coolers packed up!" Donovan barked. "You too, Kevin. Help him with that stuff! Victor, get my balls off the field! Help him, Shawn. Morris, Booker, Quincy, Trey – y'all get those tables folded up and bring them in the gym!"

He clapped his hands loudly.

SMACK!

"Come on! Get moving! We gotta clear this field!"

With that, Donovan could stay his eager legs no longer. He began to eat up the field with long strides, without looking back to see if his team was doing what he asked of them.

"Coach!" one of them yelled. "We ain't through drinking yet!"

"Hurry up!" Donovan shouted back. "And pack it up right! If I come out here and see *one football* on the ground, every one of you is running sprints!"

"Coach, wait!" Kevin hollered. "I thought you was gon' help me with my math!"

"Come to my office when you get through!" Donovan told him, and then he was too far away to answer any more of their questions.

≈ ≈ ≈ ≈ ≈ ≈

17

Donovan didn't use his computer in the gym very often. He nearly had a heart attack while waiting for it to power up. He read the message on his cellphone over and over with an excitement he hadn't felt in years. *Kyra Reynolds was alive and well.* Donovan's smile was from ear to ear. It was an unusual sight; a burly football coach hunkered over a computer with tears in his eyes.

How many times had he searched for Kyra on Facebook? It was impossible to count. When the networking site first hit the internet in 2004, Donovan was reluctant to get sucked in to another MySpace-like environment. He didn't want to post private pictures of himself, and he didn't want to be bombarded with silly updates from people he barely knew in real life.

But as Facebook's popularity grew, Donovan began to spend more and more time on the site. He reestablished contacts with people he met in college and with folks he knew way back in middle school. Donovan found that he actually liked to see updates from his long lost friends as well as pictures from their vacations or trips to the ballpark.

And the name Donovan typed into Facebook's search bar most often was *Kyra Reynolds*. In the early days he searched for her as often as once a week. Shocked that he couldn't find her, Donovan tried just her first name, thinking she got married. But he still couldn't find her among the hundred or so Kyra's who did have accounts. Sometimes Donovan searched until he had a stress headache. But he never stopped looking.

Almost every time he logged onto Facebook, Donovan wanted to know if Kyra Reynolds had a profile yet. Today his prayers were answered. Donovan was so excited when he finally got Facebook pulled up, he entered his password incorrectly three times in a row.

When he got it right, he emphatically jabbed the button that said *Yes* he would accept Kyra as his friend. *Yes, yes and hell yes!* And finally, after a full fifteen years with absolutely no contact, Donovan saw the woman who had become somewhat of an obsession. Kyra was so beautiful, Donovan stared in awe, unaware that a joyful tear rolled down his cheek.

"Oh God, thank you."

Kyra's profile was new, and it didn't offer much information about what she'd been up to since the last time Donovan saw her. But it revealed enough to make him more and more joyous at every click.

Kyra's hometown was listed as Overbrook Meadows, and her current location was also Overbrook Meadows. Donovan assumed that was a mistake, but he prayed that it was true. He longed to see Kyra with his own eyes and touch her and hug her. Donovan clicked some more and learned that Kyra wasn't just beautiful, but she was a mother now. In one of her three pictures, she was holding an adorable baby girl in her arms. The child was the spitting image of her mother.

Donovan put a hand to his mouth and sniffled. He wasn't an emotional guy, but this was not the average Facebook encounter. Kyra was Donovan's best friend ever since they met in grade school; Donovan in the fourth and Kyra in the third. There was never an attraction between them, and many were baffled by how thoroughly they bonded. When Donovan learned that Kyra lived less than half a mile from his house, he rode his bike to visit her nearly every day. During the summertime they would be together from sun up till sun down. They made tree houses and army forts in the bushes, and they loved to roll their pants up and explore creeks and ponds, in search of tadpoles and baby turtles.

Kyra's home life was rough back then. Donovan was the one person who always loved her. He never hit or talked bad to her. They became play-brother and sister, and when the abuse at Kyra's house reached a peak, Donovan did everything in his power to save her. He was only a child himself, but he stood up to adults for Kyra. He comforted Kyra when her mom went to jail, and Donovan even talked his mother into letting Kyra live with them when they were in high school.

Finding Kyra on Facebook was like finding his twin brother or a pot of gold at the end of a rainbow. Knowing she had grown into a beautiful, healthy adult was one of the greatest gifts Donovan ever received.

A sound at the door alerted him to a visitor. Donovan wiped his face quickly as Kevin entered the office with books in hand. The sweat on Donovan's face effectively masked the tear that he was much too manly to shed in the first place.

19

"What you doing, Coach?" Kevin approached and stared over his shoulder. "Who's that? She fine."

Donovan chuckled. "She's an old friend. I haven't seen her in fifteen years."

"Dang," Kevin said, studying the picture more closely. "Is that why you look so happy?"

Donovan nodded.

"How you find her?" the boy asked.

Donovan gave him a look. "I guess common sense ain't that common..."

Kevin laughed. "Oh, you found her on Facebook?"

"Yeah," Donovan said, his eyes still glued to Kyra's picture.

"You can find *anybody* on Facebook," Kevin said.

"I guess so," Donovan agreed. He went back to Kyra's profile so he could send her a personal message.

"You gon' ask her out?" Kevin wanted to know.

"Boy, go sit down," Donovan said. "This is my *sister*. She my play-sister. We used to live together and everything."

"She still fine," Kevin said as he made his way to a desk. "Y'all didn't never kiss or nothing when she was living with you?"

"Boy, I just told you she's my sister."

"You said *play*-sister, Coach," Kevin noted. "So y'all not really related. I know I wouldn't be able to live with a girl if she looked like that – especially if we weren't really related."

Ain't that the truth, Donovan thought. "Be quiet so I can send this message," he said. He sent a quick message to Kyra and then went and stood before Kevin's desk. "Alright, what are you having problems with?"

"I don't know how to graph these functions," Kevin said. He dug his math book from his backpack.

"That's what I helped you with last time," Donovan recalled. "Why do you need help with the same thing?"

"I forgot how to do it, Coach."

Donovan frowned at him. "You smoking weed, Kevin?"

"Nope," the student said right away. "I don't smoke weed, Coach."

"I know your brother smokes weed," Donovan said. "And your cousins do, too. You getting high with them, Kevin? Don't lie to me."

"I don't smoke weed," Kevin stressed. "I don't smoke cigarettes or Black & Mild's or *nothing*. I don't do nothing that's gon' take my breath away."

The *take my breath away* comment was something Donovan warned his students about all the time. But Kevin maintained eye contact when he spoke, and Donovan believed him. He pulled up a chair next to his mediocre defensive end.

"I hope some of this starts to come back to you really quick," Donovan said. "I don't want to be here all night."

"Why, you got a date with Miss Murphy?" Kevin joked.

Donovan frowned again. "If you say one more thing that's not related to math, I'ma make you do so many pushups, you won't be able to lift your arms tomorrow. You understand me?"

"Yes, sir," Kevin said, his smile gone, his nose down in his book.

CHAPTER TWO
AUNT RUTH

Two days later Kyra was still struggling to keep a positive attitude as she cleaned the blinds and windows in her bedroom on what was actually a beautiful Saturday afternoon. At bedtime Kyra's room was cramped with herself, her two year old daughter and her eight year old son, but it wasn't the crowded conditions that had her fighting off a wave of depression. It was her new landlord that made Kyra wonder if maybe she should've stuck it out in Arkansas.

When she reached out to her aunt two weeks ago, Kyra didn't think Ruth would take her in. Fifteen years ago when Kyra's mother went to jail, everyone assumed Ruth would be the one to step in for her sister's kids. But they were wrong about that. Before anyone even had time to ask her, Aunt Ruth said she was too busy. She had too much going on to be burdened with three rugrats that weren't even hers.

Kyra's brother Duke and her sister Jackie were sent to Arkansas, where most of Kyra's family was from. The only reason Kyra stayed in Overbrook Meadows was because Donovan begged her mom to take her in. But that didn't last long. Soon Kyra was shipped off to Arkansas as well, and for a long time she hated her aunt for being so cold-hearted. Kyra would've given up a kidney to stay with Donovan in Texas, but fate had other plans.

When Kyra summoned the courage to flee Arkansas fourteen days ago, Aunt Ruth was her absolute last resort. Kyra had her finger poised over the hang up button when she called her, and she was blown away when Aunt Ruth told her, "Of course you can come stay with me, child, until you get your life back together.

I'll help take care of your kids. You been gone a long time. I miss you Kyra. If you need somewhere to stay, I'm here for you."

Within a week Kyra took her aunt up on the offer. She spent her last dime on bus tickets and packed all of the clothes she could carry in two huge suitcases she got from her brother. Duke wanted her to stay with his family, but Kyra knew she had to leave Arkansas entirely. She had troubles with her ex, the police and Little Rock's child protective services. But Kyra wasn't fearful when she got on that bus. Aunt Ruth's offer of food and shelter was a light at the end of a very dark tunnel.

That light dimmed very quickly.

Kyra's first surprise when she arrived in Overbrook Meadows was that Aunt Ruth's three bedroom home actually had only *two* bedrooms. The third one was filled with junk that Aunt Ruth was in no hurry to remove. Kyra offered to clean it herself, but Aunt Ruth said she didn't want anyone going through her personal stuff. Kyra accepted that.

They decided to let Quinell sleep on the couch while Kyra and Kat shared the one bedroom, but that only lasted one night. The next morning Aunt Ruth complained that Kyra's son was a lot bigger than she thought he was. She said Quinell sleeping on the couch was messing up her cushions. He'd have to sleep in the bedroom with Kyra and Kat instead. Ruth offered Quinell an air mattress to sleep on but insisted he spread it out in his mother's room rather than clutter up the living room. Kyra accepted that, too. Unfortunately it was only the beginning of Aunt Ruth's tyranny.

≈ ≈ ≈ ≈ ≈ ≈

After cleaning the windows and making her bed and putting Quinell's air mattress away, Kyra was lured out of her bedroom by the sound and smell of frying bacon. She found her son in the living room sitting quietly on Aunt Ruth's precious sofa. The TV was tuned in to Saturday morning cartoons, but Quinell was distracted by the good smells coming from the kitchen. He was a fair-skinned boy with large hands and feet and a small mouth that was almost always closed. He countered his quietness with watching and listening, and Kyra knew he was formulating his own opinions about what was going on in their new home.

23

Kyra found her daughter Kat sitting quietly on the outskirts of the kitchen, like she knew it was something good going on in there, but for whatever reason she couldn't get close to it. Kyra hefted her daughter and went to speak to her Aunt for the first time that morning. Last week Kyra greeted Ruth with a hug and a kiss. Today she gave her a guarded, "Hey, Auntie."

"Hey," the head of the house said without turning away from the stove.

Aunt Ruth was fifty-six years old. She was tall with golden brown skin and short hair that she preferred to keep curly. Ruth wore large glasses with thick lenses. She had a burgundy robe pulled over her night gown. From the back, Kyra saw that the heels of her feet were ashy and calloused from too much time spent barefoot.

"If y'all want something to eat, I got some peanut butter in the cabinet," Aunt Ruth said.

Kyra didn't take the bait. She put Kat down and went to the cabinet to retrieve the peanut butter.

"Don't put that baby down in here," Aunt Ruth said, looking over her shoulder. She stopped smoking four years ago, but her voice was still a little manly from the four decades of damage she caused herself before quitting. "I told Kat I don't want her in here while I'm frying bacon," Aunt Ruth continued. "Don't want no grease to pop up on her."

Kyra didn't say anything, but she did pick up her child and deposit her outside of the kitchen. One of the things Kyra found strange about her aunt was how Ruth could say something mean-spirited in a way that left plenty of defense if someone tried to call her on it. She probably wasn't doing it now, but Aunt Ruth did it so often Kyra had to give conscious thought to how she responded to her.

Kyra found half a loaf of bread on the kitchen table.

Ruth turned to face her.

"Don't eat all my bread, neither. I need *three pieces* for my breakfast."

Aunt Ruth had one gold tooth, a canine, and a faint moustache above her top lip. Her nose was pudgy, as was the rest of her body. Kyra didn't think she was physically unattractive, but maybe the rest of the world disagreed. Ruth had been married three times, each one ending in divorce. She had one son who went to the military and then moved to California afterwards. Kyra hadn't heard anything about him since she'd been there.

"If y'all want some bacon, you should'a went down to the WIC office, like I told you to," Ruth said. "We would have enough food for everybody."

"We don't need bacon," Kyra said. What she needed was a utensil to make their peanut butter sandwiches, but her aunt was standing in front of the counter drawer. Kyra understood that no one was eating anything until Aunt Ruth had her say.

"Your son asked me for some bacon," Aunt Ruth informed.

Kyra looked back at him, and Quinell abruptly returned his eyes to the television.

"He's just a kid," Kyra said. "He smelled bacon, and he wanted some. I'll tell him we're eating peanut butter."

"That ain't the point," Aunt Ruth said. She turned towards the stove and began removing the crispy strips of pork. She placed them on a plate lined with paper towels. They looked and smelled delicious. "The point is," she said when she faced Kyra again, "that you didn't do what I told you to."

"I only been here a week," Kyra said. The sight of the bacon made her stomach rumble. It was loud, and she knew her aunt heard it.

"You been here long enough to get some food stamps," Aunt Ruth countered. "You got two kids and not a dime in your pocket. They can give you an emergency card the day you walk in there."

"You knew I didn't have any money," Kyra said, careful to keep her tone neutral. If Aunt Ruth put her out, Kyra knew she'd have to take her family to a women's shelter. She had no other relatives in Overbrook Meadows, and she didn't have any money to take the Greyhound back to Little Rock.

But returning to Arkansas was not an option. Even a homeless shelter was better than that.

"Yes I knew you didn't have no money," Aunt Ruth said, greasy spatula in hand. "But we also talked about getting you on some benefits, until you start working."

"I said I would go Monday," Kyra reminded.

"You could'a went yesterday," Ruth said. "You could'a went the day before that. Hell, you can go *today*. They got places open for emergencies."

25

"I didn't know it was an emergency," Kyra said. "You still got a lot of food in your refrigerator."

As soon as she said it, Kyra wished she hadn't. Aunt Ruth's eyes widened.

"That's *my* food! I'm on disability. I don't got enough money to be feeding all of y'all. I said I would give you somewhere to live. I never said I could pay for all the food your kids been eating. If you wanna know the truth, I think you being irresponsible, Kyra, not going to get those food stamps."

Kyra took a deep breath. Her face reddened, but she managed to maintain her composure. The word *irresponsible* hurt her more than Ruth knew. Or maybe her aunt did know how often the word was tossed around in Arkansas. Ruth knew about Kat's father, and she knew about Kyra's run-in with CPS. Maybe she chose the word *irresponsible* because she wanted to pour salt on the wound.

In her defense, Kyra thought getting hooked on public assistance in Texas was the irresponsible thing to do. She saw it many times: Young girls realize they can get Medicare, housing and free groceries simply by remaining unemployed and not supported by their children's father(s). Kyra knew she'd work harder to get a job if she didn't have too much help along the way, but her aunt had a valid point.

"Do you want to take me to the welfare office today?" she asked with a defeated look in her eyes.

"Naw. We got enough food to make it through the weekend," Ruth said right away. "It's gon' be too damned hot today. And that place is always packed on Saturday. You'll be in line for hours. But we do need to go first thing Monday morning. I'll take you then."

"Okay," Kyra said.

"Y'all can have that bacon," Aunt Ruth said, wiping her hands on a wash cloth. "It's some eggs in the refrigerator, if you wanna cook 'em. You wanna go out tonight? Want me to watch the kids?"

Kyra frowned. "No."

"Alright," Ruth said and promptly left the kitchen.

Kyra was left standing there, wondering if that was what this breakfast argument was about. Did Aunt Ruth really just torture two children with the smell of bacon just so she could get Kyra to do her bidding?

Kyra pushed the thought away. When you have nowhere else to go, why burden yourself with complaints about how bad your situation is? It's better to look on the bright side, like how everyone had a roof over their head last night, and no one in the house was getting high. Plus Kyra could feed her children a hot meal this morning. That was something to be grateful for.

"You want some bacon and eggs?" Kyra called to the living room.

"Yes!" Quinell jumped off the couch and headed her way.

"Hold on, I haven't made the eggs yet," Kyra said with a grin. "I'll let you know when it's ready."

≈ ≈ ≈ ≈ ≈ ≈

By eleven o'clock Kyra had her kids fed and dressed and on the bus stop down the street from Aunt Ruth's house. Quinell didn't talk much as they waited for the #8 to round the corner. Kyra hoped he wasn't getting depressed about their new environment.

"You ready to go back to school on Monday?" she asked him.

Their bus stop didn't have a roof or clear, plastic walls like the fancy ones downtown. There was just a fiberglass bench that was thankfully beneath a tall pecan tree. The shade it provided was a welcomed blessing. Quinell was busy trying to coax ants into an ant lion's trap, but he dropped his poking stick and stood before his mother.

"I guess so."

Kyra held her daughter in her lap. Kat's hair was freshly styled with ten shiny plaits that had the pleasant aroma of Royal Crown hair grease.

"You nervous?" Kyra asked her son. "I know I used to get nervous when I had to move to a new school."

"You moved a lot when you were little?" Quinell asked her.

"I did," Kyra said. "But not as much as you. When I was little, I grew up not too far from here. I went the same school you're going to on Monday."

Quinell's eyes brightened. "You went to Sunrise?"

27

Kyra nodded. "Sure did."

"Is it fun?"

Kyra smiled. "I don't remember it that much. The teachers are all different now anyway. It won't be the same for you. I remember I climbed up on the roof one time during the summer. That was fun."

Quinell's smile grew wider. "Really?"

"They used to have a covered walkway in the back," Kyra recalled. "It had these poles holding it up. Me and my friend used to climb them like monkey bars. Once we got on top of the walkway, we could follow it to the school and then climb on it."

"What was up there?" Quinell asked, his eyes glistening.

"I don't want you trying to get up there," Kyra said quickly. "It was stupid for us to do it. We could'a fell off and broke our neck."

"I won't try to get up there," Quinell promised.

"I'm serious." She gave him a stern look. After her trouble in Little Rock, Kyra found herself over-thinking everything about her parenting. She couldn't bear to get call from more social workers because of a curiosity she ignited.

"I'm not," Quinell said. "Was it toys up there?"

"That's what we went looking for," Kyra confirmed. "We thought we'd find all kinds of cool stuff. But mostly it was just rocks they had all over the roof. It was some Frisbees and tennis balls the kids threw up there, but they were all old and ugly from being in the sun and the rain for so long. Lord knows I shouldn't have had my butt up there in the first place."

But as she spoke, Kyra couldn't stop a wistful smile from brightening her features. The voyage to the summit of Sunrise Elementary would forever be one of her fondest memories. She and Donovan were big time explorers when they were little. Their imagination was often the only escape from a reality that was much too ugly for eight year old Kyra to see every day.

"Are you glad we came back?" Quinell asked, noticing his mother reminiscing.

"I didn't come back for me," Kyra said. "I did it for you. I know things don't look too good right now, but it'll be better here in Texas. Do you like living with your auntie?"

Quinell took too long before he nodded.

"Do you like it better *here* or in Arkansas?" Kyra asked.

Quinell answered right away this time. "Here."

Kyra nodded. She looked up and was happy to see their bus coming to a squeaky stop in front of them.

≈ ≈ ≈ ≈ ≈ ≈

The bus was fairly empty, so Kyra didn't have to squeeze her family into two seats. She took a window seat and sat Kat in the empty spot beside her. Quinell got two seats by himself across the aisle. He faced the windows, smiling with his sneakers dangling a foot off the floor. Kyra was happy to see him happy. But she knew she wouldn't be free of her nagging guilt until she righted all of her wrongs. The problem was, some dated back to before Quinell was born.

When she first left Texas in 1999, Kyra went to live with her Aunt Joyce in Little Rock. Joyce already had five kids of her own, including four year old twins. Joyce did the best she could to care for her sister's brood, but she lived in a bad neighborhood, and Kyra's brother Duke was the oldest man in the house. Kyra only had three years left in high school, and Joyce knew that she'd been fending for herself for quite a while. Aunt Joyce left Kyra to her own devices, for the most part, and she was thankful that Kyra graduated high school *before* she got herself pregnant.

After graduation, Kyra found a job as a waitress. Shortly afterwards, she fell in love with a boy she met at a neighborhood house party. Tommy was tall and skinny with rich, dark skin and a pocket full of dope money. He only used a condom three quarters of the time, and Kyra was not surprised or particularly upset when she learned that his *withdrawal* method was not effective. She was only nineteen, but most of the other girls in Kyra's neighborhood had babies by that age. Not one person in Kyra's life told her she should've waited when they noticed her belly growing bigger and bigger.

Kyra went to live with her grandmother because Aunt Joyce didn't have the time or patience to help raise a brand new baby. Kyra's relationship with Tommy continued as usual, even though the bun in her oven began to garnish negative attention. Kyra heard rumors that Tommy was still with his ex-girlfriend Alisha. Alisha even confronted Kyra a few times. When Alisha called Kyra a *ho*, Kyra called her a ho right back. And when Alisha wanted to meet up to fight, Kyra was down for that, too. But thankfully others intervened when they saw how far along Kyra was at that point.

"You can't be fighting no pregnant girl!" an older bystander warned.

"Her face ain't pregnant," Alisha had said. "I can slap the shit out of her." She had her rings removed, her weave removed and her shoes off already. Alisha had a razorblade hidden in her mouth as well, but Kyra wasn't afraid of her. She brought half a dozen cousins with her to rival the half a dozen hood rats Alisha brought as backup.

The tension reached a boiling point on Christmas Eve, two months before Quinell was born. Incensed that Tommy was really going to stay with Kyra and start a disgusting *family* with her, Alisha went to Kyra's grandmother's house and knocked calmly on the door. She wanted to rip Kyra's hair out when she answered, but Alisha maintained her cool until Kyra summoned Tommy to the door.

Tommy called her a bitch, and then Alisha punched him in the chest. She ran away, and Tommy stumbled back into the living room. Tommy tried to tell Kyra that Alisha had something in her hand when she punched him, but Kyra could see for herself. There was a steak knife sticking out of his bony chest. At first Kyra thought he was holding it in his arm pit (*Ha ha, you so funny!*) but she saw the blood, and she saw the look of shocked confusion in her baby-daddy's eyes.

She laid him on the couch and watched in horror as Tommy yanked the knife from his wound. The blood began to flow in earnest then. Kyra's screams brought her grandmother running from the main bedroom. The ambulance responded within ten minutes, but Quinell's father was pronounced dead an hour after being stabbed. Tommy was only eighteen years old. The doctors said he would've died whether he pulled the knife out or not, but Kyra never believed that.

Alisha was arrested, but she managed to get her murder charge dropped to second degree because no one actually saw her stab Tommy and no one could prove she took a knife to the residence specifically to kill the love of her life. Kyra had her bastard child in February, and once again she was right on par with the other girls in her neighborhood. Whether they lost their daddy to the grave or the penitentiary, there were enough fatherless black children in Little Rock to fill several high schools.

≈ ≈ ≈ ≈ ≈ ≈

When they got to the library, Kyra had to wait nearly an hour for a computer. But that was okay. She found a couple of romance novels to check out as well as a few DVD's to watch with the kids this weekend.

When she was able to get online, Kyra checked her career builder site. But by then she couldn't deny that she was too preoccupied to care about a job at that moment. It had been two days since she sent Donovan a friend request on Facebook. Kyra was dying to know if he accepted it yet.

She abandoned her job search and logged onto Facebook, surprised to see fifteen notifications this time. Most were to inform her that people accepted her friend requests. The last person on the list was Donovan Mitchell. Kyra's heart shot up in her throat when she saw that Donovan sent her two personal messages as well.

She worked to steady her breathing as she clicked on his name. Kat was trying to talk to her, but Kyra was so excited she wouldn't have noticed if her daughter recited the whole Gettysburg Address. Two seconds later Donovan's profile popped up. Kyra found herself staring at the same screen she accessed the other day – except now it was virtually uninhibited.

Kyra's eyes were wide and nearly frightful. She wiped her mouth and noticed her fingertips were cold. She chuckled nervously, trying to shake off the jitters. She clicked on Donovan's "Photos," and then she clicked on the first album labeled "Profile Pictures." A page full of small images appeared. Kyra clicked on the first one, and *finally*, after more years and dreams and prayers than she could keep up with, Kyra saw the boy who ascended Mount Sunrise Elementary with her and never tried to steal a kiss when they got to the top.

Donovan was a grown man now.

Kyra took a deep breath and blew it out slowly, her eyes quickly filling with tears.

The last time she saw him, Donovan was a junior in high school. He was skinny and athletic with brown skin like cognac and one of those high-top haircuts that were all the rave in those days. Kyra could see that this was the same Donovan, but the differences were nearly as shocking as reconnecting with him in the first place.

The biggest dissimilarity was the sheer bulk Donovan added to his school-boy physique. As Kyra clicked from one picture to the next, she noticed at least one hundred pounds of new Donovan that completely dwarfed the old Donovan images in her mind. The added weight was mostly muscle. It was stacked oh so perfectly on his chest and arms and shoulders and thighs. He wasn't too muscle-bound. He was just right.

As Kyra clicked away, she saw that he accomplished his dream of playing college football. She saw that he coached high school football, and he still had a good relationship with his mother, Ms. Beverly Mitchell.

Kyra backed out of his profile pics and noticed Donovan had eight more photo albums. The largest one was labeled "Vacation Pics." It had more than fifty photos. Kyra was both nervous and elated as she explored the albums one by one. It almost felt like she was peeking into Donovan's personal life, but she noticed comments on a lot of his pictures and figured this type of snooping was acceptable.

With the Facebook photos, Kyra was able to trace much of Donovan's life, from his graduation from Western Hills to his football days in Ohio and his subsequent return to Overbrook Meadows. Kyra didn't know why he didn't go on to play for the pros, but Donovan looked successful and fulfilled in his recent pictures, and Kyra was increasingly happy for him.

One thing Kyra didn't like was her omission from Donovan's high school photos. But she knew she shouldn't get upset about that. The few high school pictures Donovan posted were from his senior prom and graduation. Kyra was long gone by then. But still, she couldn't help but wonder if Donovan missed her, because he looked so happy with his other friends from Western Hills. Kyra forced the silly thoughts from her mind.

Her smile didn't slip again until Kyra came across more recent photos of Donovan in the presence of (and sometimes the arms of) a beautiful woman. Kyra didn't believe she was jealous of the brown-skinned girl who kept appearing, but she couldn't think of a better explanation for the unease she suddenly felt.

She never expected to return to Texas and spark a relationship with her old friend. She and Donovan never attempted a relationship before she left, as a matter of fact. And why would they? He was her best friend. They introduced themselves as brother and sister so often, a lot of people thought that actually was the case.

Kyra closed the photo album she was looking at, but she opened it again a second later and stared at the woman Donovan was embracing. Her hair was long and curly. Her waist was slimmer than Kyra's, but Kyra thought her curves looked better. The woman definitely had better hair than Kyra, but it was probably a weave. If Kyra had money to go to the beauty shop, she could–

What the hell? Kyra caught herself and chuckled. Why was she comparing herself to Donovan's (apparent) girlfriend? Was she really sitting there fantasizing about being with her play-brother?

Ewww!

Kyra shook her head and returned to Donovan's Profile Pictures. She found the photo she liked the best, which was a simple shot of him from the waist up. Donovan's hair was short, his shirt tucked in. He would've looked preppy in the collar shirt, but his physique screamed *athlete*. His chest was awesome, his eyes smiling, but still piercing. His neck and shoulder muscles begged for a slow massage. His lips were perfect, and they begged for something too, but Kyra wouldn't allow those thoughts to take hold.

After nearly thirty minutes of her photo-investigation, Kyra finally backed out of Donovan's albums and read the messages he sent her. They were both sent two days ago, the day Kyra found him on Facebook. Kyra's blood flowed hot in her veins as she read the first one:

"Kyra! OH MY GOD! I can't believe it's really you! You have no idea how many times I searched for you on Facebook. I thought I would never find you. I looked for you just a few weeks ago, but I could never find your profile. I'm so happy to finally see your pictures. I can barely sit still. I been worried about you for the last fifteen years. Your profile says you're back in Overbrook Meadows. Is that true? I know that can't be true. I would love to see you! I'll fly to Arkansas if I have to. Write me back soon! P.S. I see that you're a mommy now! That is so awesome, Kyra! Hurry and write me back!"

Kyra's brain was racing when she finished reading. Her heart was racing as well. She always knew Donovan missed and cared about her as much as she missed and cared about him, but seeing it with her own eyes gave her joy like nothing else.

She quickly read Donovan's second message:

"Kyra, I've been waiting like crazy for you to respond, but you won't! I feel like I'm chasing a ghost again. When you get this message, please call me. Don't bother responding on Facebook. Just call me. Please." He gave her his number.

Kyra pulled her cellphone from her purse. She added Donovan's number, but she didn't call him – not right away. There were too many people in the library who were already giving her strange looks because of her *extra-excited* computer time. Kyra knew that her first talk with her best friend after two and a half decades would be much too rowdy for this hushed environment.

CHAPTER THREE
BRIANNA

On the way out of the library, Kyra spotted a few cushioned chairs in the lobby. Her bus stop was right outside of the door, so she decided to wait inside. She dug her cellphone from her purse and told Quinell, "Come sit down," before she called Donovan.

"Is the bus coming?" her son asked.

"It'll be here in ten minutes."

"Can I go look at some more books?" Quinell asked.

"No. I might need you to run out there and stop the bus if no one gets off," Kyra said. And then she heard Donovan's phone ringing. Her mouth was completely dry. Kyra got up to wet her whistle at a nearby fountain. Kat got up to follow her, and the toddler dropped her sippy cup on the tiled floor. Nine out of ten times nothing would've come of that, but today the lid popped off the cup, splashing red Kool-Aid on the bone-white tiles.

Kyra barely had time to look back before someone answered her call.

"Hello?"

"Uh, hi," Kyra said.

"Uh-oh," Kat said.

"Mama," Quinell said.

A couple of patrons entered the library at that moment. They stared at the spilled juice and gave Kat a wide berth. Kyra was mortified. She sighed in exasperation.

"I, uh, I'm sorry. I have to call you back," she said into the phone.

"Who is this?"

"I'm sorry. I, uh..." Kyra put a hand to her face and rubbed her forehead. She took a breath and let it out slowly. "This is Kyra. Quinell, go in that bathroom and get me some paper towels."

"Kyra?"

Quinell hurried to the bathroom.

"I'm sorry," Kyra said. "My daughter just spilled Kool-Aid in the library." She shook her head as she pulled Kat away from the mess. "I should've waited until I got home to call you."

"Is this, did you say *Kyra*?"

She was so stressed, Kyra barely noticed that the person she was speaking to had a rich, baritone voice. "Yes. Is this Donovan?"

He sighed and chuckled at the same time. "Kyra Reynolds. I don't believe it."

Kyra took a seat. She had to. Her legs were trembling.

Quinell returned with a fistful of paper towels. He went to work on the spill and found both parts of Kat's sippy cup. The toddler squirmed out of Kyra's arms and tried to help put her cup back together. Kyra tilted her head back on the wall behind her and took another slow breath, trying to calm her nerves.

"It's good to hear from you," she said.

"Same here," Donovan said. "You just don't know. Where are you?"

"I'm at the library."

"Where?" he said. "Your Facebook says–"

"I'm in Overbrook Meadows."

"Really? Since when?"

"Last week," Kyra said.

"Do you know how many times I looked for you on Facebook?" Donovan asked. She could hear the elation in his voice. "Do you have any idea?"

Kyra smiled. "I read your messages."

"A lot," Donovan continued. "A lot, Kyra. I been so worried about you. I almost cried when I got your friend request."

"Me, too," Kyra said. "It's been a long time."

"Too long," Donovan said. "Too damned long."

"You sound different," Kyra noticed.

"You do, too," he said. "And you look different, too! I see you're a mother now. That's so awesome, Kyra. You changed a lot."

"No, you're the one," Kyra said. Her smile was big and beautiful. She had a warm glow in her chest that wasn't embarrassment this time. "I saw those pictures you had on there."

"Which one," he asked.

"All of them."

"You saw all of my pictures?"

"Just now," Kyra said. "I couldn't stop looking." She thought about her favorite pic and blushed. She was glad he couldn't see her. "You're a grown man now," she said with play-sisterly pride. "All big and stuff."

"Whatever," Donovan said.

"You played for Ohio?" Kyra asked. "I always knew you were gonna go far. I'm so proud of you."

"Aw, man. I didn't do too much."

"I'm serious," Kyra said. "Not too many people from my past made something of themselves."

"I'm just a teacher," Donovan said. "And a football coach."

"That's something to be proud of," Kyra countered. "A lot of black men your age are in prison by now."

"Thanks," Donovan said, and after a short pause, "I wanted to say I'm sorry, Kyra. For what happened."

"Please," she said. "That's not your fau—"

"I know," Donovan said. "But the way it went down... I never got a chance to say I was sorry. And then I never heard from you again."

"We, just... Are you trying to get me crying?" Kyra asked. She looked up to the ceiling to keep the tears in.

"No," Donovan said. "I'm sorry. It's just... Never mind."

After an awkward silence, Kyra said, "So, you coach for Finley High?"

"Yeah," Donovan said. "How do you, oh yeah."

Kyra chuckled. "Is that stalking? I felt like I was stalking you when I looked through your pictures."

Donovan laughed, too. "No. That's what they're there for. It's all good."

"Why didn't you teach at Western Hills?" Kyra asked.

"I thought about it," Donovan said. "But they didn't have an opening when I got out of college. Plus I didn't really want to work with any of the teachers who taught me. I still put them on a pedestal. I don't wanna know what they're like in real life."

"Oh, and I see you're still a mama's boy," Kyra said.

"No, I'm not," Donovan said. Kyra could tell he was amused.

"Yeah you are. You had around a dozen pictures with her."

"*She* posted those and tagged me," Donovan offered.

"You'll always be a mama's boy," Kyra said with a grin. "It's all good. I noticed a lot of students in your pictures, but no babies that looked like you..."

"I don't have any kids," Donovan said. "You have a daughter."

"And a son. He's eight."

"That's awesome," Donovan said. "I can't wait to meet your family. Are you married?"

"No. And you?"

"No," Donovan said.

There was another break in the conversation. Kyra wanted to ask about the beautiful woman in his pictures, the one with the long, curly hair, but she didn't know how to bring it up.

"So when can I see you?" Donovan asked. "Where are you staying?"

"With my aunt in Berry Hill."

"Close to where you used to live?"

"Yep. Walking distance."

"Can I come see you today?" Donovan asked. "Can I pick you up, take you out for dinner?"

Kyra's heart leapt at the thought, but she didn't have a thing to wear. Actually she had *one* outfit that was suitable for such an occasion, but it wasn't clean.

"How about tomorrow," she said. "I can see you tomorrow."

"Okay," Donovan said. "But I would really—"

"Q, go catch that bus!" Kyra blurted.

"Huh?"

"Sorry, I gotta go," Kyra said.

"Where are you?" Donovan asked.

"At the library, on Bolt Street."

38

"You're riding the bus?"

He didn't sound like he was putting her down, but Kyra still felt self conscious.

"I came down here with pretty much nothing," she said as she gathered their books and tote bags. "I don't have a job or a car. I can't even get on the internet with my cellphone. That's why I couldn't accept your friend request until I came back to the library."

"Oh," Donovan said. Kyra was glad she couldn't see his expression. She knew he'd be looking down on her, like she was an abandoned puppy or something. "That's cool," he said. "Will you call me later?"

"Yeah," Kyra said, heading for the door.

"This is your phone, right?" Donovan asked. "I can call you on this number?"

"Yes," Kyra said. "I'm sorry, but I gotta get on this bus, or I'll be stuck here another forty minutes."

"I can come get you," Donovan offered.

"No, that's alright," Kyra said. "I'm sorry. I gotta go."

"Okay, bye," Donovan said, but she had already hung up.

≈ ≈ ≈ ≈ ≈ ≈

Donovan sat back in his recliner with a broad grin, but it was short-lived. The woman sitting on the sofa next to him had been waiting most impatiently for the call to end so she could ask him, "Who the hell was that?"

Donovan gave her a look. "Don't trip."

"What do you mean, *don't trip*?" The woman rose to her feet and took a step closer. "Who the hell was that, Donovan?"

"I said her name at least fifty times," Donovan stated. "That was *Kyra*. Her name is Kyra."

Donovan wore long basketball shorts with a sparkling clean, white tee shirt. It was twelve-thirty on a warm, Saturday afternoon. Donovan began his day with a two mile run with his German shepherd Wyatt and his pit bull dog Doc. When he returned to the house, he showered and had a simple breakfast of grapefruit and granola bars. He planned to grade papers and watch a few MMA fights during the hottest part of the day, but his

39

visitor thought that was boring. She wanted him to take her to the movies instead.

That was fine. But one thing Donovan *did not* want to do today was try to explain himself to someone who would probably never understand the intangibles of his and Kyra's relationship. But his visitor wasn't just anybody. She was the woman from his Facebook photos (who couldn't possibly have made Kyra jealous because she and Donovan were like brother and sister).

Ewww!

The woman stood six feet even. She wore skinny jeans with three-inch heels that boosted her height even more. She was thin and beautiful with long, curly hair that was worth every cent she paid for it. Her name was Brianna, but at times like this she preferred to go by her other title, which was *Donovan's woman.* His *only* woman.

"Baby, sit down," he told her.

"I don't want to sit down, Donovan! You just sat there and talked to some other woman like I wasn't even here!"

"Exactly!" Donovan said, trying not to give in to frustration. "I just had a conversation with her *right in front of you.* I didn't go to another room, and I didn't tell her I'll call her later."

"Yes you did tell her you'll call her later."

"You know what I mean," Donovan said. "I took the call in front of you because I have nothing to hide, Brianna. Now, if you'll sit down, we can talk about this like calm individuals. You don't have to scream every time you don't understand something."

Brianna folded her arms over her chest, and Donovan knew they were going to argue anyway. Something he would never understand about his woman was how she could be so beautiful, yet so insecure. Brianna had smooth skin the color of cinnamon. She was fit and stylish. Her face had classic angles, and she knew how to accentuate her beauty with very little makeup.

But when it came to not understanding, Brianna was in the same boat. She didn't get how Donovan could remain cool and collected when she was at her hottest – especially when you considered what a brawny and aggressive guy Donovan was. He played football for the better part of his life, during which time he was constantly trying to rip the opposing quarterback's head off.

He had to tone it down a little when he started coaching, but he was still a big, tough guy.

Looking at the two of them, you'd never expect Donovan to be the one to say, *Sit down. We can talk about this like calm individuals.*

"Explain yourself," Brianna said. She tried to match his poise. Even while angry, most people would think she was still gorgeous. Donovan was not one of those people. He sighed.

"Kyra is my best friend from back in the day."

"How far back?" Brianna asked. "I never heard of her."

"I've known Kyra since the fourth grade," Donovan said. "She moved to Arkansas when I was a junior in high school."

"Why is she all of a sudden calling you now?" Brianna wanted to know. "She found you on *Facebook*?" She said it like it was a porn site.

"Yes," Donovan said. "She said she moved back to Overbrook Meadows."

"That's just great."

"I know you're being sarcastic, but yeah, it really is."

Brianna had a small, pointy nose. Her nostrils flared, but you could barely tell. She took a seat. Her arms remained folded in a defensive gesture.

"Me and Kyra met at Sunrise Elementary," Donovan said. "I was in the fourth grade, and she was in the third. I don't remember how we started talking. I think it was at recess or something. We got along really good. When I found out she didn't live that far from me, I started visiting her house, and we became close. She was my best friend."

"A *girl* was your best friend?"

"I know it doesn't make sense," Donovan said. "A lot of people didn't understand it – especially my mama. But we were little kids, and it really was innocent, so no one told us we *couldn't* be friends."

"Did you ever kiss her?"

"No," Donovan said. "I just told you we were kids."

"You said she didn't leave until you were in high school. You weren't kids then."

"Yeah, but after you call someone your sister for so long, you can't turn around and start dating them. It would've been weird."

41

Brianna didn't look like she believed that.

"Plus Kyra really is like a sister to me," Donovan said. "You know I don't have any real brothers or sisters. Maybe that's why things worked out so well with us. Plus Kyra needed help back then. I was always there for her."

Brianna's frown intensified. "What do you mean she needed help?"

"Her family life," Donovan said with a slow shake of his head. "Her mom was on dope, and Kyra didn't know her father. She had so much against her. She used to say I was the only source of peace in her life."

Brianna's eyes widened. Her mouth fell open, too.

"No, not like that," Donovan said. "It wasn't that big a deal."

"How is that not a big deal?" Brianna wondered. "You were her *only source of peace*? What the fuck, Donovan? That's a big fucking deal!"

"Okay, but–"

"Why are you trying to downplay it?"

"Alright, Brianna. Okay. You're right. She didn't have a lot of hope, and I was a good friend when she needed one the most. Yes, it was a big deal."

"Sounds like it still is."

"I am excited to hear from her," Donovan confirmed. "I can't deny that."

"I know you can't deny it. You were practically jumping up and down when she called."

"I didn't leave my seat," Donovan said. "Anyway, we're both grown now, so it's not like we're going to fall into the same situation we had back then. This means a lot to me because it's been so long, and I don't know what happened to her when she left. I've been worried sick."

"You never told me about her."

"It wasn't something that was on my to-do list every day, Brianna. But I did look for Kyra a lot. A whole lot. I never forgot about her."

"Why did she leave?" Brianna wondered.

Donovan already lied to his girlfriend twice in this conversation. He didn't want to do it again, but he couldn't tell her the *real* reason Kyra got sent to Arkansas. Brianna would surely blow a fuse.

"When Kyra's mom got arrested, her brother and sister had to go live with relatives in Arkansas," he said. "That's where most of her family is from. I begged my mom to let Kyra stay with us, and she did. But it didn't last long."

"Beverly let her live with y'all?" Brianna couldn't believe it.

"Yes, but my mama never really trusted her," Donovan explained. "She thought Kyra would mess up my life just because hers was messed up. The longer Kyra lived with us, the more my mom didn't like her. It only lasted about five months.

"One day we came home from school, and Mama had all of Kyra's stuff packed. She said Kyra's family wanted her to go to Arkansas to be with them. I didn't believe it, and Kyra didn't either. She cried so much. I did, too."

Brianna was still against Kyra's return to her boyfriend's life, but she couldn't help but feel sorry for her after that story. She could imagine Beverly dragging Kyra's suitcase to the door while Donovan and Kyra cried in the background.

In her mind's eye, Brianna could see Donovan and Kyra holding hands until the last moment. The awful adults in their lives had to pry them apart. Kyra was forced to live without her *only source of peace* for the next fifteen years.

Brianna caught herself before she started feeling *too* sympathetic for Donovan's supposed play-sister.

"Pull her up on Facebook," she said. "I wanna see what she looks like."

Donovan pursed his lips, but he reached for his cellphone on the coffee table.

"No, do it on the computer," Brianna said, getting up. "I wanna see her on a *big* screen."

Donovan considered not complying, but then he rose from his recliner. Brianna watched him closely. She didn't know if he was hesitant because he had something to hide or because he didn't like being ordered around. She knew she'd find out which one it was in a few short moments.

≈≈≈≈≈≈≈

Kyra was so beautiful, Brianna almost started crying. She bullied Donovan out of his computer chair so she could navigate Kyra's profile at her own pace. Donovan stood next to her, his patience growing thinner by the second.

"You know I'm only allowing this because I care about you," he said, "and I understand that this might be a little weird for you. But if you don't start acting like you trust me—"

"You didn't tell me she was gorgeous," Brianna said, her eyes on the computer screen. "How many kids does she have?"

"Two."

"Is she still with her *baby-daddy*?" Brianna asked with a pompous tone. "Or should I say *baby-daddies*?"

Donovan grunted. "You were sitting right there when I talked to her. Did you hear me ask about that?"

"Why you getting an attitude?"

"Why you trying to put her down?" Donovan asked.

"What do you care?" Brianna said, her eyes on the computer.

Donovan couldn't answer right away. Why was it his job to defend Kyra? He couldn't answer that question fifteen years ago, either.

"*You sent her messages*?!" Brianna's voice was nearly a shriek.

"Of course I sent her messages. How do you think she got my number?"

"'*Oh my God, I can't believe it's really you!*'" Brianna read. "What the hell, Donovan?"

"What do you mean?"

"You got it in caps and everything!" Brianna's eyes skated across the screen, her scowl growing deeper by the second. "'*I can barely sit still*?!'" she read. "'*I'll fly to Arkansas if I have to*!?'"

"You said you wanted to see what she looked like," Donovan said. "Why you reading my personal messages?"

"You're writing personal messages to another female," Brianna said. "I have a right to see this!"

"*A right*? What the...?" Donovan shook his head in exasperation. He wanted to physically remove Brianna from his computer. She was a skinny girl. It wouldn't take much. But Donovan never manhandled a woman. His mother would pass out at just the thought of it. "See, this is why..." He mumbled something and then turned, heading for his recliner.

"This is why *what*?" Brianna yelled at him. "This is why *what*, Donovan?"

Why I don't wanna live with your crazy ass, Donovan thought – but of course did not say. Brianna was out of control now, but she really had her panties in a bunch a month ago when Donovan pressed the PAUSE button on her marriage plans.

Brianna was 27 years old, and she already had life figured out. She believed Donovan was the man she wanted to spend the rest of her life with. He was tall, dark and any woman within a mile radius knew he was handsome. Donovan's teaching job was rather *blah* by Brianna's standards, but she was an executive at the General Motor's Las Colinas office, so she didn't need her man to bring in a lot of money.

Brianna hoped they could shack up on their ninth month together, start planning a marriage by their tenth month and be on their honeymoon a few months after that. Donovan burst her bubble when he refused to move in with her. He wouldn't let Brianna come and live with him, either. He told her that was a huge step, and he wasn't sure if he was ready.

Truth be told, Donovan didn't know if their relationship would survive if he never had any private time AWAY from Brianna. She was a beautiful girl – a great catch, very career-minded and focused. But she was also the most insecure woman Donovan ever dated. He didn't understand it. Brianna could have any man she wanted. Rather than take comfort in that, she constantly stressed over losing the man she had.

Brianna didn't come and join him in the living room until she searched every bit of Donovan and Kyra's Facebook profile and found no evidence of an ongoing or potential relationship. She stood next to his recliner. Donovan ignored her and kept flipping channels with his remote.

"I'm sorry," she said.

How many times have I heard that before? Donovan wondered. At some point or another, Brianna had accused him of having eyes for nearly every pretty girl he knew.

"This is different," she said, reading his mind. "You know this is different, Donovan. You never told me you were *missing* some girl for fifteen years."

"It's not *some girl*," Donovan said. "Kyra's my sister."

"No. She's not," Brianna said. "But I don't want to argue anymore. She placed a hand on his shoulder. "Can I show you something, in the bedroom?"

Donovan frowned without looking up at her. "You think that's the solution every time? You get mad and I get mad, and then we have sex and everything's cool?"

"I didn't think we had sex," Brianna said, speaking softly now. "I thought we made love, Donovan. You still love me, don't you?"

"Whether it's sex or making love, it's the same scenario," he said. "You got issues that you can't fix. Every time you realize you're wrong about one of your wild accusations, you try to get me in the bedroom so I'll forget about it."

"Everybody does that," Brianna said as she kicked off her heels and unbuttoned her pants. "They don't all take it to the bedroom, but husbands buy their wives flowers when they screw up. They take them out to eat. I don't know what wives do, probably make meatloaf or something. I would try that, but I'm not a good cook."

She slid her jeans past her hips and then stepped on the cuffs so she could pull her long, slender legs out of them. Donovan didn't want to look, but Brianna's legs were a thing a beauty. She didn't have much hips or ass, but those legs belonged on a fashion runway. Her panties were black lace. She was standing close enough for Donovan to feel the heat between her legs.

She pulled her blouse over her head as she positioned herself between his legs. Brianna's bra matched her panties. Her stomach was completely flat, with nary a stretch mark. Her breasts were perfect for her size. Her long, curly hair flowed an inch past her shoulders. Her legs were spread slightly. Donovan felt blood rushing to his manhood as he stared at her slight camel toe.

Brianna reached for his shorts and tried to pull them down. She couldn't do it without Donovan lifting his hips. He didn't want to at first, but he couldn't deny his attraction. He licked his lips as he facilitated the removal of his shorts and boxers. When she got them off, Brianna dropped to her knees and kissed him on the belly button. Donovan inhaled sharply, and his manhood sprang to life. It pulsated, already hard and throbbing against Brianna's jugular vein.

She lowered her head and took him into her mouth without using her hands. She backed out and devoured him again, working her tongue magically along the way. She watched him the whole time. Donovan's expression was stuck somewhere between surprise and bliss. Brianna's eyes were dark and seductive.

She backed away. She kissed the tip and then sucked the head rhythmically, until Donovan's legs began to fidget. He reached for her with both hands and buried his fingers in her beautiful mane. Brianna didn't stop until she felt his toes digging into the carpet. She licked him slowly from bottom to top and then asked, "Are you still mad at me?" as the fat head glistened and jumped against her lips.

Donovan shook his head. "Get me a condom," he breathed.

Brianna smiled and stood and turned away from him so she could reach into her purse. Donovan stared at her thong panties. She didn't have tons of ass hanging out of them, but when she bent over Donovan desperately wanted to slide between her moist folds. He didn't think it was possible to *fuck some sense into her*, but there was certainly no harm in trying.

Brianna faced him again and tore the condom wrapper with her teeth. She gave Donovan the contraceptive and slipped her panties off while he rolled the condom down the length of his shaft. Donovan wanted her on all fours, but he wasn't upset when Brianna climbed on top of him. She positioned herself carefully and placed a hand on either side of Donovan's neck. Donovan took hold of her hips and guided her down slowly. Brianna's bottom lip disappeared inside her mouth as he invaded her moistness.

Donovan gripped her ass more firmly. Brianna threw her head back and moaned softly. She relaxed her muscles to accommodate his length and girth. The feel of her tight, slick walls clutching his manhood made Donovan's heart sigh. The sight of his dark meat disappearing inside her was even better. Brianna kept her pubic hair shaved, leaving just a small patch. When Donovan's bush mingled with it, he emitted a primal grunt that made the hairs stand on every part of Brianna's body. Her legs quivered. She lowered her head, and her hair fell into her face.

"*Feels so good,*" she purred. "*You feel so good.*"

Donovan wanted to tell her that this was not a solution. They had serious problems in their relationship that needed to be addressed. This passion they shared would change nothing. But Brianna started working her hips to a rhythm that was only in their souls, and Donovan pulled her close and sucked her throat. And he began to wonder if maybe he was wrong about all of that.

CHAPTER FOUR
MAMA'S BOY

The next day was Sunday, August 17th. Donovan picked up his mother for church at ten a.m. sharp. This was usually the only day of the week he could spend time with her.

Donovan's father, Darrell Mitchell, used to be the one to escort Beverly to services at Greater Missionary Baptist on Seminary. But he passed away when Donovan was in college. Coming home for that funeral was one of the hardest things Donovan ever had to do. Going back to school afterwards and leaving his mother alone in the home she shared with Darrell for nearly 30 years was just as tough.

When he graduated, Donovan never considered staying in Ohio or moving to any of the other states he was fond of. His mother wasn't needy, but she loved him dearly. It would break Miss Beverly's heart if Donovan had to get on a plane each time he visited her.

Plus Donovan loved Overbrook Meadows, so he didn't feel like he was passing up on any opportunities when he returned. It wasn't like he moved back into his mother's home and was still driving her car. Donovan had his own *everything*. So despite what Kyra said yesterday, he knew he wasn't a mama's boy.

≈≈≈≈≈≈

That morning Pastor Ricky Williams spoke to the congregation about volunteering more for the many church activities they had going on – and doing it with a grateful heart. He stressed that good deeds alone would not guarantee anyone a spot in the kingdom of heaven, but not offering any good deeds at all was just as bad.

After service Donovan waited while his mother spoke to the pastor and a few women at the church she'd grown close to over the years. When Miss Beverly was done with her goodbyes, Donovan led her into the bright sunlight outside and helped her into his new F-150. Beverly was a small woman, totally dwarfed by her tall and stout son. She was thin enough for Donovan to hoist into the truck like a child, but she only needed to hold his hand while she climbed into the cabin.

"Was Brianna busy this morning?" Beverly asked when Donovan got settled behind the steering wheel. He started the truck and rolled slowly out of the parking spot.

"I didn't talk to her," he told his mother.

"Was she out partying last night?"

Donovan grinned.

Brianna came to church with him and his mother only twice this year. Last year she tagged along once. Donovan thought that was a clear indication that Brianna wasn't the church-going type, but Beverly felt the need to bring it up again each week.

Donovan's mother was fifty-eight years old. She wore her hair short; it was more salt than peppery. She was spry and quick-witted. She wore wire-rimmed glasses and preferred slacks over skirts or dresses. Her skin was smooth and dark. Donovan had never seen her put on any makeup – not even a thin coat of lipstick. Beverly was retired from the DMV, but she maintained a lot of the impatience and sarcasm she perfected after more than three decades on the job.

Donovan loved his mother dearly. His only complaint was that she wouldn't take another man or even make room in her heart for a lonely puppy after her husband died. Donovan knew she had a lot more love to give. But Beverly was stubborn when she made up her mind about something. She knew no man could ever measure up to Darrell, and she cherished her home too much *to let some mangy dog chew it up*. Donovan offered to find her a cat, declawed. Beverly was not interested.

"Why don't you give me a grandbaby?" she'd asked instead. "If I got more love to give, I'll save it for my grandbaby."

Donovan made a left on Seminary.

"Brianna didn't go out partying last night," he said. "She just doesn't like to wake up early on Sunday."

"That's part of the sacrifice," Beverly preached. "Sometimes you have to do things your body doesn't want, if you want to follow Jesus."

"Why you telling me?" Donovan asked. "I got up this morning."

"I was thinking maybe you could pass the word along to your girlfriend," Beverly suggested.

"But I don't care if she goes to church," Donovan said honestly. "I thought you liked Brianna."

"I do," Beverly said. "She's beautiful, and she's smart. But if she was a heavy-praying woman, too..." She held a finger in the air. "That would seal the deal for me. I'd be proud to give you away at your wedding."

Donovan chuckled. He told her countless times that a mom does not give her son away at a wedding, but Beverly wouldn't give up the dream.

"You're my only child," she had replied. "I got to have *some* role in your wedding – besides just sitting there. Why does the bride's family get to do everything?"

Donovan drove past the Golden Corral they usually stopped at after church.

"Where you going?" Beverly asked.

"I forgot to tell you, I can't have lunch with you today, Mama. I'm meeting someone."

Beverly frowned. "Someone like who?"

Donovan smiled. "Kyra."

Beverly frowned some more. "Kyra *who*?"

Donovan fought hard to keep from cracking up. "You know which Kyra."

Beverly's eyes widened. She removed her glasses and fixed a serious look on him. "Kyra *who*?"

"Reynolds, Mama. Kyra Reynolds."

Beverly's mouth fell open. "Aw hell."

Donovan laughed. "We just left church, Mama."

Beverly didn't give a damn. "Don't tell me that girl is back in this city."

"She is," Donovan said. "And she's not a girl anymore, Mama. Kyra's a grown woman."

51

Beverly stared at her son like his nose just fell off. "Donovan, don't play with me."

"I'm not," he said. He couldn't wipe the smirk off his face. "She moved back last week. And she found me on Facebook. I talked to her yesterday."

Beverly stared in silence for a moment, and then she brought a hand to her face and rubbed her forehead. "Jesus," she muttered.

"It's been fifteen years," Donovan said. "I know you're not still mad at her."

"Are you trying to give me a heart attack?" Beverly asked. "Do you want to send me to an early grave?"

"No, Mama. Of course not."

"What the hell is Kyra doing back in this city?"

"She can live wherever she wants to, Mama."

"Did she come back for you?"

Donovan frowned. "No."

"Then why she look you up?"

"She was my best friend," Donovan reminded. "Why wouldn't she look me up? I've been looking for her, too."

"Looking for her *when*?"

"All the time," Donovan said. "Tell me you're not still mad at her."

"I'm not mad. I just can't stand her," Beverly said matter-of-factly.

"Mama, that's cold."

"Donovan, don't sit there and act like this is brand new. You know I can't stand that girl. Never could. She ain't never brought nothing but trouble."

"She never caused me any trouble, Mama. You're exaggerating."

"I remember when she used to follow you home," Beverly said. She was staring at the traffic, but what she saw was a memory tucked deep inside a recess of her mind. "When y'all were kids, I remember thinking, *Aw, look at my baby trying to help that poor, homeless girl.* But I made the mistake of feeding her ass, and she wouldn't go away. She was like a bad fungus infection, just, just always there! Always knocking on my damned door: *Is, is Donovan here?*" Beverly scrunched up her face and mocked Kyra with a childish voice. "I wanted to tell her *Hell no! Not for you! Not never!*"

"Wow." Donovan watched his mother in amazement. It was hard to believe they had totally different recollections of the same person. "Kyra never did anything to harm you," he said. "Why you acting like that?"

"It's not what she did to me. It's what she almost did to you! Had you in all types of trouble over there."

"No, Mama. Kyra never got me in trouble."

"What about when you called the police over to her mama's house? Got yourself in all that *mess*! You were in the 8th grade then."

"You just said it," Donovan noted. "*I* called the police over there. Kyra didn't tell me to do that. And I didn't get in trouble for calling the police."

"And what about when you got in a fight with that man over there?"

"Again that was something *I* chose to do, Mama. You can't blame Kyra for that."

"How come I can't? Your name wouldn't have been in no police reports if it wasn't for her. Her whole family was all messed up, and you was right in the middle of it. Wasn't nothing I could tell you to get you to leave that girl alone."

"I always wondered why you weren't proud of me for trying to help somebody."

"How can a little boy help somebody?" Beverly wanted to know. "That's what I was trying to tell you, way back then. The only thing that can happen is you get pulled down right along with her."

"But I didn't get pulled down, Mama. As you can see, I'm not on drugs or in prison."

"Did you tell Brianna about her?" Beverly asked.

"Of course I did," Donovan said. "You think I'd go see another woman without telling my girlfriend?"

"And she's okay with it?"

"Well, she ain't great," Donovan admitted. "But she does trust me."

"Did you tell her why I put Kyra out my house?"

Donovan's smile slipped. "I, uh…"

"Yeah." Beverly nodded fiercely. "That's what I thought."

"I told her everything else, though."

"If you didn't tell her you was fixing to have sex with that girl, then you lied," Beverly accused.

"All we did was kiss," Donovan said.

His mother's mouth fell open, and she got upset all over again. "Boy, don't sit there and tell me that bull! I saw it, Donovan! Did you forget that? I saw it with my own eyes!"

Donovan pulled into the driveway of his childhood home. He didn't kill the engine right away. He turned and looked at his mother.

"You saw us kissing," he said. "Not getting ready to–"

"In *my house*," Beverly nearly shouted. "Y'all played me like a fool. Whew!" She fanned herself. "I don't know why you got me thinking about that girl again. Gon' have my blood pressure up."

"We didn't play you, Mama."

"Yes you did. Told me y'all was *just friends. She's like my little sister*," she mocked. "I knew it wasn't no way a boy and a girl could live together like that, but I believed you. And y'all stabbed me in the back! *Both of you!*"

"It was just one kiss," Donovan reasoned. "That was the first time we ever did that. And it wasn't planned. We didn't lie to you. I didn't know that was gonna happen."

"It wasn't *just a kiss*," Beverly growled. "Y'all were touching on each other, tongue all in each other's mouths!" She grimaced. "If I didn't come home from work early that day, I'd have my grandbaby by now. She'd be fourteen years old already."

Beverly leaned back in her seat and fanned herself. It was already chilly in the vehicle, but Donovan reached to turn his AC up more.

"I swear I feel my pressure rising," Beverly said.

Donovan shook his head, not sure how to respond to her. He knew *the kiss* was bad, but he didn't think his mother would harbor this much resentment after so much time.

≈ ≈ ≈ ≈ ≈ ≈

The incident occurred on October 7th, 1999. Donovan was a junior at Finley High. Kyra was in the 10th grade at the same school. She'd been living with Donovan's family for five months,

since the day her mother went to prison for her 4th forgery
conviction. At school Donovan and Kyra referred to each other as
brother and sister or cousins. The other students didn't know
what to make of them. They knew Donovan and Kyra lived
together, and they never saw the best buds hugging or holding
hands or showing any sexual interest whatsoever. Whatever they
were, boyfriend and girlfriend wasn't it.

At that point, Kyra and Donovan had been friends for
seven years. They were both on cloud nine, since Beverly trusted
them enough to take Kyra in. She didn't have to move all the way
to Arkansas, and Kyra was now safe from her neglectful and
sometimes dangerous home environment. With Donovan's family,
Kyra was happier than she had ever been.

When they got home from school that day, nothing was out
of the ordinary. Kyra had developed most of her womanly features
by then. But Donovan seemed uninterested. His mother warned
them that Kyra would have to go if they started any funny
business. Donovan knew was at stake. But it didn't matter
because he didn't have those kinds of eyes for Kyra. When some of
his friends at school asked if he noticed Kyra's steadily bulging
breasts, Donovan responded, "Yo, that's nasty. That's like me
looking at my *mama's* chest!"

Donovan still felt that way on October 7th. But that was the
day he learned that you can go from having zero interest in
somebody to having a blinding yearning for them in the blink of an
eye – depending on the situation. The situation for them was the
family den, with dark curtains on the windows, and a new music
video on BET. The feature was *"We Can't be Friends,"* by R.L. and
Deborah Cox.

The song was about a couple who broke up and realized
they couldn't remain friends afterwards because they were still in
love. The video matched the lyrics precisely. When it went off,
Donovan was surprised to see tears in Kyra's eyes.

"What's wrong with you?"

The teenagers sat next to each other on a long sofa. They
weren't supposed to have any alone time together, but Donovan's
father went to help a friend with a flat tire. Kyra had her legs
tucked under her. Her stretchy Capris put her supple thighs on
display. Beverly took Kyra to get her hair done last weekend, and

she had managed to keep her 'do in place since then. She was very attractive, even as she wiped her tears.

"That's a sad song," she said. "You didn't think it was sad?"

Donovan grinned. "He got with her in the end. They're both happy now, right?"

Kyra shook her head. "I don't think they got back together. They're just saying they can't be friends. It sounds like they have to break up and not talk to each other at all."

Donovan thought about that. Both singers were crying at the end of the video, so maybe Kyra was right.

"Do you think that could ever happen to us?" Kyra asked. "Do you ever think about us not being friends anymore?"

Donovan shook his head. "How could that happen? You were never my girlfriend, or nothing like that."

"But what if I was?" Kyra proposed. "What if we did decide to be boyfriend and girlfriend, and then we broke up and couldn't be friends?"

"I don't think that's possible," Donovan said, not sure where she was going with this.

"Why?" Kyra asked. "Why couldn't it happen?"

Donovan stared at her. He chuckled nervously. But Kyra wasn't smiling. Donovan's head tilted in confusion. "You mean why we couldn't be boyfriend and girlfriend or why we couldn't be friends anymore if we broke up?"

"Both," Kyra said, then, "boyfriend and girlfriend."

Donovan forced a grin. Kyra remained very serious. Her bottom lip was red from a Now & Later candy she had earlier. Donovan found himself staring at it. At that lip.

"Well, first of all my mom would kill us," he said.

"But do you ever think about me, like that?" Kyra asked.

Donovan knew they were wading into dangerous waters, but there was nothing he and Kyra couldn't talk about. "Wh, why? Do you ever think about me like that?"

Kyra nodded. "Since I was little."

Donovan was stunned by that. His whole body went numb. But he was also a little relieved. For years, ever since Kyra's lovely lady lumps began to sprout in the 7th grade, he'd been mesmerized by her journey into womanhood. Given the nature of their relationship, he knew he had to repress those feelings. But lately he'd been listening more and more to the little devil on his other shoulder, the one reminding him that Kyra was not his relative. There was no blood between them. So it was okay for her to give him a boner.

Up until October 7th discretion won out because Donovan knew Kyra didn't feel the same way about him. But her admission opened a floodgate of emotions and opportunities that Donovan could not put the lid back on.

Even as he told her, "I think like that sometimes, too," Donovan's eyes rolled down to Kyra's breasts. He'd been sneaking glances at those big humps of mystery for months. He longed to stare at them openly.

When Kyra saw his change in demeanor and the direction of his gaze, her nipples hardened like pebbles. At their ages, they had more hormones than good sense. They were both virgins, too. Right then and there Kyra decided that she wanted Donovan to be her first. It made perfect sense. She loved him more than anyone in her life – even her family, and she knew that Donovan loved her, too. Not brother-sister love. It was full grown adult love.

And it was a beautiful thing.

Neither remembered who leaned in first. They met eagerly in the middle. The moment their lips touched, a fire ignited in both of their souls. They knew this is what their relationship was meant to be all along.

Kyra's bottom lip tasted like cherry Now & Later's. Donovan would never forget that taste. It was so sweet. He hummed as he sucked it. Kyra emitted a breathy moan. Donovan stole the opportunity to explore her mouth with his tongue. Kyra had never been kissed like that before. She had no idea Donovan was so skillful. Or maybe his prowess was all in her mind. Either way, she was in bliss.

When he felt her breast beneath his hand, Donovan was surprised because he didn't remember reaching for it. Kyra arched her back in appreciation, and Donovan didn't slow up at all. He gripped her flesh softly, like he wanted to so many times. Kyra moaned again. Donovan left her mouth and sucked her fiery neck as his hand snaked under her shirt and under her bra.

The feel of her bare flesh and hard nipple was overpowering. Donovan's manhood jumped in his pants. He felt the moistness of his pre cum. He was harder than he had ever been in his entire life.

Kyra began to lie back on the couch. Donovan was obliged to follow. Kyra's legs spread on their own accord. Donovan fit so nicely between them. They kissed again, this time with an animalistic urging that begged to be quenched. Donovan grinded his hips, and Kyra felt his hardness trying to get in. There were two layers of denim between them; his and hers. Donovan reached down, maybe to unbutton his jeans, maybe hers, maybe neither. They would never know because the next sound they heard was a horrified scream that changed both of their lives forever.

"What the hell is going on?!"

Donovan jumped off of Kyra, and she yanked her shirt down. They tried their best to look normal with their hair messed and their breathing ragged. But Beverly had seen the dirty deed. She stood in the doorway with shock and fury battling for dominance of her expression. Her chest began to heave up and down.

The next five minutes were very unchristian, to say the least. Beverly called Kyra horrible things, things a teenage girl shouldn't know the definition of – let alone have directed at her. Beverly also accused her only son of betraying her. She said both of them played her like a fool.

Donovan tried to plead their case. Kyra really was like a sister to him. This was the first and *last* time something like this would ever happen. But even he didn't believe that. Maybe things were innocent before Kyra moved in, but they weren't now, and it could never go back to the way it was.

It wasn't like Beverly was taking any chances. She contacted Kyra's relatives that night and bought her a plane ticket the next morning. When Donovan and Kyra got home from school, Donovan's father was waiting to take Kyra to the airport.

Donovan cried himself to sleep that night. But he couldn't hate his mother for what she did. Instead Donovan blamed himself for surrendering to the desires of his flesh. Kyra may have initiated it, but she was young. Donovan was the one who should've known better.

≈≈≈≈≈≈≈

Donovan turned his truck off and got out so he could help his mother down from the elevated cab. He walked her to the door and unlocked it with the same key he had since he was in high school.

"Alright, Mama. I'll see you later." He gave her a kiss on the cheek.

"If you don't tell Brianna about that kiss, then you're lying to her," Beverly warned. "It ain't right to lie to her about what you and Kyra had going on."

Donovan knew his mother was right, but he also knew he wouldn't listen to her. He couldn't. Brianna would never allow him to see Kyra if she knew.

"Love you," Donovan said as he headed back to his truck. "I'll come by and cut your grass later, when the sun starts to go down."

"Can you bring me a slice of buttermilk pie?" Beverly asked. "That's the one thing I really wanted from Golden Corral today."

"Okay," Donovan said with a smile. He didn't think he'd be near any restaurants that sold single pie slices, but he would make it happen – not because he was a mama's boy, but because he was a good son. *There is a difference*, Donovan told himself.

CHAPTER FIVE
BFF'S

Twenty minutes later Donovan stood on Aunt Ruth's porch wearing the black slacks, gray shirt and black tie he wore to church that day. His heart was racing, and his palms were moist. He hadn't been this nervous since he was in high school. He rang the doorbell and wiped his hands on his pants and then stuffed them in his pockets. He pulled them out and adjusted his tie and cleared his throat. He took a step back so that whoever answered could see him in the peephole. But then he thought it would look weird; him standing way back there, so he returned to his original spot.

Get a hold of yourself, man.

That was easier said than done. It wasn't possible at all when the door opened and Donovan came face to face with the object of his fascination. Kyra wore a black skirt with a sleeveless pink blouse. She had her hair styled in a short bob with one bang concealing her left eyebrow. The skirt was form-fitting, clutching her curves like an insatiable lover. The blouse didn't offer more than a glimpse of her cleavage, but it didn't have to. Kyra's breasts were vast and luscious. She wore a light coat of lipstick and a little mascara. Her eyes were as big and beautiful as Donovan remembered them. Her lips were full and moist, much more enticing than they were fifteen years ago.

While Donovan stood stiffly, unable to get his *Hello* out, Kyra found herself in similar disarray. She studied all of his Facebook pictures and thought she knew every muscle and contour of Donovan's physique. But seeing him in real life was a totally different experience. The pictures didn't do him justice.

They failed to capture the intensity of his presence, the fire dancing in his dark eyes.

Donovan was a few inches taller than Kyra in high school, but he must have had another growth spurt after she left. He now looked to be six-foot-four inches tall, maybe six-five. Donovan was slim in the waist, compared to some of his Facebook photos. But even with a long-sleeved shirt on, Kyra could see that his upper body was massive, especially his chest. His trapezius muscles were like two fist-size knots on either side of his neck.

I wish he dressed more casual, Kyra thought. But she knew she'd swoon at the sight of him in a tight tee shirt – or a tank top. Or maybe they could go to a pool, and she could have him *completely topless.*

Whoa there.

Kyra tried to get her thoughts in check as her eyes swam up his torso, towards his face. Donovan was clean-shaven. The boyish good looks Kyra admired when they were young had evolved into a strong, manly jaw line, dark brown eyes that were almost intimidating even though his lashes might have been the longest Kyra had ever seen on a man. Donovan had a crew cut with a slight fade. His edge-up was impeccable. His lips were delectable.

Before Kyra could formulate a greeting for the Adonis that stood before her, Donovan closed the distance between them and wrapped his strong arms around her. Kyra felt a surge of electricity shoot from his hands to deep inside her core. She gasped, totally unprepared for the energy in his touch. Donovan pulled her closer, close enough for Kyra's breast to press against his hard stomach. She felt her legs giving way. Donovan's sweet fragrance filled her nostrils and intoxicated her further.

She grabbed hold of him – she had no choice, and they held on to each other for hours. Or maybe it was only seconds. It was hard to tell. Nothing mattered at that moment except for him and her. Neither of them realized how badly they missed each other until there was nothing between them but heartbeats, heavy breaths and a few layers of clothing that were the *only* thing stopping this hug from being something much more than friendly.

When he finally released her, Kyra's head was spinning. She took a step back and wobbled slightly in her pumps. Donovan took her hand to brace her. Thank God she didn't wear taller

heels! She would've fallen for sure. That would have been awful –
not just because Donovan would've seen it, but Kyra looked
around and noticed that her whole family had joined her in the
living room. Her face flushed with crimson.

"Hey, Donovan," Kyra said as if she'd just opened the door.
"This is my Aunt Ruth and my two kids, Katavia and Quinell." She
turned to introduce them.

"Nice to meet you," Donovan said to the children. "Good
afternoon," he told Kyra's aunt.

Kyra's kids were more shy than usual. Quinell had only
taken one step into the room. Kat sought shelter behind Aunt
Ruth.

"Come on, ya'll. Come say hi," Kyra implored. "Donovan's
a good friend of mine. I've known him since I was your age," she
told Quinell.

Q stepped forward out of obedience, but Kat was still
unsure about this hulk of a man who somehow squeezed through
their front door.

"Girl, get over here," Kyra said with a chuckle.

She went to retrieve her daughter. Donovan struggled to
keep his eyes off Kyra's derriere when she turned away. She filled
out that skirt like nobody's business. Donovan had been with
Brianna for so long, he nearly forgot what a real, southern woman
looked like – one who didn't eat rice cakes or pull out a calorie
counter before she ordered at a restaurant.

Donovan knew he'd never place his hands on Kyra's
lusciousness, but he had a sudden craving for a woman her size.
Definitely not Kyra, he told himself, but if he was lucky enough to
meet a totally different woman built exactly like her, Donovan
might have to trade-in his Skinny Minnie.

"Hi."

Donovan looked down and saw a young boy standing there.
Donovan squatted so he could look the child in the eyes.

"Hello. My name is Donovan."

His voice was deep and rich, creating a roll of bass that
seemed to bounce off every wall before dissipating. He stuck out a
hand to shake, and Quinell obliged. Kyra watched her son's mitt
get totally swallowed up in Donovan's paw. She smiled. She
walked over to them with Katavia in her arms.

"And this is my daughter, Kat," she said.

Donovan stood and grinned at the baby. "Hello there."

Kat stared at him for a moment, and then she smiled and buried her face against her mother's shoulder.

"Oh, stop being shy," Kyra said. She tried to get the baby facing the right direction, but it was no use. No matter which arm Kyra switched her to, Kat wouldn't meet Donovan's eyes. "I'm sorry," Kyra said. "She's usually not like this. I don't know what's gotten into her."

"She's fine," Donovan said. "I think she'll like me once she gets to know me."

Kat looked up at him, and Donovan winked at her, and the baby turned away again giggling. Kyra laughed. Donovan looked up and then crossed the floor to greet the last person in the room. Aunt Ruth eyed him suspiciously, even when Donovan reached to shake her hand.

"Hi, I'm Donovan Mitchell."

She shook it, but Ruth was clearly guarded.

"You Kyra's old friend, from when she used to live down here?"

"Yes," Donovan said. "And she lived with my family once, for a little while, a long time ago."

"Hmph," the older woman said. "Y'all have a good time."

She didn't look like she meant it. Kyra didn't know what was going on with her grumpy aunt, and she didn't care. She deposited her baby on the sofa and went to wait for Donovan at the door.

"We'll be back in a couple of hours," he said as he backed away from Aunt Ruth. When he turned to face Kyra, Donovan smiled big and dopey. Kyra did, too. She hadn't been this excited since the day Donovan's mom let her move in with them.

≈ ≈ ≈ ≈ ≈ ≈

When they got in his truck, Kyra quickly fell in love with the cozy seats and cool air-conditioning. It's strange, the things people take for granted. Kyra never thought a new truck would be so impressive, but after riding the bus and in her aunt's '96 Camry, Donovan's pickup felt like the lap of luxury.

63

The childhood friends couldn't take their eyes off each other as Donovan backed out of the driveway and headed for a restaurant downtown.

"What?" Kyra said after catching a few of his glances.

"I don't know," Donovan said. He shook his head and tried to keep his eyes on the road. "You look so different. I'm glad to finally see you again."

"Different how?" Kyra asked. She couldn't wipe the smile off her face, either.

"You're all grown up," Donovan stated. "You've become a beautiful woman, Kyra."

She blushed and coyly looked away. When did Donovan's eyes become so damned piercing? When did his lips get so freaking suckable? Donovan moistened his puckers while she watched, as if he could read her mind.

"You did a lot of growing yourself," she said. "You had some little muscles back in the day, but they're all full-sized now. I see you."

Donovan grinned. "Thanks, but my most important muscle will always be the one between my ears. The rest are superficial."

Kyra heard him perfectly, but she still thought he said *the one between my legs.* Her eyes even swam in that directly. She caught herself.

Dammit woman, get a grip!

"I worked out to get bigger for football," Donovan explained. "Especially when I got to college. Those guys are NFL-size. You gotta be strong to compete. But I'm a lot slimmer now."

"I saw your college pictures," Kyra said. "Your body does look better now. I mean *you* look better. Not your body. You know what? Let me shut up."

Donovan chuckled. "Well, as a friend, I can say that your body looks better now, too. *As a friend*, I noticed that you got it going on."

"Thanks," Kyra said, blushing again. The AC was blowing perfectly, but it still felt warm in the truck. She fanned herself. "I don't know why I'm so nervous around you."

"Please don't be," Donovan said. "You used to be able to talk to me about anything. I hope we can still be like that, even though it's been a long time since we talked."

"Me too," Kyra said. "I miss that. I miss you. Thanks for picking me up."

"I said I'd fly to Arkansas to see you," Donovan stated. "I meant that."

"Thank you," Kyra said. Her heart was filled with happiness.

"So tell me about your kids," Donovan said.

"Okay. My son is eight years old. His name is Quinell. My daughter Katavia is two. Everyone calls her Kat."

"They're beautiful," Donovan said. "You said you've never been married?"

"No." Kyra thought she'd feel self-conscious about that, but she didn't, not with Donovan.

"Are you still with their father?"

Kyra shook her head. "Quinell's dad died before he was born. He got stabbed." Her eyes glazed over as the bloody memory filled her mind.

"That's terrible," Donovan said. "I'm, I'm sorry that happened to you."

"A lot of bad stuff happened," Kyra said with a shrug.

Donovan thought that was a dreadful and cryptic comment, but he let it go for now.

"What about Kat's father?" he asked instead.

Kyra sighed. "His name is Leonard. He's still alive. He's a hustler, and he does drugs, too. I didn't know how bad he was at first. He's in jail now. We're not together anymore."

Donovan didn't know what to make of what he was hearing. He thought Kyra's life was bad before she left Overbrook Meadows. He always assumed things got better for her in Arkansas.

"What about you, Mr. Mitchell?" Kyra asked. "I know you're not married, but there's got to be some woman trying to get her hooks in you."

Donovan chuckled. "Yeah, there is someone. I've been with my girlfriend for almost eight months."

Kyra couldn't explain why her heart grew heavy at that moment. She already knew Donovan had a girlfriend. Even if he didn't, it wasn't like she and he could ever be more than friends. The one time they tried, all hell broke loose. That ill-advised shot at love literally ruined Kyra's life.

"Is she pretty?" Kyra felt foolish for asking, but Donovan didn't notice her inner turmoil.

"She is. Her name's Brianna."

"Is she in any of your Facebook pictures?" Kyra tried to sound like she was barely interested. "I think I might've seen her."

"She has long, curly hair," Donovan said. "She looks like a model. She actually could be a model. If you saw her pictures, you'd know because she kinda takes center stage, no matter who she's posing with."

"Yeah, I think I saw her," Kyra said. *Ha!* Who was she kidding? She had practically memorized Brianna's facial features. Kyra was pretty sure she could give a perfect description if someone wanted to do a composite drawing. "Eight months is pretty serious," she said.

"It can be," Donovan agreed.

Kyra didn't know how to respond to that, so she changed the subject. "I see you took Regina Bryant to the prom."

Donovan laughed. "You saw my prom pictures?"

Kyra giggled, too. "Is that stalking? I promise I wasn't stalking you!"

"No, it's all good," Donovan said. "I forgot I had those pictures up."

"I didn't know you liked Regina."

"I didn't," Donovan said. "Not like that. I know *you* didn't like her."

"I never said I didn't like her."

"Whatever. I know you didn't like her," Donovan insisted. "You didn't have to tell me."

Kyra wondered where he got that bit of insight from. But Donovan was dead-on, as usual. The strange thing was Kyra never had a good reason to *not* like Regina when they were in high school. It might have been because Regina revealed her fondness for Donovan one day when Kyra was a freshman. Kyra hadn't expressed any attraction to Donovan at that point, and she convinced herself that she was just being protective of her big brother.

"I didn't think she was good enough for you," Kyra admitted.

"You were probably right," Donovan said. "I only went to the prom with her because she asked me. And don't worry, we didn't do anything afterwards."

Kyra was happy to hear that, but she said, "I wasn't worried. That's your business."

"You don't care?" Donovan asked. He looked skeptical.

"Uh-uhn," Kyra said, shaking her head. "Why would I?"

"I dunno," Donovan said. "I just thought since you didn't like her, it might have upset you if you thought we had sex or something."

"You mean like *jealousy*?"

Donovan shrugged. "I don't know. Maybe."

"We're just friends," Kyra said. "Friends don't get jealous. Right?"

Donovan nodded. "You're right."

"But it is good to know that I don't have to find Regina and punch her in the mouth for something she did so long ago," Kyra said.

Donovan cut his eyes and grinned.

"I'm kidding," Kyra said. "You know I'm just kidding."

≈ ≈ ≈ ≈ ≈ ≈ ≈

Donovan took her to Red Lobster, and they dined on lobster tails and so many crab legs Kyra thought she should send an apology letter to PETA. While they dined, they talked more about what Kyra missed out on during Donovan's junior and senior years at Finley High. And then he wanted to know what happened to Kyra when she moved to Arkansas. Kyra was eager to talk, but she didn't want to dampen the mood with her war stories.

"Why do you want to hear about that?" she asked. "Didn't nothing good happen in Little Rock."

"Because it's a part of your history," Donovan said. "I know it wasn't bad 24-7. Even the slaves had *some* happy times."

Kyra laughed at his analogy. "You know what, that's a good way to describe it. Everybody in the hood knows they're in the hood. They know they're poor, and the neighborhood stinks, and you can get killed for cashing your paycheck at the corner store. But at the same time, we always found time to party. A lot of people live every day like it's their last, because it might just be."

"I don't want to know about everybody," Donovan said. "I wanna know about you."

Kyra's smile slipped for the first time since they arrived at the restaurant. "I don't really wanna talk about it," she said. But just as quickly she offered him a brief recap: "When I left your mama's house, I was hurting. I didn't want to live in Little Rock. But I had to accept that's where I was gonna be, and I might as well get used to it. It was hard. It got real bad sometimes. I used to wish you were there. I wished you were with me."

"I'm sorry my mama kicked you out," Donovan said. He never realized how big an impact that decision had on Kyra's life.

"Please," she said. "That wasn't your fault."

"I feel like it was," Donovan said. "I never forgave myself."

"Stop, please," Kyra said. She shook her head and then batted her eyes. But the tears pooled and fell anyway. She quickly reached to wipe them away with her napkin. "I don't wanna cry," she said. "I'm having fun. Please. I don't wanna talk about that."

"Okay," Donovan said. His heart was suddenly sick and heavy. He never wanted to see Kyra cry. Ever since he was a child, he would do anything to make her happy. "Hey, do you remember the time we beat up Jimmy and his sister?" He offered a hesitant smile.

Kyra's eyes lit up, and she smiled, too. "Big-lip Jimmy and that *stanky* Rochelle!" She laughed loudly. "We tag-teamed the hell out of them!"

It was good to see her laugh again. Donovan leaned forward with his elbows on the table while Kyra retold the harrowing tale.

≈ ≈ ≈ ≈ ≈ ≈

Twenty minutes later, Kyra was reluctant to leave the restaurant. She hadn't eaten that well in a long time. But returning to the comfy confines of Donovan's truck was nice, too. Kyra hoped she'd meet a handsome man in Overbrook Meadows who had a nice car. It didn't have to be anything flashy, so long as the seats were cozy and he had a loud sound system like Donovan did. Better yet, Kyra dreamed of the day she would have her own ride.

"So, what are your plans?" Donovan asked as he exited the restaurant's parking lot. "You got some short term goals?"

Kyra grinned. "I was just thinking the same thing."

"About your goals?"

She nodded. "Yeah. The first thing I need is to get me a car. Wait, the *first* thing I need is to find a job. And then a car and my own place."

"Do you have anything lined up?" Donovan asked.

She shook her head. "I'll take whatever job I can find at this point."

"What kind of work have you done," Donovan asked, "in Arkansas?"

Kyra frowned. She knew he was going to ask about that. "I never had a real good job. I've been a waitress. I worked at some other restaurants, as a cashier and stuff. I had a job as a customer service rep. That one was cool."

"Have you ever worked as a receptionist?" Donovan asked.

"No," Kyra said. "But I know I can do it. The customer service job was kinda like a secretary."

Donovan didn't say anything, but he was watching her carefully.

"Don't look at me like that," Kyra said.

"Like what."

"I know that look."

Donovan's eyes narrowed. "What look?"

"That *I wanna help you* look," Kyra said. "That's the way you used to look at me when I was little; when you thought you could fix all my problems."

Donovan smiled. "I do want to help you, Kyra. I didn't know you could read my mind, though."

"I know you, Donovan."

"Yes, you do."

"And you think you know me, too. But a lot has changed since I been gone."

"I know," Donovan said. "I want you to tell me everything. I don't care how long it takes."

"Okay, but not today."

"Okay." Donovan smiled. "You know, I think you just need somebody in your life to encourage you and look out for you."

"That doesn't have to be you," Kyra said. She regretted her comment when she saw a flash of pain in Donovan's eyes. "I mean, you don't feel like you have to keep saving me, do you?"

"I don't know what I feel," Donovan said honestly.

"I know that's how it always was with us," Kyra said. "But that's not why I came back to Overbrook Meadows. I don't want to depend on people anymore."

"You didn't come back for me?" Donovan was glad he was driving. He kept his eyes on the road rather than look at Kyra. This was the question Brianna and Beverly were most concerned about. Donovan wanted to know as well, but he was afraid of her answer.

Kyra swallowed and held her breath when she said, "No."

Donovan's heart stopped beating completely as he processed the rejection. But he didn't know why that should upset him. He was in a relationship, and he hadn't spoken to Kyra in fifteen years. Of course she didn't come back for him. She didn't even know that he still lived in the city until she contacted him on Facebook.

"Okay," Donovan said. "I'm not asking you to depend on me, but will you at least let me assist you?"

"Assist me how?"

"I might be able to help you find a job," Donovan offered. "And if I'm not working, I can give you rides to the library – or if you just wanna hang out and talk. I know things have changed, but I still consider you my best friend, Kyra. We're still BFF's, right?"

BFF's. That put a genuine smile on Kyra's face. How many people pledged to be *Best Friends Forever* only to lose touch after graduation?

"I don't deserve you," she said. "I don't deserve to have someone like you caring for me. I told you that before, haven't I?"

"Yes, I believe so."

"But you never listen."

"You shouldn't have come back to my city if you didn't want my help," Donovan said.

It was a joke, but Kyra knew he was serious. And she took comfort in his words, despite the fact that she really did want to be independent.

Ten minutes later Donovan pulled into the driveway at Aunt Ruth's house. It was late afternoon, still warm and sunny.

"Your girlfriend didn't have a problem with you seeing me?" Kyra asked before she got out of the truck.

"Like I told my mom, Brianna ain't great, but she's okay with it," Donovan replied.

"Your mom, Wow." Kyra brought a hand to her face. "You already talked to her about me?"

"I took her to church this morning."

"Mama's boy." Kyra snickered.

"Whatever."

"Is she still mad at me?"

"She, um. She ain't great, either," Donovan admitted.

Kyra thought about the last time she saw Miss Beverly. Bad idea. She felt mortified and turned on at the same time. It was an awkward mix of emotions. She wondered if Donovan ever thought about their kiss. She would love to talk to him about it, but she knew it would be improper to bring it up because of his girlfriend.

"What about your aunt?" Donovan asked. "I feel like she doesn't like me."

"I have no idea what her problem is," Kyra said. "I can't wait to move from over here." She eyed the front door of her aunt's house much like she did when she was a child, looking at her own home.

Donovan was hit with a powerful sense of déjà vu. It was clear they weren't meant to have a sexual relationship, but Donovan believed God put him in Kyra's life to be her protector. They may have lost contact for a decade and a half, but his concern for her was one thing that remained the same.

"Please tell your girlfriend that I never asked you to help me with anything," Kyra said as she opened the door.

Donovan grinned mischievously. "Will do."

Kyra stared into his beautiful, brown eyes. "Thanks for lunch, and everything."

"You're welcome," Donovan said. "I'll call you tomorrow."

CHAPTER SIX
DONOVAN THE PROTECTOR

Brianna sent Donovan two text messages during his lunch with Kyra. He read them when he stopped at a light down the street from Aunt Ruth's house.

Hey, baby. Just wanted to know how things were going. Are you still with her? Where'd you take her? What are y'all doing?

In the second one, sent an hour later, Donovan knew his woman was losing her resolve.

Hey, baby. How long is your lunch going to be? I don't want to call you. I'm trying real hard. If you don't call me soon, I'm going to call you. Call me as soon as you can!!

Donovan almost didn't call her back. Why'd she have to go overboard with the exclamation points? He had a lot on his mind. He didn't want to explain things to Brianna until he knew what was going on. He had to remind himself that although his girlfriend was insanely jealous, this was a unique situation. This time Brianna's concern was understandable. Donovan dialed her number, and she answered right away.

"Hey," he said.

"Hey," she said. "Is your date over? You on your way home?"

"It wasn't a date."

"Whatever. Is it over?"

"Yes."

"I have a lot I want to say about this. Are you on your way home?"

Donovan cringed. "Yes."

"Can I meet you there, so we can talk?"

"Alright."

"Where'd you take her?" Brianna asked. "What did y'all talk about? What have you been doing all this time?"

And so the inquisition begins. Donovan sighed. "I thought you were coming to my house so we can talk in person?"

"Yeah. Okay."

"Alright, I'll see you there."

≈ ≈ ≈ ≈ ≈ ≈

Brianna's new Jetta was parked in his driveway when Donovan got there. He pulled in beside it and locked eyes with Brianna. She was already trying to read his expression. Donovan offered her a smile as he got out of his truck. He went around to open Brianna's door for her, but she hopped out of her ride just as quickly. She met him halfway.

She stood with her arms by her sides, her eyes darting slightly as she searched her man's eyes for the truth his mouth might not give her. She checked his lips and collar for foreign makeup. Donovan's expression was unreadable.

Brianna wore black leggings with a small tee shirt. Her slender limbs were long and sexy. Her hair was flawless. But she was so unsure of herself, her attractiveness sank from a 10 to a 7½.

"So, how'd it go?" she asked.

Donovan shrugged. "Okay, I guess."

"What's wrong?" Brianna asked. "You look upset. What'd she do?"

Donovan didn't think he was, but now that she mentioned it, he did feel a little gloomy.

"Just thinking about some stuff."

"About *her*?" Brianna's chest hitched.

Donovan already felt bad for Kyra. Now he had to offer more empathy to his girlfriend. "What are you so nervous about?"

73

"I've been going crazy," Brianna admitted. "I didn't know what was happening, on your little date. I imagined the worst things."

"Jeez, Brianna. This is why..." He caught himself.

"This is why what?" she demanded.

"Nothing."

"Are you going to tell me what happened with her or not?"

"Yes. Could we go inside, please?"

"Yeah," Brianna said. "I'm getting hot. I can tell you right now, I don't like this, Donovan. I don't like anything about it."

≈ ≈ ≈ ≈ ≈ ≈

When they got inside, Donovan gave his woman a long, comforting hug and they sat together on the sofa. He told her about his lunch with Kyra, from the moment he picked her up to the worry he felt when he dropped her off.

Brianna wanted more details, like what went through his mind when he saw Kyra and how he felt when they hugged. Donovan was as open as possible, but he drew the line at letting Brianna play psychiatrist.

When he was done talking, she asked the same question Kyra asked when Donovan dropped her off.

"Why do you feel like you have to do something to help her?"

"I don't know," Donovan said. "I just do."

He kicked off his church shoes and pushed them to the side of the coffee table. His tie and button-down were already draped over the arm of his recliner.

"That doesn't make sense," Brianna said. "I understand a friend wanting to help a friend, but you haven't heard from her in fifteen years. Why are y'all still so close?"

"I know," Donovan said. "No one does. You would have to understand what it was like when we were kids. What she and I went through together."

"Then tell me."

This is senseless, Donovan thought. There was nothing he could say that would make Brianna feel better about him spending time with Kyra or any other woman. But he didn't mind reliving some of the memories. Maybe if he talked about it out loud, he could help himself understand why he needed to be Kyra's guardian. Why him? Did God really assign Donovan this role, or did he take it upon himself, way back in the day when he was too young to know any better?

≈ ≈ ≈ ≈ ≈ ≈

He told Brianna about meeting Kyra in grade school. She was quiet and small for her age. Kyra didn't have nice clothes. Sometimes she came to school with her hair half done, like she styled it herself without an adult around to give her a once-over before she left the house. Kyra had a brother named Duke who was two years older. Her sister Jessica was a year older than Duke. Every now and then Kyra was fortunate enough to attend the same school as one of her siblings, but for the most part she was on her own.

Donovan and Kyra weren't in the same grade, either. They only saw each other at lunchtime and occasionally before or after school. The first time they spoke was during recess when Kyra was in the 3rd grade. Donovan noticed her walking alone near the gym while most of her peers were involved in games with at least one other person.

Donovan approached Kyra and asked if she wanted to play with his yo-yo. The smile that lit up her face changed Donovan's heart in ways he still didn't comprehend. He would never forget how awkward and vulnerable Kyra was. For the next twenty minutes Donovan's only intention was to keep a smile on the quiet girl's face. The following day he sought her out again with the same goal in mind.

The first time Donovan walked Kyra home from school, it was because a clique of bad girls tried to attack her. Kyra allegedly stole a dollar from one of them. Donovan was more sympathetic than upset when they arrived at Kyra's home and she admitted to stealing from her classmate's purse. Donovan gave her all of the money he had in his pocket (a buck fifty), and told her to ask him the next time she needed money. She never did, but Kyra would take a bag of chips or the desert from his lunch whenever Donovan offered.

What Donovan found most endearing about Kyra was the beauty and joy she possessed on the inside despite the obstacles in

75

her daily life. Kyra's mother, Deidra, smoked crack cocaine. Kyra never met her father. Kyra's brother Duke was a budding criminal, spending the bulk of his adolescence in juvenile detention centers and alternative schools.

Kyra's big sister, Jessica, had seen way too much. She was hardened and bitter about life. Jessica barely reacted to the hell their mom put them through. The only comfort she offered Kyra was the certainty that after awhile she'd get used to it.

With Donovan, Kyra found one person who never criticized her about her hand-me-down clothing or her dopefiend mom. Donovan was there for her when Kyra wanted to talk about the most dreadful situations, like when the dope boys came to her house and threatened to kill her mom over an unpaid debt. And Donovan had the *regular* life Kyra dreamed about every night. Donovan's father still lived with him, and his parents were married. There was food in the refrigerator at Donovan's house, and he even had cable television.

But the thing that made Kyra love Donovan so much was that he genuinely cared for her, though he had absolutely no reason to do so. Donovan never judged her. He rarely had solutions to her problems, but his encouragement lifted young Kyra's spirits.

"It won't be like this forever," he would tell her. "When you grow up, you'll have a normal family. Until then, you can come visit me whenever you want to. I'll help you anytime I can."

He was only a child himself, but Donovan was serious about being there for Kyra. The first time he helped her out of a jam was when she was in the 7th grade. Donovan was in the 8th. Kyra's mother's addiction was going strong, and she came up with a boneheaded idea to move a drug dealer into her home. In exchange for living there and selling dope out of the house, the dealer paid Deidra *rent*, which was never cash; always drugs.

The dealer was known as *FourFive*. He was 35 years old with long hair he kept in cornrows most of the time. He set up shop in Duke's room because Kyra's brother was locked up or running the streets most nights. FourFive was respectful of Kyra and her sister, but they feared for their safety the entire time he was there. FourFive had beef with several dealers in the city. There were more goons who wanted to take FourFive's life because he supposedly killed one of their relatives. FourFive didn't fear his enemies. His signature weapon, a .45 semi-automatic, was never out of reach.

Despite the obvious dangers, the main problem FourFive brought to Kyra's home was traffic. FourFive's new dope house was open twenty-four hours a day. Junkies knocked on the front door when the sun was up and went around back when it got dark outside. FourFive had two good friends who were always there. They played loud music and smoked weed into the wee hours of the morning. Sometimes they brought female crackheads inside for sex if the women couldn't afford their high.

After a month, FourFive was comfortable and established in his new spot. Unfortunately his new spot was Kyra's home, and she barely slept at night. Donovan listened to her complaints day after day. He walked Kyra home so he could see FourFive himself. Donovan knew the drug dealer was dangerous, and he was too young to tackle the problem on his own.

Without telling anyone, Donovan began making anonymous phone calls to the police regarding the drug activity on Bishop Drive. On his sixth call, Donovan was told that he had to give them his name and address if he wanted to file a formal complaint. Donovan was only 13 years old. He knew his information would be filed in a police report. He also knew that snitching was a capital offense on the streets of Overbrook Meadows.

But Donovan cared enough about Kyra to take the risk. Two days later a SWAT team invaded Kyra's residence while she was at school. When Donovan walked her home that day, her house was in disarray. The door had been kicked in. Every room was ransacked. Kyra's mother sat on the porch looking lost and depressed. Kyra's eyes lit up when she heard that FourFive was in jail, and he was never coming back.

Donovan didn't tell her that he was the one who summoned the police until the next day. Kyra hugged him so hard Donovan had to beg her to, "*Let me go. I can't breathe!*" Donovan waited three months before he told his mother about the incident. Beverly was furious. She truly disliked Kyra from that point on, but Donovan never doubted that he did the right thing.

≈≈≈≈≈≈≈

The second time Donovan put himself in harm's way on Kyra's behalf was in 1997. He was in the 10th grade at Finley High. Kyra was a freshman, and they were as thick as thieves. Kyra was doing well in school. She was even a better math student than Donovan. Typically the best friends went to Donovan's house after school to do their homework. Beverly wasn't happy about that, but she was supportive because it kept Donovan safe at home.

Kyra had developed most her womanly physique by then, and she had quite a few admirers, both in and outside of school. Donovan was not among them, and he didn't mind talking to Kyra about some of the boys she liked. She didn't tell Donovan about the one crush that made her uncomfortable until things nearly got out of hand. This admirer was bad news from the start because Marvin was already in a relationship with Kyra's mother. And he was 38 years old.

Sometimes, late at night, Marvin had a look in his eyes that chilled Kyra to her core. She was so frightened, she started barricading her bedroom door before she went to bed. Unfortunately she could only block her door with items she could lift or drag herself, and Marvin was much stronger than she was. He pushed her door open twice already. Kyra was awakened both times. She stared wide-eyed at the door, and she saw Marvin's ugly face in the opening. But he didn't walk in. Not yet anyway.

When Kyra finally told Donovan about the way her mother's boyfriend watched her and always felt the need to use the bathroom when she was in the shower, Donovan was upset that she didn't tell him sooner. His concern became anger when Kyra told him that she complained to her mother several times, but she wouldn't listen. Marvin was a dopefiend, too. He provided Deidra with a mostly free source of drugs. Kyra's mother wasn't willing to give that up just because her youngest daughter might get raped. Hell, a lot of things *might* happen.

Less than a week after Kyra confided in Donovan, her troubles at home reached a boiling point. Marvin broke through Kyra's barricade one night after he sent Deidra to score their next high. Egged on by the hard liquor he'd been consuming, Marvin stepped into Kyra's room for the first time and tried to pull the sheets off her body. She held on to them with all her might and screamed at the top of her lungs.

Spooked, Marvin retreated and didn't bother her anymore that night. Kyra lay in bed trembling until her mother returned. When she heard Deidra's voice, Kyra summoned the courage to confront Marvin in her mother's presence. But nothing happened.

Marvin said he thought Kyra barricaded the door so she could sneak out of her bedroom window. He said he lifted Kyra's sheet to if it was really her under there, rather than a pile of clothing. He said he was startled and confused by her scream. He never did anything to harm her. He didn't know why she didn't like him.

Surprisingly, Deidra sided with Marvin. She threatened to kick Kyra out if she continued to lie on her boyfriend. Deidra told Kyra to stop barricading her door at night. She said she wanted to be able to check to see if Kyra really was trying to sneak out of her room. Plus Kyra's barricade might prevent someone from saving her if there was a fire, Marvin added.

Kyra told Donovan what happened when she got to school the next morning. He was in a foul mood for the rest of the day. She had never seen his eyes so dark. The best buds usually went to Donovan's house after school, but he insisted on visiting Kyra's home instead. She was against it, but Donovan marched on alone when she tried to stop him. Kyra caught up and pleaded with him along the way.

Donovan was only sixteen at the time, but he'd been playing football since the fourth grade. He had the build of a college freshman. When they arrived at Kyra's house, Donovan knocked on the door while Kyra paced anxiously in the front yard. Marvin answered. His expression was quizzical. Donovan dropped his backpack and grabbed a fistful of the man's tee shirt. He yanked him out of the house so quickly, Marvin stumbled down the steps and face-planted on the dry lawn. Kyra screamed. Deidra rushed from the house, her eyes spooked from cocaine. She started yelling, too.

Marvin scrambled to his feet with anger quickly replacing his confusion. He went after Donovan with his fists raised. Kyra started crying. The difference between their sizes looked astronomical. Deidra demanded to know what was going on. Kyra wanted to know, too. She talked to Donovan about everything, and he never reacted like this.

"What the hell's your problem?" Marvin barked. His tee shirt was ripped. Dead blades of grass clung to his nappy hair.

"Quit messing with Kyra!" Donovan told him. He stood defiantly with his little fists balled.

Marvin shook off the rest of his shock and sneered at him. "Boy, I'll beat yo bitch ass!"

"Stop!" Kyra wailed. "Please, stop!"

"Come on!" Donovan said. "I ain't scared!"

"Get that boy away from my house!" Deidra shouted.

"*Come on, you pervert!*" Donovan yelled. His eyes were locked on Marvin's.

Kyra had never seen him fight before, but Donovan's boxing stance was official. For a brief moment she thought Donovan would be able to stand his own. But Marvin had been in plenty of fights during his life as a junkie. He grinned and closed the distance between them with quick, purposeful strides.

"You gon' do something about it, little punk?"

"Kyra, get that boy–"

WHAP!

Deidra was cut off by the sound of palm hitting cheek. Donovan didn't see it coming. And when it connected, he couldn't see anything past a blinding flash of red and white. Donovan stumbled backwards. The side of his face exploded with blistering pain. Kyra screamed again, and so did a couple of street people who were drawn to the fight like moths to a flame.

"You come to my goddamned house starting shit!"

PAP!

Marvin berated Donovan as he whooped him. But he wasn't fighting him like he would a man. The second blow was another slap that connected with the side of Donovan's head. His world spinning, Donovan dropped to one knee. He didn't feel the blood leaking from his split lip, and he couldn't hear any of the people shouting around him. Vaguely he caught sight of a loose brick in the lawn. He reached for it instinctively.

But Donovan's senses were slurred. His movements were telegraphed. Marvin saw him go for the weapon, and he decided to put an end to this. He reared back with his right leg, planning to punt the runt's face like a football, but Donovan's brain cleared up for a fraction of a second, and he saw the sneaker coming.

Donovan blocked the kick with his arms, and then he grabbed Marvin's leg and threw all of his weight at him.

Marvin fell to his back with the teenager on top. Donovan knew he'd lose the fight if he didn't take full advantage of his superior position. He swung blindly, as hard and as fast as he could. Marvin blocked the first eight punches, but the ninth one landed square on the chin. Donovan didn't notice Marvin's face grow slack, and he didn't see the man's eyes roll to the back of his head. Donovan did realize that all of his subsequent blows were landing flush, but he didn't slow up.

If I stop, he'll get me, he told himself. *If I stop, he'll get me.*

The warning played over and over in his head like a mantra. Donovan's heart was jack-hammering. Blood began to leak off his chin. He had Marvin fully mounted. The dopefiend's limbs were stretched limply in the grass. After five more blows, Donovan felt his fists starting to bleed. A few punches later, Donovan realized it was Marvin's face bleeding, not his hands.

By then Donovan knew the man was unconscious, but he was still too afraid to stop. The two blows Marvin delivered were the hardest Donovan had ever been hit in his life – and he knew the dopefiend wasn't really fighting him at the time. If he let up, Donovan fully believed Marvin would kill him. So he hit him again and again. He didn't stop swinging until one of the bystanders grabbed him from behind and pulled him off his opponent.

"Stop, man! You killing him!"

Donovan broke free of the stranger's grip, but he didn't go after Marvin again. Everyone could see that Kyra's tormentor was no longer a threat to her or anyone else – not for the rest of the day at least.

Kyra rushed to Donovan's side. He turned to retrieve his backpack while the crowd surrounded Marvin. Most gawked. A couple of people took pictures with a new gadget called a "camera phone." One person had the sense to roll Marvin onto his side so he wouldn't swallow his tongue while unconscious.

"Cuh, come on," Donovan told Kyra. His chest rose and fell rapidly. His face was a mess with sweat and blood. His hands and knuckles were throbbing with pain. But Donovan didn't acknowledge what just happened. "We gotta, we gotta go do our homework," he panted. "Go to my mama, go to my mama's house."

81

He started walking in that direction. Kyra was stunned stiff for a second, but she broke out of it and ran to catch up with him. Her mom yelled, "Kyra, where the hell you going?!" but she didn't slow up or even look back.

When they got to his house, Beverly nearly had a heart attack at the sight of her sweet baby. She didn't calm down much when Donovan told her why he had to fight. That night Beverly forbade Donovan from hanging around Kyra. But of course he wouldn't listen. He started taking Kyra to the library after school rather than bring her home. This was the first time he openly defied his mother. When Beverly found out, she was the one who conceded. She told Donovan to bring Kyra to their house after school like he'd been doing, so at least she would know where he was.

Kyra's mother didn't stop smoking crack after that, but they never saw Marvin again. Later, whenever Kyra tried to talk to Donovan about what happened, he downplayed his heroics. He didn't agree that he *put his life on the line* for her. But he didn't have to. Kyra saw it with her own eyes.

Donovan wasn't sure if fate led him to Kyra on the playground of Sunrise Elementary. But he knew that she needed him in her life. If he wasn't there for her, who would be? He couldn't think of one person.

≈≈≈≈≈≈

The house became completely silent when Donovan finished his story. Brianna stared at him, her heart fluttering in her chest. There were a million thoughts swirling through her head. She didn't want to vocalize most of the things her subconscious was telling her, but it was so black and white. There was no way she could pretend not to see.

"Donovan, tell me the truth. Do you love her?" Brianna felt her heart ripping in two before he opened his mouth to respond.

"I do love her. But it's not like you think. I'm not in love with her."

"But, how can that be? After all you've been through with her."

"If she was a boy, you wouldn't ask that."

"But she's not."

"Why can't a boy and a girl be close without falling in love?"

"I'm not saying it can't happen, Donovan. But I don't think it's possible with you two. I don't like this, Donovan. I don't like the idea of you hanging around other girls."

"I'm a teacher, Brianna. I'm around mostly women everyday."

"I know, and I don't like that, either," Brianna said frankly, as if it was the most normal thing in the world. "Tell me why your mother put her out."

Donovan's heart froze. *She knows.* A chill enveloped his whole body. But Brianna was worried and unsure, not accusatory. Donovan wanted to tell her about the kiss, but he knew she wouldn't believe it was a one time thing.

"I told you, my mom never trusted her."

"Then why would she let her live with y'all in the first place?" Brianna wondered. "That's a terrible thing to do to a child; take them in, and then kick them out after a few months."

"She didn't do it to be mean," Donovan said. "My mama wanted it to work. She gave it her best shot. But she thought me and Kyra were going to start *liking* each other. It started to drive her crazy. She couldn't do it. She thought she could, but she couldn't."

Brianna nodded slightly, and Donovan knew she accepted that. The lie made him feel sick to his stomach.

"Did Kyra come back to Texas for you?" Brianna asked.

Donovan's eyes lit up. He was happy he could be completely honest with this answer. "I asked her that today, and she said no."

"You asked her if she came back for you?"

"Yes," Donovan stated. "I asked her that exact question."

Brianna frowned. "Why did you ask her that? Did you want her to come back for you?"

"Now you tripping," Donovan said with a shake of his head. "You're on a fault finding mission."

"What if she said yes?" Brianna asked. "What if she did come back for you?"

"She didn't."

"But what if she did?"

"What if the world ends in an hour?" Donovan said. "I have no idea what I would do. Why are you worried about something that didn't happen?"

"You have no idea what you would do if Kyra said she came back for you?"

"Brianna, I'm with you. And I love you. I wouldn't leave you for Kyra – not even if she told me she came back for me. I'm not an asshole. Now please, stop."

He reached for her, and Brianna allowed him to pull her into his arms. Donovan's embrace was as warm and wonderful as it had ever been.

Despite what he told her, Brianna's vision blurred with tears. She knew it wasn't wrong for her to want him all to herself. The thought of losing this man was unbearable.

CHAPTER SEVEN
RUTH THE SCHEMER

The following Wednesday Donovan was surprised that there were no students waiting for him after football practice. There was usually at least one member of the team who needed tutoring or a ride home or just a man they could talk to about man stuff. Roughly half of Donovan's players lived in a home without a father-figure. Donovan didn't mind filling in the gap for them.

He called Kyra before he locked up the gym.

"Hello."

"Hi. Busy?"

"No," Kyra said, "just looking at this paper."

"How are the kids?"

"They're fine."

"Q started at Sunrise, didn't he?"

"Yeah, he started Monday. He likes it."

"I loved that school," Donovan said. "Do you remember when..." He trailed off because Kyra was giggling. "What?" Her laughter put a smile on his face.

"*Do you remember when*," Kyra said. "How many times have you said that since I've been back?"

Donovan chuckled. "I don't know. A lot, probably."

On Sunday night Donovan and Kyra stayed on the phone until well after midnight. Donovan paid for it the next morning when he had to get up at 6:30 for work, but he didn't mind the baggy eyes. He loved reliving the past with Kyra.

"Do I remember what?" she said.

"Forget it. I'm not telling you now."

"Come on."

"Uh-uhn. You shouldn't have laughed at me."

"Come on, Donovan. Now I'm gonna keep wondering what it was."

"Maybe later," he said. "Can I come over?"

"Yes. Why?"

"I want to bring you some papers I printed out. There are a few openings in the school district. I think you should apply for them."

"That's what I'm doing right now," Kyra said, "looking in the newspaper for a job."

"You see anything hopeful?"

"I found a lot of hopefuls. It's just a matter of whether I want to flip burgers or not."

"You don't want to flip burgers."

"Honestly, I wouldn't mind. I just need to save up some money so I can get out of here."

"That's fine, but you can't move out of your aunt's house with a minimum wage job," Donovan warned. "Unless you want to keep struggling, or stay on public assistance."

"I'm not tripping on public assistance," Kyra said. "I used to think I didn't want it, but now I don't care what it takes to get my own place."

"Why are you in such a rush," Donovan wondered. "Did something happen?"

"No." Kyra sighed. "Nothing in particular. It's an everyday thing, with my aunt."

"I'm on my way to bring you these papers. I'll be there in twenty minutes."

"Wait. I don't have anything to wear."

"What? Are you serious?"

Kyra's face grew warm. "I didn't bring a lot of clothes down here, Donovan. I had to make sure I got all of the kid's stuff first."

"What are you wearing now?" Donovan asked.

"Just some jeans and a tee shirt."

"Then you're fine. *I don't have anything to wear?..*" He frowned. "Kyra, that's ridiculous. You used to come to my house in flip flops and sweat pants."

"I'm not a little kid anymore."

"But you're still my best friend, and I don't care what you look like. I'm on my way."

He hung up, which was a good indication that was non-negotiable.

≈≈≈≈≈≈

Donovan knocked on Aunt Ruth's door twenty minutes later. Kyra answered wearing the blue jeans and tee shirt she promised. What she failed to mention was how well the outfit accentuated her figure. Her jeans weren't that tight, but her tee shirt was. It clung to her flat stomach and stretched over her perky bosoms.

Donovan's eyes widened. He already ironed out his feelings for Kyra, but every time he saw her she looked more stunning. *Why couldn't...*

"Thanks for stopping by." Kyra cut off his train of thought with not only her words. She also stepped to him and gave him a brief hug.

Why does he always smell so good? Kyra wondered as Donovan wrapped his arms around her. She knew that he showered after football practice, and he took the time to put on cologne. Or maybe it was just Axe body spray. Either way, Kyra found it irresistible.

Donovan wore a tee-shirt with canvas shorts today. His arms were as muscular as Kyra expected. His shoulders and biceps were incredible. He belonged on the cover of a Men's Health magazine. Each one of his pectorals was roughly the size of Kyra's head. She knew there was a nice crease between them. She couldn't see it, but she knew it was there.

When they separated, Kyra wondered how long these forbidden feelings would last. While it was natural for her to be attracted to a fine specimen of a man like Donovan, her conscious usually kicked in when someone was off limits. Surely she wouldn't have to go through this every time she saw him. No way was God that cruel!

"Kyra, you look beautiful," Donovan said. "Talking 'bout you don't have anything to wear."

"These jeans are a year old," she told him. "But thanks."

"I brought those papers I told you about," Donovan said.

Kyra took them and scanned the first page. "What do I do, go online to apply?"

"Yeah," Donovan said. "Have you applied for any jobs in the school district?"

Kyra shook her head.

"Then you'll have to set up an account," Donovan said. "It's pretty easy."

Kat took a step into the room, supporting herself with a hand on the doorframe.

"Hey, I didn't know she could walk," Donovan said. He grinned at the toddler. She really was precious, the spitting image of her mama.

"Of course she can walk," Kyra said. "Hey, bookie bookie." She went to retrieve the little girl. "Kat, you remember Mr. Donovan, don't you?"

The baby was not as shy today. She didn't smile at him, but she did look Donovan in the eyes.

"Hello again," he said. "I hope you're not afraid of little, old me."

He had the sweetest smile on his face. Kyra had never seen him with a child, but she knew he was good with babies.

"Hello, sir."

Donovan turned and saw Kat's older brother in the other hallway.

"Hey, what's going on, big man?" Donovan went and shook his hand casually. "I heard you're going to my old school."

Quinell nodded. "I go to Sunrise."

"You like it?"

Q smiled. "I like my teachers, so far."

"You know me and your mama climbed on top of that school one time?"

"Don't tell him that," Kyra said, but she was smiling. "I don't want him trying to do it hisself."

Quinell nodded. "She already told me."

"What?" Donovan gave Kyra a playful frown. "It's okay for you to tell him, but I can't?"

"I told him so he *wouldn't* try it," Kyra said.

"Yeah right," Donovan said. "Hey, have y'all eaten dinner yet? Wanna go to McDonalds?"

"Yeah," Quinell said.

But at the same time his mother said, "No, that's alright."

Quinell's smile fell.

"Come on, Kyra," Donovan said. "You already cooked dinner?"

"No, but we–"

"You might as well go," Aunt Ruth interrupted. "We 'bout out of food anyway."

Kyra's eyes flashed with humiliation and annoyance. She turned slowly towards her eavesdropping landlord. "Auntie, we do have something to eat in there."

She spoke calmly, but Donovan knew it was a strain. He felt like he stepped into an ongoing argument. Normally he would've backed out and let the women deal with it on their own, but he *really* wanted to get Kyra out of the house now, so she could tell him what was going on.

"Come on, y'all," he said and opened the front door. "Y'all ready? Where's your car seat, Kyra?"

"It's in the back of my car," Aunt Ruth said. "You can get it. The door's open."

"Okay, thanks." Donovan took a step outside and looked back at his best bud. "You coming?"

Kyra's nostrils flared. But other than that, she didn't look upset. "Yeah. Go put your shoes on, Q."

≈ ≈ ≈ ≈ ≈ ≈

Donovan paid for everyone's meal. Kyra appeared to be in a chipper mood until they finished eating and Quinell went to play video games. Kat headed for the bounce house.

"That was not cool," Kyra told Donovan when they were alone.

"I'm sorry," Donovan said. "Honestly, I didn't think it was a big deal."

"Not you. Her," Kyra said. "My damn aunt. Well, you too."

Donovan frowned. "What did I do?"

"Forcing us to come here with you."

"I didn't force you," he said with a chuckle.

"You didn't give me much of a choice. You were already going to get the car seat."

89

"Okay, I'm sorry. I only wanted to get you out of the house. Y'all looked like you were going to start arguing."

"I'm not mad at you," Kyra said. She sighed. "Thanks for bringing us. I'll pay you back."

"That's okay."

"No, for real."

"Kyra, I don't want you to pay me back, alright? You think I'm gonna hold fifteen dollars over your head?"

She shook her head. "Donovan... I don't mean to take it out on you."

"Tell me what's going on," he said, "with you and your aunt."

"She's trying to use me," Kyra stated. "And I don't have nothing. Ain't that something?" She laughed, but there was no humor in it.

"How is she using you?"

"She been bitching about me getting food stamps since I got here," Kyra explained. "We went to the welfare office on Monday. She woke me up at six o'clock, so we would be the first ones there. They gave me $300 on a EBT card. While we were there, Aunt Ruth started asking about other stuff, like if she can get money for letting me live with her."

"How does that work?" Donovan asked.

"It *doesn't* work," Kyra said. "At first she wanted to know if she could get money for being a foster parent for us."

Donovan narrowed his eyes.

"*Exactly!*" Kyra said. "They told her she couldn't be a foster parent because the children's mother – *that would be me* – is still taking care of them. They told her that's a totally different agency, anyway. And then she asked if she could get Section 8 money, like if she was renting her house to me."

Donovan's eyes narrowed even more.

"That's what I was looking like!" Kyra said. "I was thinking, *How you gon' bring me in here for food stamps and then start asking about all this other stuff?*"

"You asked her that?"

"I did when we got back to the car."

"What'd she say?"

"She said if they got money to give, why shouldn't she take it?"

90

Donovan shook his head, grinning. "I guess you can't blame her for trying."

"I can blame her if she's trying to use *my* kids for her scams."

Donovan wiped the smile off his face. "Okay. So you if you got groceries on Monday, why is she saying she doesn't have any food?"

"I don't know," Kyra said. "I think she sold those food stamps. I never saw her bring a bunch of groceries in."

"Didn't you get groceries when you left the welfare office?"

"No. Aunt Ruth said she had to run some other errands. She dropped us off first."

"Why didn't you keep the card, so you could get them yourself?"

"It's kinda hard to get $300 worth of groceries home on the city bus."

"Kyra, I'm trying to help you. Why you getting an attitude with me?"

"I'm sorry, Donovan." Her features softened. "I don't mean to. I get frustrated. You're the only person I can talk to about this stuff."

"It's alright," Donovan said. "Did you ask her what happened to your card?"

"I was going to, but you were there. I'll ask her when we get home."

Donovan thought for a second. He checked his watch. "Hey, let me take you to get some groceries when we leave here."

Kyra's mouth fell open. She shook her head emphatically. "No, Donovan."

"Kyra, stop it."

"No, that's not right."

"Why can't I buy you groceries?"

"'Cause she already got that card! She should've bought the damned groceries herself."

"So what do you wanna do, go home and argue with her? You gonna accuse her of selling the card? Is it really worth it? Kyra, you told me you don't have anywhere else to go."

"But that doesn't mean she can steal my money like that."

"You can't right all the wrongs in the world," Donovan said. "You just have to be the best person you can be and let God deal with everyone else. I'll get you some groceries today, and then when you get your card again, call me and I'll take you to get some more. That way it will always be food in the house for you and your kids."

Kyra's eyes glossed over. She looked towards the ceiling and managed to keep the tears in this time. "Why don't you take your own advice?" she asked when she met Donovan's eyes again.

"What do you mean?"

"You can't right all the wrongs in the world."

Donovan smiled. "I don't want to right all of them. Just yours."

Kyra's heart swelled with love and foreboding, but mostly love. "Do I remember what?" she said.

"Huh?"

"On the phone you asked if I remembered when... something. You said you'd tell me in person."

Donovan's smile grew broader. "Well, now I don't think it's appropriate."

"You said you would tell me."

Donovan snickered. He looked down at the table sheepishly. "I was gonna ask if you remembered when you stole Tabitha Spencer's dollar, and I had to walk you home because she and her friends wanted to beat you up..."

Kyra laughed at the memory. "I thought I told everybody I didn't do it."

"You did," Donovan said. He looked into her eyes. "Except me. You told me the truth."

He smiled. Kyra wanted to kiss him so badly right then. His lips had a magnetic force that was pulling her face straight to them.

Give it a few weeks, she told herself. *You'll be able to look at all of that delicious man flesh over there without batting an eye.*

"I could've beat Tabitha up," Kyra said. "If it was just her by herself."

"I know," Donovan said. "I never doubted that you could take care of yourself."

Kyra raised an eyebrow.

"It's true," Donovan said. "Now let's go get your groceries."

≈ ≈ ≈ ≈ ≈ ≈ ≈

Donovan took them to Kroger's and filled Kyra's basket with everything from fruits and vegetables to Totino's Pizza Rolls (Quinell's favorite). When they got to the register, Kyra felt sick to her stomach when Donovan swiped his debit card for the $174.35 total. It was one thing for Ruth to scheme the county out of welfare funds, but Kyra would be damned if her mean-spirited aunt would pull another slick one on Donovan.

Donovan noticed Kyra's unease as they stood at the register. He reached and put an arm around her. He gave her shoulder a reassuring squeeze. This was the first time he touched her outside of the hugs they exchanged in greeting. Kyra felt the same electricity she felt when they embraced on Sunday. She was comforted by Donovan's touch. His eyes told her, *Everything will be fine*, and Kyra believed him. As long as she'd known him, Donovan never let her down.

When they got home, the look on Aunt Ruth's face as Kyra, Donovan and Q brought in bag after bag of provisions was priceless. A few minutes later, Kyra couldn't help but grin at Donovan as she stood on the porch, bidding him farewell. Donovan stood in the lawn looking up at her.

"I like to see you happy," he said.

"I know," Kyra said. "You been telling me that for as long as I can remember."

"Don't forget to check out those papers I gave you," he said. "There's a lot of jobs in the school system that you don't need a degree for."

"I will," Kyra promised, then, "What's your girlfriend going to say about you spending $200 on me?"

"I reckon she won't like it," Donovan admitted. "I hope she doesn't ask."

"Aren't you going to tell her?"

"I, I don't think I'll volunteer the information," Donovan said. "Why, do you think I should?"

Kyra shrugged. "I don't know. That's *your* woman. I just don't want her getting mad at me, like I'm the one who told you to do it."

Donovan laughed softly. "I don't think she can dislike you any more than she already does."

Kyra pondered his dilemma. "Nope. I wouldn't be able to do it."

"Do what?"

"Let my man spend time with another woman like that. Like *this*. If I had a man."

"What if she was your boyfriend's best friend?"

"I don't care who he said she was. Ain't no haps."

"What if you still lived in Arkansas," Donovan ventured, "and I was the one who came to your city. And I looked you up on Facebook, and I didn't have any friends in Little Rock except you. You wouldn't spend time with me?"

Kyra smiled big and bright. "Of course I would!"

"What if your boyfriend told you not to hang around me?"

She smacked her lips. "Please. If he don't like it, he don't have to stay with me. I wouldn't choose him over you."

Donovan's heart glowed. "But you just said–"

"I said I wouldn't let my man do it," Kyra stated. "I never said I wouldn't do it myself, if I was in your position."

"So you understand why I'm here."

"Yes. But what if your girlfriend decides to put her foot down, like I would?"

"Well, I hope she will understand that I can't turn my back on someone I've known ten times longer than I've known her."

"I don't wanna be the cause of your relationship going bad," Kyra said. She wasn't smiling now.

"If it goes bad, I assure you you're not the only cause," Donovan said as he headed to his truck. "I'll call you tomorrow."

"Wait."

Donovan looked back, and his eyes bulged at the sight of Kyra hopping off the porch. Her breasts were 100% real. They had plenty of bounce to them.

Wow.

She ran up and gave him a big hug.

"Thank you, for everything."

Donovan thought he had things under control, but the feel of her boobs pressed against his torso sent a jolt from his chest, down his stomach and right between his legs. He pushed her away gently when he felt himself becoming aroused.

Why is this happening?

"Girl, get those things off me," he joked.

"What?" Kyra said, and then she looked down at her chest. "Boy, shut up." She giggled as she pranced back to the porch.

Donovan saw that her body was bouncy in the front and in the back.

"I can't help the way God made me," Kyra said, and she slipped inside the house.

No, you certainly can't, Donovan agreed. *And I thank Him. Well, not me, but some lucky guy will!*

CHAPTER EIGHT
THE ALMOST ULTIMATUM

Donovan called Brianna on his way home from Kyra's house. She tried to reach him when he was at McDonalds, but Donovan didn't answer. He sent her straight to voicemail. He was surprised Brianna only sent him two text messages since then. The first one read: Still at practice? In the second one she asked: Where are you?

Brianna answered her phone on the second ring.

"Donovan?" She sounded worried.

"Hey, baby. What's up?"

"What's going on?" she asked. "Where are you? Did practice run long?"

It was 8:30 pm. Donovan kept his team on the field as late as 7:00 pm every now and then, but that was not the norm. He figured he could tell Brianna, *Yes, that's exactly where I was*, and they'd get through this day without an argument. But Donovan didn't want to lie. He never liked being dishonest, especially with a girlfriend. It was bad enough he hadn't told Brianna about his and Kyra's ill-fated kiss. Donovan didn't want to get into a pattern of telling half truths where Kyra was concerned.

He bit the bullet and said, "I just left Kyra's house."

Brianna mulled that over for a moment. "What did you go over there for? How long have you been there? Why didn't you answer your phone when I called?"

Donovan sighed. Was this it? His next answer could end their relationship or lead to one of the biggest fights they ever had.

96

Was Kyra worth it? Donovan answered his question before it even sank in. Of course she was.

"I didn't answer when you called because I knew you'd give me the third degree, and I didn't want to go through that while Kyra was sitting there. I don't want her to know how bad things are between us; how much you don't trust me."

"You put your phone on silent?"

"No, I just didn't take your call."

"Because of her?"

"Because I didn't want to argue in front of her, yes."

"What'd you go over there for? I don't want you going over there."

"I had to take her some papers about some jobs I think she should apply for."

"What jobs?"

"In the school district."

"So now you're trying to get her a job, so y'all can work together? I don't like this, Donovan."

"No, not with me. Just somewhere in the district."

"And you couldn't have *called* her and told her about those jobs?"

Donovan grunted. He wanted to tell her to get off his damn back. But a part of him still felt that her curiosity was warranted. If Brianna started to pal around with an old guy friend, Donovan figured he'd interrogate her as well – but not like this.

"Yes I could've called her," he said. "But Kyra doesn't have a computer. I wanted to give her the papers so she would know the exact job titles and reference numbers and stuff."

"You couldn't have read that to her on the phone?"

"I suppose so. And do you see why I didn't answer when you called? You think I wanted to answer all of these questions while I was with her?"

Brianna ignored his comment and pushed forward with her inquisition. "If you could've read it to her on the phone, why'd you go over there? Why didn't you call me *first* and tell me you wanted to go over there."

"It would've took too long to read all of that. And I didn't realize I needed your permission to get in my car and drive somewhere."

Brianna ignored his sarcasm. "Did you want to see her?"

That question had plenty of obvious and hidden booby traps. Donovan didn't want to go anywhere near it.

"I told you why I went over there."

"What time did you get there?"

Donovan pursed his lips. He'd been fair and open, but she wasn't letting up. How much more of this did she think he would put up with? Brianna heard him exhale roughly.

"You don't wanna answer my questions?" she asked.

"Who the hell *would* want this, Brianna? I'm not in jail. I don't have to put up with—"

"Yes you do have to answer my questions, Donovan! I'm letting you spend time with that, that—"

"Be real careful," Donovan warned.

"What?"

"I don't know what you're about to call her, but you should be real careful."

"What? What the?..." Brianna lost it.

Donovan heard her sniffling. She uttered a soft wail that was drowned in grief. It broke Donovan's heart to hear her like that. He didn't think he was a bad person. And he didn't think he'd done anything wrong with Kyra. But there was no doubt he was hurting his woman. He had a strong urge to end their relationship right now, so at least he wouldn't cause her anymore pain.

"*Why are you so worried about her?*" Brianna cried. "*What about **me**, Donovan? What about your girlfriend? Do you care anything about me?*"

She was full-out crying now. Her words cut like a knife. Donovan winced and found himself doubting his decisions. Was he doing Brianna wrong? Was it okay for him to care about and spend time with Kyra? Even Kyra said she couldn't do it, if she was in Brianna's shoes.

Donovan accepted that he wasn't handling this situation well, but he also wasn't doing the things Brianna thought he was. He had no intention of starting a relationship with Kyra. And nothing he'd done for Kyra was to impress her or make her want to be more than friends. He was attracted to Kyra, at times, but he wouldn't make a move on her – not even if he was single.

His mind made up, Donovan knew it was time to take a hard line with his woman. Kyra thought Brianna would be the one to put her foot down. But Donovan knew he had to do it himself.

"Stop crying, Brianna. I do care about you."

"*No you don't!*"

"Yes I do. But you're too upset to talk. I'm going to hang up the phone."

"*Don't hang up on me!*"

"Brianna, if you want to talk about this in a calm manner, I'll try my best to explain the situation again. But right now you're not listening. You're mad, and I understand that. I think you need time to cool down."

This was how Donovan spoke to his students when they got out of line. He didn't think it would work on an adult, but Brianna tried to get herself together. She stopped sniveling and gradually her breathing slowed.

"Where are you? Are you almost home? I want to come over."

"No," Donovan said. "I don't want to see you tonight."

"Wh, *why*?"

"Because I don't like this pattern," Donovan said. "I don't think you need to see me every time you get upset."

"But I want to see you," Brianna said. "*I do need to see you, Donovan!*"

"It's almost nine o'clock on a Wednesday night," he reminded. "We both got work tomorrow. You need to try to get some sleep. And I do, too."

"*Donovan, please...*"

"No, Brianna. Damn!"

"Is, is she still with you?"

"Who?"

"You know who."

Donovan took the phone away from his face and stared at it. He almost hung up on her. "You're asking if I'm taking Kyra home with me?" he growled.

After a pause Brianna said, "Are you?"

Donovan took a deep breath, realizing he needed to calm down just as much as she did. "I'm going to hang up now," he said. "But for the record, *no*, I'm not taking Kyra home with me. She's just my friend. And also, for the record, I'm not going to stop being her friend just because it hurts you. You need to accept that she's not a threat, and she's not going away. And you need to make a decision: Do you still want to be with me, or not?"

"I don't think I can do it."

Donovan's whole body went cold. He had been with this woman for eight months. Brianna was needy, but she loved him dearly. But lately Donovan wondered if Brianna had the wrong kind of love. Sick, obsessive love is not good for anyone.

"Why don't you think about it and let me know tomorrow."

"I want you to stop seeing her."

"I can't do that," Donovan said.

"If you don't stop, then I can't be with you."

There it was. He forced her hand, and Brianna gave him the ultimatum he'd been dreading. Donovan gave his response all the reverence it deserved, but his feelings didn't change.

"I'm sorry to hear that. I guess we have to break up then."

"*No!*"

Donovan frowned. That wasn't one of the replies he expected. What did she mean *no*?

"What do you mean?"

"I don't wanna leave you," Brianna cried. "*I never want to lose you!*"

Donovan exited the freeway with his eyes narrowed in confusion. How does someone not let you break up with them? And *never want to lose you* sounded a little psycho.

"Brianna, this ain't working out."

"*Please, let me come over there,*" she begged.

"No. Why would... No, Brianna."

"Then let me think about it," she said. "I don't wanna lose you, Donovan. Okay?"

That actually was not okay. Donovan felt like he was free from her tears and accusations just a few seconds ago. Was she trying to get back with him already? He wanted to tell her no, but there was a chance Brianna could change. It was a long shot, but they had been together for eight months. She deserved another chance.

"Alright," he said. "I gotta go now."

"Donovan, wait."

"No, Brianna. I'm getting off the phone. For real this time."

"Call me before you go to bed."

"Okay, bye."

He disconnected and drove the rest of the way home with his radio off. Donovan was a spiritual man, and he knew he didn't have to be in church to have a powwow with his maker.

"If I'm wrong, God, please tell me." He spoke aloud in the quiet confines of his truck. "I don't think I'm wrong, but she makes me feel like I am. You know I don't want to hurt her. I don't wanna hurt nobody..."

≈ ≈ ≈ ≈ ≈ ≈ ≈

When he got home, Donovan took his dogs Wyatt and Doc for a two mile jog. He didn't normally run at night, but working out had always been his best stress reliever. The night air was warm, but there was a decent breeze blowing in from the north that cooled the sweat on his face and chest.

When he returned to the house, Donovan felt a lot better about his argument with Brianna. He had a sense of peace, knowing that whatever happened with them was meant to be. He took another shower and crawled into bed at eleven o'clock wearing only his boxers.

He had already dozed off when his phone rang at eleven-thirty. He reached for his cellular and frowned at the bright display. He forgot to call Brianna before he went to bed, and she was no doubt upset about it. But the incoming call was from Kyra, not his girlfriend. Donovan's aggravation quickly dissipated.

"Hey."

"Hey," she said. "You sleep?"

"I was laying down."

"I'm sorry. I be forgetting you have to wake up early. I can let you go."

"No, it's cool. What's up?"

"Nothing," she said. "Just sitting here watching TV. I can't sleep."

Kyra's voice was calming. Donovan didn't think they'd ever had a real argument. He rolled to his side and closed his eyes. "The kids up, too?"

"No, they're in there sleep. I had to come in the living room so I wouldn't wake them up."

"What's up with your aunt? Did y'all have it out when I left?"

"No. I did like you said," Kyra replied. "I didn't even ask about the food stamp card I gave her. I did tell her not to disrespect me in front of my company, though."

Donovan grinned. "What'd she say?"

"Nothing. What could she say? She know she wrong."

"Cool. I'm glad that worked out."

"What about your girlfriend?" Kyra asked. "Is she mad at you?"

"No. Why you say that?"

"That wasn't her who called while we were at McDonalds?"

Donovan chuckled. "How'd you know?"

"I saw the look on your face," Kyra said. "I figured it was either her or your mom. Did you tell her where you were?"

"Yeah. I don't lie to her, well I try not to."

"You told her about the groceries?"

"No."

"Was she okay, though, about you coming by here?"

"Don't worry about it," Donovan said. "That's *her* problem. It doesn't have anything to do with you."

"Alright." Kyra had so much to say about Donovan's woman. And she wanted to know exactly what the long-haired beauty had been saying about her since she returned to Overbrook Meadows. She knew she could get Donovan to tell her. But Kyra also knew that any advice she gave him about his girlfriend was biased at best and out of line at worst. She decided to stay out of it completely.

"Do you remember when Bo robbed that ice cream truck?" she asked instead.

Donovan laughed. That incident occurred when they were in middle school. Bo was a knucklehead, had been since he was in diapers. He was only thirteen when he told Donovan and Kyra that he planned to rob an ice cream truck with a pellet gun that was so realistic it looked like a 9mm. Donovan thought he was pulling their leg until they heard an ice cream truck round the corner a few minutes later. Bo took off in its direction with the fake pistol in his pocket.

"You know he's in prison now," Donovan told Kyra.

"No, but I'm not surprised," she said. "What'd he go for?"

"Robbery," Donovan said. "It was another ice cream truck."

"Nuh-uhn!"

"For real." But Donovan couldn't keep a straight face. "Nah, I'm just kidding."

"I knew you was lying!" Kyra cracked up. "Do you remember his sister? You know she used to like you."

"Ewww, stinky Stacy?" Donovan hadn't thought about her in years.

"Yeah!" Kyra laughed. "She always used to come around when y'all were playing street football. She used to sell candy that she stole from the grocery store. I wonder what happened to her."

"Stacy got married to a dope boy," Donovan informed. "She had four kids by him, and she had the nerve to look surprised when the police kicked in their door and hauled her man off to jail. Funny thing is, I taught Stacy's oldest boy when he was a freshman. I had to go to her house a couple of times because of his attendance."

"Did she remember you?"

"She did," Donovan said. "While I was there, she started flirting with me. It was sad, to see her down and out like that."

"I've been there," Kyra said. "Hell, I'm there right now."

"At least you still have hope," Donovan countered. "And you want your kids to do well. That's one thing that separates you from women like Stacy..."

≈≈≈≈≈≈

The best friends were still on the phone an hour later. Talking to Kyra was the highlight of Donovan's day. He missed having a friend he could say anything to. Kyra was eager to hear about everything she missed when she went to Arkansas. She listened to Donovan's stories in wide-eyed amazement.

Donovan didn't realize how late it was until he received another call. He glanced at the caller ID and got a sinking feeling in his gut.

"Damn."

"What's wrong?" Kyra asked.

"Brianna's calling me. I was supposed to call her before I went to sleep, but I forgot."

"Ooh. You in trouble."

"I know. Thanks."

"I'm sorry. Don't tell her you were on the phone with me. Good night."

"Goodnight," Donovan said and accepted his other call. "Hello?"

"What you doing?"

"Brianna?" She sounded so stuffy, Donovan wasn't sure it was her.

"I thought you were going to call me before you went to bed." Her voice was rich with sorrow.

"I'm sorry. I forgot," Donovan said. "What's wrong? Have you been crying?"

"What were you doing?" she asked, ignoring his question. "Were you asleep?"

"No, I was..." Donovan stared into the darkness. Once again the little devil on his shoulder urged him to lie. But Donovan's conscious was already eating him up because he didn't tell Brianna about buying Kyra groceries. If he continued to hold things back from her, that would mean he and Kyra did have something secret going on.

"I fell asleep, but Kyra called and woke me up. I was talking to her." Donovan's heart raced while he waited for a response. Brianna didn't say anything right away, but Donovan noticed her breathing became labored. "I'm sorry," he said. "I know I should've called you before I went to sleep. I don't want you to think I was talking to her instead of you on purpose."

Brianna's breath hitched. Donovan could hear the moisture in her nose. He rubbed his face, his expression pained. Earlier he asked God for a sign. Surely this was it. Brianna's suffering was God's way of telling him to end their relationship, because for whatever reason she was unwilling to do it herself.

"Look, Brianna, I'm sorry, but we—"

"It's okay," she said.

"Huh?"

"That you were talking to her. It's okay. I understand."

Bewilderment replaced Donovan's worry. "Obviously it's not okay, Brianna, if you're crying like this."

"I've been thinking about it," she said. Her voice was grief-stricken, but he could tell she was trying to be strong. "I thought I couldn't be with you anymore. I was ready to let you go. But I took some time to really think about it, and I realize it's *me* not you. I'm worried about your friend because I don't trust you around her. But you never gave me any reason not to trust you. I've been acting like a fool. I know Kyra needs to be in your life, and I won't say anymore negative things about her. I'm the one who has to change, not you. I love you, Donovan. I don't want to lose you."

What? Donovan sat up in bed, blinking wildly. *Did she just stop me from breaking up with her twice in four hours?* He almost told her *Nah, it's too late for that*, but how coldhearted would that be?

If Brianna was willing to accept his friendship with Kyra, maybe she could shed her jealous ways entirely. That's all he ever wanted. It was now up to Donovan to make sure his and Kyra's relationship remained as innocent as he described it. He had to put an end to the attraction he sometimes felt towards his best friend. And he had to be completely honest about *all* of their interactions from now on.

"Okay, baby. That's great. That's a big load off my shoulders."

"I know it is. I'm sorry I put you through this."

"Alright. I gotta go to bed now. Do you wanna have dinner tomorrow?"

"Yes. That would be nice."

"I'll give you a call after work. I'll end practice early."

"Okay."

"Goodnight, baby."

"I love you." *And I never want to lose you!*

"I love you, too," Donovan said. "Talk to you later."

CHAPTER NINE
MOTHER KNOWS BEST

A week and a half later the blistering heat of summer was still blazing a path through the Lone Star State. But there was a change in the air. The Dallas Cowboys were midway through their preseason games, which was a welcome precursor to Donovan's favorite time of year: Football Season.

Within a month cool winds from the north would drop the average temperatures in Central Texas a full twenty degrees. The pecan and oak trees would liven up their wardrobe with dashes of yellow and orange, and every Friday night fans would flock to the high school football stadiums to cheer their team.

Donovan loved football as a child, he loved it as a player, and he was still in love with the sport as a coach, even though his Mad Stallions were off to a 0-3 start this year. Donovan knew winning wasn't everything, but it did mean a lot to a lot of people. Thankfully he took the Stallions to the state championship three years ago, so the Western Hills boosters weren't coming down too hard on the coach. They understood that great players will eventually graduate and move on to bigger and better things. Another great player is not promised with the new batch of incoming freshmen.

One person who did blame Western Hills' coach for this season's pitiful start was the coach's very own mother, Ms. Beverly Mitchell. She sat behind a plate of rotisserie chicken, macaroni and cheese and broccoli and gave Donovan suggestions for how he could turn things around. Donovan listened politely because his mother probably knew more about football than he did. Beverly was a fan before his birth, and she never missed a game when her son played for Finley High. When Donovan returned to Overbrook Meadows and took a position at Western Hills, his mother started attending every game he coached. Neither rain nor icy roads could keep Beverly away.

The date was Sunday, September 20th. Donovan took his mother to church and was pleased to dine with her afterwards at Golden Corral. Donovan didn't think he would implement any of the changes she suggested for the team, but he admired his mom's tenacity. He grinned at her over his meatloaf.

"Don't look at me like that," Beverly told him. "I know you're not listening to me."

"I am listening."

"Well, are you going to start that funny-looking boy or not?"

The funny-looking boy was Patrick Miles. He was the best running back at the school, hands down. But Donovan kept him on the bench for most of their last game because Patrick thought it was fun to pick on people.

"Patrick knows what he has to do to get his starting spot back," Donovan said.

"You said he was passing his classes and coming to practice," Beverly recalled. "What does it matter if he picked on a few people?"

"Bullying is a big deal these days, Mama. Who knows where it could lead?"

"If it was that bad, they would've kicked him out of school by now," Beverly noted.

"No, it's not that bad," Donovan agreed. "But last week Patrick was picking on my quarterback after practice. That first fumble last game was because they don't get along. If Patrick doesn't want to be a leader *on and off the field*, then he can ride that pine, 'til he grows up a little more."

"And while he's *riding that pine*, your record is getting worse and *worse*."

Donovan laughed. "Mama, did you bet money on us or something?"

"No, of course not," Beverly said. "I just don't like to lose. You know that. I don't like to be sitting up in them stands when those dumb parents start talking about the team. They talk about you, too. This Friday I had half a mind to sock one of them."

The thought of Beverly sticking up for him like that made Donovan laugh again.

"You'd better pull out at least an *even* record," Beverly threatened, "while you're over there laughing."

"Yes, Ma'am. We'll get things turned around."

"Does this got something to do with your two girlfriends?" Beverly asked. "Is that why you're not focusing on the team?"

"That's cold, Mama."

"Whatever, Donovan. I know they been running you ragged. You know it, too."

That was true, but "Kyra's not my girlfriend, Mama. We're just friends. I finally got Brianna to come around, and you should, too."

"Come around to what, Donovan? Come around to accepting her? I did that once before. Remember? Remember what happened when I trusted Kyra?" She fixed a hard gaze on him.

Donovan looked away.

Beverly rolled her eyes. "Did you find her a job yet?"

"No," Donovan said. "But I did find her a car. And she applied for a few jobs with the district. I think she'll get a call back from at least one of them."

"You found her a car?"

"Yeah, I did. We picked it up Thursday."

"You bought that woman a car?" Beverly was incredulous.

"No, I didn't buy it, Mama. I found a charity organization that donates cars to, you know, poor families. I got Kyra an application, and she qualified. They gave her a '99 Escort. The fuel pump didn't work. Had to get it towed to the shop, but we should get it out this week."

"I hope you're not paying for that repair bill..."

"Mama, you know Kyra doesn't have any money. Who else would pay for it?"

Beverly put her fork down and stared at her plate in disgust. Donovan knew it wasn't the food she was upset with. "And when were you planning on telling me all of this?"

"I just did," Donovan said. "But to be honest, Mama, it's none of your business." He downed a spoonful of potatoes and meatloaf and smiled at her, hoping to soften the sting from his comment.

"You're right." Beverly nodded. "It is none of my business. But you're my son, and I'm not going to stop caring about your well-being."

"I know," Donovan said. "And I appreciate that."

"I won't stop trying to warn you when you're about to fall off a cliff, either."

"I know," Donovan replied. "But maybe you should, especially if that cliff is all in your head."

Beverly cleared her throat and took a sip of tea. "So how much are you spending on Kyra's auto repairs?"

"That's none of your business, Mama," Donovan said, still eating.

Beverly took a long inhalation through her nostrils. Donovan pretended not to notice.

"Aren't you gonna finish eating?" he asked her.

"No, son. I'm not hungry anymore."

Donovan chuckled. "Mama, you tripping."

"How much time are you spending with Kyra?" she asked. "Do you talk to her every day?"

Donovan nodded. "Yeah, I think so."

"And you see her, too?"

"Not that much," Donovan said. "Maybe once or twice a week."

Beverly gasped.

"That's only because we've been taking care of this business with the car and her applications," Donovan explained.

"And you've been giving her money?"

He shook his head. "No, Mama."

"That girl never asked you for money?"

"She never asked me for anything. She thinks I'm doing too much as it is."

"And Brianna? I guess you're keeping all this secret from your girlfriend?"

Donovan smiled. "No, Mama. I don't keep secrets. Brianna knows about everything. It used to be a problem, but it's not anymore. I don't hide anything from her. I feel free."

His mother stared at him in awe. "*Free?*"

"Free to be Kyra's friend, without it interfering with my relationship with Brianna."

"I can't believe this, Donovan."

"I know. It's crazy. I never would've thought it possible."

"Brianna knows you go over to Kyra's house?"

"Yep."

"And the job? And the car? You told Brianna you bought Kyra a car?"

"I told you; I didn't buy Kyra a car. She got it for free. I'm just paying the repair bill."

"Which is how much?"

"Not that much."

"Did you tell Brianna how much it was?"

"Yes."

"And she's okay with it?"

"Yeah. It's not like I asked *her* for the money."

Beverly was baffled. "I don't understand this, Donovan. How can Brianna be cool with all of this?"

"She trusts me." That wasn't true, but Donovan kept a straight face when he said it.

"She's not a stupid girl," Beverly said, lost in her own thoughts. "I like Brianna. She's so smart – and *beautiful*! That girl is drop dead gorgeous, Donovan. Why would she let you carry on with another woman like that? Do, doesn't she know you're working on her replacement; getting Kyra all fixed up so she can slide right into Brianna's spot?"

Donovan laughed. "That's not what's happening, Mama. I'm, honestly I can't believe you think so little of me. I'm not the kind of guy who would do something like that. And Brianna's not that great of a catch. I know you want me to marry her, but you got to believe me when I tell you that girl has issues."

"I'd have issues too if my man was running around town, flaunting his girlfriend, claiming they just friends."

"No, Mama. Brianna had issues *way* before Kyra came back. That's why I didn't want to move in with her. She's insecure and jealous as hell."

Beverly raised an eyebrow.

"As *heck*," Donovan conceded. "But as far as Kyra, don't think we came to this understanding without a lot of arguing and crying."

"Donovan, I know you're not gonna leave Brianna over that, that..."

"Don't do it."

"Over *Kyra*," Beverly said. "I know you're not going to leave Brianna over Kyra."

"If Brianna didn't stop tripping about her, then yes, I would have. I almost broke up with her twice. But it wasn't so I could start a relationship with Kyra. Me and Kyra are just friends."

Beverly was clearly in shock about all of this. Donovan didn't know why she found it so hard to believe.

"Do you have any idea what you're doing?" his mother asked. "Brianna has everything you need in a wife. Kyra has absolutely *nothing*. She ain't got two dimes to rub against each other."

"Regardless of what happens with me and Brianna, I'm not interested in Kyra," Donovan insisted.

"What do you mean *regardless of what happens*? Are you still thinking about breaking up with her?"

Donovan shrugged. Brianna did tolerate his and Kyra's friendship, but she did so grudgingly. She was like a ticking time bomb. Donovan sensed they were headed for another meltdown.

"What about the kiss?" Beverly asked. "If you're so honest with Brianna, then surely you told her about you and Kyra's kiss..."

Donovan lost half of his confidence in the blink of an eye. "I, well, we uh..."

Beverly shook her head slowly.

"That was a one time thing," Donovan stated. "And it was a long time ago. It's in the past, Mama. Let it go."

"If it's not a problem, why don't you tell Brianna?"

"I don't see the point in that."

"There's a reason you won't do it," Beverly speculated.

"Is there any chance that if I don't ask you what the reason is, you won't tell me?"

Beverly's eyes narrowed. It was a look that used to incite fear when Donovan was a child. It still scared him a little today.

"Don't sass me, boy."

"Yes, ma'am."

Beverly never finished her comment, and she only picked at the rest of her meal. Donovan wished he didn't have to disappoint his mother, but he didn't feel too bad when he dropped her off thirty minutes later. As a matter of fact, he felt pretty good about his life.

Donovan already stood up to Brianna in regards to Kyra, and now his mother knew where he stood as well. Beverly responded with her typical drama, but Donovan knew that eventually she would accept his decision and love him anyway. She had no choice. He was her only child, after all.

≈≈≈≈≈≈

Donovan hadn't made it home yet when he got a call from his girlfriend. He didn't think anything of it, although Brianna rarely called him at this time of day. She knew this was when he spent time with his mom.

"Hey, baby." Donovan answered the phone happy and full from his buffet at Golden Corral. Brianna changed his mood entirely with just seven words:

"Why did your mom kick Kyra out?"

Donovan played dumb, but already knew what had transpired. "Wh, what you mean?"

"When you were in high school," Brianna said. "You told me Kyra lived with you, and your mom put her out. I asked why she put her out, and you didn't tell me the truth. I want you to tell me the truth now. Why did your mom kick Kyra out?"

Brianna was mostly calm, but her breaths came hard through her nostrils. It sounded like she was speaking through clenched teeth. Donovan knew a huge part of his life was about to change, but he wasn't as upset as he thought he would be.

"Why are you asking me this?"

"Why are you not answering the question?"

"Did you, have you talked to my mother?"

"She just called me," Brianna hissed.

Donovan felt his anger rising, but he wasn't upset with his girlfriend. "So what happens now?" he said.

"You haven't answered my question!"

"Brianna, I don't want to argue. I'm sorry I didn't tell you the whole story."

"You're sorry? *You're sorry*? Is that all you have to say for yourself? *You lied to me, Donovan!* All this time, you *been* lying!" She was crying now.

Donovan stared at the road until his vision blurred. "I'm on my way home. If you want to—"

"I'm on my way over there!" Brianna yelled and hung up on him.

Donovan took a few calming breaths before he called his dear, old ma.

"Hello?"

"Why, Mama?"

"Because you can't keep lying to that poor girl, Donovan. Brianna loves you, and I like her. She wants to get married – right now. Did you know that? She has her own house and her own car and a good job in Dallas. I don't know why you wanna mess that up over somebody like *Kyra*."

"It's not your business what I do what my life!" Donovan snapped.

"Boy, don't raise your voice at me."

"Or what, Mama? You got some more skeletons you wanna drag out of the closet?"

Beverly was stunned silent.

"You don't have the right to interfere with my relationships!" Donovan barked, a lot more aggressively than he meant to. He caught himself before he got too out of line. "I don't know what you thought was going to happen–"

"I want somebody to put an end to this Kyra nonsense!" Beverly cried. "I been telling you to leave that girl alone since you was a little boy, Donovan. Why won't you listen? I'm not scared to admit when I need some help. I was hoping that if Brianna knew how you and Kyra really feel about each other, maybe she can say something that will make you come to your senses."

"You don't know how me and Kyra feel about each other!" Donovan shouted. "Even if we were doing something wrong – *which we aren't* – you don't have the right to butt into my life like that! What is it gonna take to get that through to you? Maybe it's my fault for telling you so much in the first place. Maybe I shouldn't call you at all."

Donovan was bluffing, but Beverly didn't know that.

"I, I'm sorry, Donovan. I didn't mean any harm." Beverly was frightened and uncharacteristically demure.

Donovan knew he couldn't hold a grudge against his mom, but he let her simmer on the hot seat, so she would know how royally she screwed up this time.

"Bye, Mama," he snapped.

"Donovan, wait. What are you gonna do?"

"Why should I tell you? So you can run and tell my business again?"

"Donovan, I said I was sorry. Please don't be angry with me."

"Alright, fine, Mama. I gotta go. I'll talk to you later."

"Will you call me today, to let me know what happened?"

"I'll call you when I'm not mad anymore. Better yet, I'll call you when you stop hating on Kyra. How about that? Goodbye!"

Donovan disconnected. He was pretty sure God didn't approve of him hanging up on his mother, but damn it felt good.

CHAPTER TEN
LIAR LIAR

Donovan pulled into his driveway ten minutes later. He barely had time to change out of his church clothes and feed the dogs before Brianna rang the doorbell. Donovan answered wearing canvas shorts with a tee shirt. Brianna wore tight Capris with a little, pink tee shirt that showed her midriff. She didn't have on any makeup, but her hair was flawless. And to Donovan's surprise, she wasn't crying. She looked angrier than a swarm of killer bees, but her eyes were dry and piercing. Overall, she looked very sexy.

Donovan stepped aside and Brianna sauntered into the living room. She had the air of a woman who finally had the confidence and ammunition she needed to accomplish her goals. She'd been thwarted multiple times in the past, but the cat was out of the bag now. Donovan lied to her, and she had him dead to rights.

The situation with Kyra had been a thorn in her side from the moment Donovan mentioned her wretched named. *We're best friends. She's like my little sister*. Yeah right! Brianna went along with that nonsense for nearly a month, although every day was like her personal torture chamber. Each time Donovan called and told her he was going to stop by Kyra's house, Brianna bared her teeth. Her claws sprang to action. She almost slit the tires on her man's car when Donovan told her he put Kyra's hooptie in the shop and was footing the repair bill.

And when he tried to break up with her... that had to be the worst day of Brianna's life. Donovan told her point blank that Kyra was going to be in the picture, and if Brianna didn't like it, he would dump *her* – not Kyra. It was humiliating and it was ludicrous. Who did Donovan think he was? Didn't he know that he belonged to Brianna? Nothing was over unless *she* said it was.

There were two things that kept Brianna sane during the days Kyra casted her dark cloud over their relationship. The first was that Brianna knew she was more awesome than Kyra in every way. She had the looks, the finances, her own home, and no rug rats! There was no way Donovan could be interested in a basic chick like Kyra. The second thing that kept Brianna from going completely bat shit was Donovan's promise that he wasn't attracted to Kyra and that he had never been. Brianna asked him specifically if he and Kyra ever kissed, and Donovan gave her an emphatic *No.*

But that was a lie. And even though it hurt like hell to find out she'd been deceived, Brianna wasn't terribly upset with her boyfriend. She could actually thank him, because Donovan's gigantic lie gave Brianna the power she needed to regain control of their relationship, like in the old days. She felt like Maury Povich with an envelope filled with DNA results. She felt like Johnny Cochran waving a bloody glove at the jury.

She took a seat on Donovan's couch and stared into her boyfriend's eyes. He warily sat next to her with the classic *BUSTED!* look stamped on his face. The only thing that kept Brianna from smiling was the fact that she was supposed to feel hurt and betrayed right now rather than haughty.

"Okay," Donovan said with a sigh. "What did my mom tell you?"

"What do you think she told me?"

Donovan frowned. It was clear Brianna was getting a lot of satisfaction out of this.

"You came all the way over here to play a riddle game?" he asked.

"Yes, I like riddles," she said. "Here's another one: What starts with '*You*' and ends with '*Lied*'?"

Donovan shook his head. That was a good one. If he wasn't sure that one of them would be crying within the next five minutes, he might have laughed.

"Okay." He nodded. "I did lie to you."

"About what?"

"About Kyra. I told you my mom kicked her out because she didn't trust us together. Obviously you now know that wasn't the whole truth."

"That wasn't the truth at all."

"No, it wasn't."

"Say what you did."

"You sure you don't want to do it yourself? You seem to have a flair for dramatics."

"Actually you're the one who's been giving the performance of a lifetime," Brianna countered. She offered three very sarcastic hand claps. "Bravo."

"I kissed Kyra," Donovan said, growing tired of her antics.

"When?" Brianna asked. "Yesterday? Last week?"

"I kissed Kyra fifteen years ago," Donovan stated, "when she was living with us. It was only one time. My mom caught us, and that's why she made Kyra leave. That was the only time we ever kissed."

His confession did little to slow Brianna's roll.

"The only time you're admitting to now..."

"What do you mean by that?"

"If you lied to me all this time about that kiss, who's to say you're not still lying? Who's to say you didn't kiss her yesterday, or the last time you saw her?"

"You, um, I guess you have to trust me."

"Ha!" She laughed in his face. "Trust *you*?"

Donovan felt like he was applying for a loan at the snobbiest bank in the country.

"Uh, yeah. You have to trust me."

"I don't get how you can say that with a straight face," Brianna replied. "Trusting you is the *last* thing I can do right now, Donovan. Maybe never again."

He didn't have a response for that.

"And according to your mother, it wasn't just a kiss," Brianna continued. "Do you want to tell me what else happened that day?"

"You mean fifteen years ago?"

"Or yesterday, or the day before. Whatever. Who knows what you and your little girlfriend have been up to?"

Donovan shook his head. "Okay, Brianna. I know you're having fun with this, but you need to get to the point. Yes, I lied to you. I kissed Kyra a long-ass time ago, and both of us have regretted it ever since. We've never touched each other again since that day, and we aren't kissing or sleeping together right now. I lied because I knew you wouldn't like the truth. But now you know. Fine. What's the bottom line? Where are you going with this?"

Brianna's blood boiled. How dare he rush her? But Donovan was right. This was all leading to a final solution, a *real* ultimatum this time: "Obviously I can't trust you around Kyra anymore," Brianna said. "I want you to stop seeing her."

Donovan didn't miss a beat. "I can't do that."

"What?" Brianna didn't expect that at all.

"Listen," Donovan said. He reached into her lap and held her hand. Brianna looked down, expecting him to slide an engagement ring onto her finger. That was about the only thing that could save him at this point.

"I did lie to you," Donovan said. "But Kyra and I are just friends. I'm not lying about that. I promise you."

"But I can't trust you."

"I know," Donovan said. He rubbed her hand tenderly. "But the truth is you couldn't trust me before Kyra moved back down here. That's why I didn't want to move in with you. You make me feel crowded, always on guard, like I did something when I know I didn't. Things spiraled out of control with Kyra in the picture, and that's when I saw how truly ugly the situation is. That's when you lost the little bit of control you had over your emotions."

What the hell? Brianna's eyes narrowed. Was he trying to turn this shit around?

"The bottom line is this," Donovan said. "You want to use Kyra as a scapegoat, but I know that your insecurities have nothing to do with her. Even if I stopped being Kyra's friend, nothing would change. That's why we have to break up. I care for you, Brianna. But we're not good for each other. I'm sorry."

Brianna stared into his eyes, her big, brown orbs widening by degrees. She couldn't speak right away. She couldn't breathe, either. Did he break up with her? This was not the solution she had in mind when she came here. This wasn't even on the radar. Brianna felt her heart rattling in the back of her throat. Her eyes blurred, and she had a tick in the corner of her mouth. The tick grew bigger until it pulled her lips down into a scowl.

Donovan continued to hold her hand as Brianna's pompous attitude dropped from 100% to negative 150. It hurt him to watch. It was like an abstract artist took her beautiful visage and turned it into something weird and melancholy. Brianna's eyes began to squirt tears, but Donovan steeled his heart, knowing this would be the last time he ever caused her pain.

"No!" she wailed.

Donovan pulled her hand towards him, and gradually Brianna fell into his arms. She laid her head on his chest and sobbed loudly. Donovan put his arms around her. His hand moved to the back of her head and disappeared into her lovely mane. He rubbed her head tenderly.

"I'm sorry, baby."

"Please, Donovan." Brianna's voice was muffled against his shirt. "I'm sorry. I didn't mean it. You can still be friends with Kyra."

Donovan held her tightly. "I'm sorry, Brianna. But there's no going back this time. We're not good for each other. We have to break up."

"Why, so you can be with *her*?" she wailed.

"Brianna, I know you don't believe me, but Kyra and I are just friends. We made a mistake when we were kids, and we've regretted it ever since. If we tried some mess like that now, it would ruin our friendship."

"Okay, I believe you, Donovan. Let's, don't break up with me."

"Brianna, are you, would you look at yourself?..."

He took hold of her shoulders and gently pushed her away. Brianna resisted. Being in Donovan's arms was the best security blanket in the world. But he was stronger than her, and resistance was futile. Brianna kept her face down rather than meet his eyes.

"Brianna, do you not know how beautiful you are?" Donovan asked. "That's why your behavior is so baffling to me. You got a great career. You're an independent woman. You got it going on on so many levels."

She looked up at him tentatively. She wiped her face, knowing she looked a mess.

"You should be with a baller," Donovan said, "or some rich business owner. Your man should be picking you up in a Lamborghini. I know guys are lining up at your feet. Why are you getting so upset over me? I'm a school teacher. I don't make a lot of money, and I drive a truck. That's not your lifestyle. Maybe if I would've made it to the NFL, I'd be on your level. But I didn't."

"I don't care about that stuff," Brianna said. "I love you."

"And I love you, too," Donovan said. "But that doesn't mean your life will stop if we're not together. Brianna, you need to look deep inside yourself and try to figure out why you have such low self esteem. Why are you insecure? Maybe you should consider counseling."

Brianna sighed. This is why she loved this man so much. Where she was wild and irrational, Donovan was calm and assertive. He always knew what was best for her.

She dried the last of her tears and offered him an embarrassed smile. "I guess there's no chance of us staying together, if I go to counseling?"

Donovan returned her smile, but he shook his head. "No. We've already done irreparable damage to our relationship – me and you. But I'd like to still be your friend."

Brianna chuckled at that. "Sorry. That's not gonna work."

Donovan expected as much. "I understand."

"But I would like it if you held me again," Brianna said. "For old times' sake."

Donovan's heart melted. He quickly pulled her into his arms. She fit so comfortably. He nuzzled the top of her head and kissed it, too. Her hair smelled nice. But even as he fought off his own tears, Donovan knew he made the right decision.

≈ ≈ ≈ ≈ ≈ ≈

Brianna didn't leave for another thirty minutes. After seeing her out, Donovan collapsed on his recliner. He was emotionally drained, and he felt physically spent, too. He almost didn't answer his cellphone when he heard it ringing, but he thought it might be Kyra. Hearing from her always brightened his mood.

Donovan rolled his eyes when he saw his mother's name on the caller ID, but he took the call. He was furious the last time he talked to her, and he wanted to take back some of the mean things he said.

"Hello, mother."

"Baby, I know you said you'd call me when you were feeling better. I just wanted to let you know how sorry I am for telling your business to Brianna. I was one hundred percent out of line, and I understand if you're mad at me for a long time. I don't know what got into me. That was disrespectful and stupid, and, and I was only doing what I thought was best for you. That's the only thing I ever worry about; what's best for you. I would never–"

"Mama, it's alright."

"–ever do anything to interfere with your relationships – no matter who you want to be with. It's not my business. Lord, I don't know what came–"

"*Mama*, did you hear me?"

"No, baby. I'm sorry."

"I said it's alright. I forgive you."

"Thank you, Jesus!" she exclaimed. "Thank you too, baby. I'm sorry for calling Brianna. Have you talked to her? Did you work it out? I want to apologize to her, too. I don't know what possessed me to call that girl. It's just, I was worried about you, baby."

"I know, Mama. And I love you for that."

"Did you talk to Brianna yet? Did y'all work everything out?"

"Yes," Donovan said. "She came over here."

"Oh, thank God!" Beverly sighed. "Baby, I thought I ruined everything for you. I been so worried."

"We broke up, Mama."

"Wha, *why*?"

"I told you me and Brianna had problems," Donovan said. "It didn't have anything to do with you. I tried to break up with her two times already, but she wouldn't let me. This time I wouldn't let her stop me."

"But, but Donovan, she was so good for you! Let me call her and apologize. Maybe you two can still fix this. When I talked to her, she told me how much she loves you. I think–"

"*Mama...*" Donovan warned.

"Oh, okay, baby. You right. If you don't wanna be with her no more, that's your decision. I won't interfere."

"Why thank you," Donovan said with a grin.

"Are you sure it didn't have nothing to do with me?" Beverly asked. "I don't think I could live with myself if I broke you two up."

"I assure you it didn't," Donovan said. "This has been a long time coming."

"Alright," Beverly said. "I mean, if that's what you want. I just want you to be happy."

"I am happy," Donovan said, but that wasn't true. He was quite gloomy and stressed-out about the whole ordeal.

"So, I guess this means you and Kyra can be together now."

Donovan chuckled. "Mama, me and Kyra are just friends. I know you find that hard to believe, but it's true. I didn't break up with Brianna for Kyra, and I'm not going to get in a relationship with Kyra now that I'm single. She's my best friend. The one time we kissed turned out *horribly*, and we'll never do that again."

Beverly finally accepted what her son had been telling her all along. And it was painful. "Oh my God, Donovan. I'm sorry. I was so wrong about y'all."

"It's okay."

"No, Donovan. I don't think it is. I feel bad about what I did. I feel like I should do something to make up for it."

"Do you really want to make it up to me?"

"Yes, baby. I'll do whatever you want. Tell me."

"Stop hating on Kyra," Donovan said. "That's what you can do for me. She's had a rough time, pretty much her whole life. She has always respected and looked up to you. When you let her live with us, that was the best time of her life. She loved you like her own mother. She loved the time you spent with her, taking her to get her hair done and stuff like that. The only thing she ever did wrong was kiss me *one time*. And if you want to know the truth about that, *I* was the one who kissed her, Mama. My life would be so much better if you stopped hating on Kyra."

After a pause, Beverly cleared her throat and said, "Alright, baby. I'm sorry I was mean to her. I won't do it again."

Donovan noticed a change in the quality of her voice. If he didn't know any better, he'd swear she was crying.

"Thanks, Mom. I love you."

"I love you too, baby. And, could you tell Kyra I said I'm sorry."

Donovan smiled. His whole body was warmed by her comment. "Sure will. She'll be glad to hear it."

≈≈≈≈≈≈

Donovan didn't talk to Kyra until later that night. He knew she was upset from the moment she said, "Hey, what you doing?"

"Nothing," he said. "What's wrong?"

"My damn aunt," Kyra said and blew out a sigh.

Donovan was grading papers. He pushed them aside and reclined in his computer chair. "What'd she do?"

"Just bitching about *everything*," Kyra complained. "She said I wasn't keeping my room clean, but I do clean it. I clean it every day. It's just that we got three people in one room, so obviously it's gonna look junky, especially with Q's school papers and stuff.

"I asked her again if I could clean out that spare bedroom so we could get some breathing room, but she won't let me. And she won't do it herself! She don't like nobody going in there. Why would she keep a room full of junk when it's three people squeezed in one little bedroom?"

"That doesn't make sense," Donovan agreed. "Did she tell you she only had one room available before you moved down here?"

"No! She said she had a three bedroom house, and she had plenty of room for us."

"Where are you?" Donovan asked, noticing Kyra wasn't trying to keep her voice down.

"Down the street," she said. "Just walking."

"Just walking?" It wasn't completely dark yet, but the street lights were on. Donovan immediately feared for her safety.

"I can see the house from here," Kyra said. "I just walked to the corner. I'm on my way back. Just had to get out of there for a second, get some fresh air."

"Oh, alright."

"I can't wait to move out of here," Kyra grumbled.

"I know you can't," Donovan said. "Have you heard back from any of the schools you applied for?"

"No."

"Did you apply for the office clerk job at J.T. Elder?"

"Yeah."

"I know the vice principal there. I'll call him and put in a good word for you."

"Thanks," Kyra said.

"As far as your aunt, I think she's just a hater," Donovan said. "She doesn't have anything good going for herself, and she don't like to see other people trying to make something of themselves. I saw it in her eyes when we brought groceries that time. She didn't look like she appreciated it *at all*. It was like she wanted to have something to complain about."

"I think you right," Kyra said. "That's why she doesn't like you."

"Me?"

"I know, right. How could she not like you? You're the most likeable person I know."

"Aww, gee, thanks. But for real, she doesn't like me?"

"She hasn't came right out and said it. But you can tell by the way she acts every time I bring up your name."

"Like when?"

"Like when you're coming over or when I was telling her about my new car. I have to thank you again for helping me with that, Donovan."

"I didn't do much. I found out about that charity through our counselor at school."

"You're so modest. You won't take praise for anything."

Donovan grinned. "Okay, you're welcome. I'm glad you like the car. But you're probably the only person I know who would refer to a '99 Escort as '*new*.'"

"It's new to me."

"Yes it is. You know, if your aunt doesn't like me, and the only thing I've ever done is try to help you, maybe she doesn't want you to get too independent. She wants to hold you down, which is worse than a regular hater."

"For real," Kyra agreed. "I think she wants me to stay here so she can keep getting food stamps and whatever else she's trying to scheme on. Yesterday she asked if she could put my kids on her tax return next year. I haven't even been here two months, and she's already thinking about tax returns!"

"Damn," Donovan breathed. "Yeah, you got problems."

"What else is new?" Kyra said. "Anyway, I don't mean to be calling you with this mess all the time."

"No, it's okay."

"What about you?" Kyra said. "How was your day?"

"It was fine. I'm good."

"How's your girlfriend? Is she feeling any better about, you know, me?"

Donovan considered his response. He wanted to tell Kyra what happened, but there was a chance Kyra might do the unthinkable and say she had more-than-friendly feelings for him. Donovan would have to come clean about his feelings for her, and then they'd prove everyone right by jumping into a (most likely doomed) relationship.

It was silly, but Donovan needed to prove to himself and his mom and even to Brianna that he didn't break up with her so he could be with Kyra. The best way to do that was to keep Kyra in the dark about the breakup, for now at least.

"Brianna's fine," he said. "I haven't had any problems with her."

"That's good," Kyra said. "Did you take your mom to church today?"

"I did," Donovan said. "It was nice."

"I want to go to church sometimes."

"Really?"

"Yeah. Why you say it like that? Don't you think I should go?"

"Of course," Donovan said. "I didn't mean to sound surprised. I'm happy to hear that."

"I would go with you," Kyra said, "but me and your mama should probably never be in the same building at the same time."

Donovan chuckled. "You can come to church with us if you want."

"Please!" Kyra said with a smack of her lips. "I know Miss Beverly don't like me."

"As a matter of fact, I talked to my mom about you today. She told me to tell you she's sorry."

Kyra's mouth fell open. "Sorry for what?"

"I don't know," Donovan said. "Kicking you out, treating you bad when we were kids."

"She apologized?" Kyra never expected that, not in a million years. "*Why?*"

"Because I told her she was wrong for hating on you. I told her you were my friend, and you weren't going anywhere. And you never did anything wrong in the first place. I got sick of her talking noise about you."

Kyra made it back to her aunt's house. She sat on the front porch with a huge smile on her face. "You're such a good friend, Donovan. You're too good to me."

"I just want you to get yourself situated, so you can be happy."

"Me, too," Kyra said. She stared at the purplish sunset disappearing behind her neighbor's house. "I can't wait 'til I have a normal life like you. I wanna sit on the porch at my own house, have a good job so I don't have to struggle anymore. I want to start going to church. Maybe I'll meet a man..." *Like you! A man just like you!* Kyra giggled at her subconscious. That was silly talk. There was no chance of her meeting a man *just like Donovan*. He was as unique as the stars that were starting to appear in the sky above her.

"You'll have all those things," Donovan assured her. Deep down it hurt to think of Kyra in the arms of another man. But Donovan would never interfere with the desires of her heart. "Everything will work out for you," he promised.

CHAPTER ELEVEN
THE FORGOTTEN STORY

The next few weeks were filled with progress for Kyra. It felt like God finally took her off the bench and put her in the game of life, saying, "Alright, baby. Show me what you got."

Kyra got her car out of the shop the day after Donovan's breakup (which she still didn't know anything about). With her car came a huge slice of freedom that was better than Kyra ever imagined. No longer did she have to wait in the hot sun for a city bus that was filled with all sorts of strangers, some friendly, some not. Quinell's school was only ten blocks away, but Kyra now had the option to take him or pick him up on bad weather days.

Best of all Kyra didn't have to ask her aunt for a ride to the social services office or to the grocery store. Aunt Ruth was a little riled up about that, but Kyra began to care less and less about offending her shifty relative/landlord. When she was in her car, Kyra felt like she could drive anywhere. She felt like she could get away at anytime. She still didn't have anywhere to go if things reached the boiling point with Aunt Ruth, but at least Kyra could pack up all of her things and leave at a moment's notice.

And that felt good.

The only thing better was a phone call Kyra received on Wednesday, September 24th. It was Robyn Powley, the principal at J.T. Elder Elementary. She invited Kyra to the campus to interview for an office clerk position. Kyra called Donovan when he got off work that day. Donovan confirmed that he spoke with the vice principal at J.T. Elder and asked him to pull Kyra's file.

Kyra was a nervous wreck when she interviewed for the position, but Mrs. Powley was funny and friendly. She put Kyra at ease, and she didn't stumble when explaining her spotty work history. She and Mrs. Powley hit it off, and the principal offered Kyra the position before she left the school. Kyra went to the administration building on Thursday for more paperwork and a background check, and she started work at J.T. Elder the following Monday.

It was such a humbling experience, all that had happened since she returned to Overbrook Meadows. Kyra felt like her life was essentially over in Little Rock. Her eyes welled with tears each time her daydreams took her back to those dark and reckless days. She knew things had to be better in Texas, but Kyra never imagined she'd have a job and a car within two months.

She knew she didn't deserve the favor God continued to show her. And there was no doubt Donovan was an extension of His holy grace.

≈ ≈ ≈ ≈ ≈ ≈

On Saturday, October 11th Donovan pulled into Aunt Ruth's driveway and parked behind Kyra's Ford Escort. He got out and walked around her car, quickly inspecting the vehicle before he went to the door. The Escort had an okay paint job and nice tires. It needed a trip to the car wash, and Donovan saw that one of the screws holding the back license plate was loose. He knelt and tightened it as best he could with his fingers.

Donovan knocked on the door and was greeted by a handsome young man with a broad grin on his face.

"Hello, Mr. Mitchell."

"What's up, Q?" Donovan rubbed the top of his head as he stepped inside the house.

A moment later Kyra appeared in the hallway looking like a ray of sunshine, as usual. She wore a purple cocktail dress that had a cinched waist and a low neckline. She had her hair pulled back in a ponytail, drawing Donovan's eyes to her lovely face. She smiled at her best bud as she put on one of her earrings.

"Hello, sir."

Donovan wore a blood red button-down with faded jeans and casual loafers. He was clean cut. His jeans fit him just right. Kyra didn't think he could get any more handsome, especially when he smiled. She loved to go out with Donovan.

128

"You look lovely," he said.

"Thanks." Kyra blushed. "Let me tell my aunt I'm leaving."

"Alright."

Kyra disappeared down a different hallway, and Donovan took a seat on the couch.

"How you doing in school?" he asked Quinell.

"Fine, sir."

"You play ball?"

Quinell shook his head.

"You look like you'd be good at football," Donovan said. "You ever played?"

He shook his head again.

"If you want, I'll ask your mom to bring you to some of my games," Donovan said. "My team isn't any good, but they're fun to watch."

The boy smiled.

Kyra entered the room again a lot less cheery than she was a moment ago. "You ready?"

"Yeah." Donovan rose to his feet. "What's wrong?"

"Nothing. We'll be back," she told Quinell. She gave him a kiss on the forehead and headed for the front door. "Make sure you brush your teeth before you go to bed, if I'm not back by ten. But I should be."

"I will," Quinell said.

Donovan gave the boy a pat on the shoulder before he followed Kyra out. "Hey, what happened?" he asked when they were outside.

"My aunt," she said. "But I don't want to let it ruin my night." She smiled. "Thanks for picking me up. I wish I could pay for dinner, but I haven't gotten paid yet, from my job, 'cause, you know, I have a job now." She was beaming, the troubles with her aunt already pushed out of her mind.

"You do have a job, don't you?" Donovan said as they stepped off the porch. "When you get paid, I want you to take me to one of those fancy steak houses."

"Okay," Kyra said. "I get paid next month."

Donovan opened the door for her and helped her inside his truck.

"I'm just kidding," he said before he closed it. "I wouldn't waste your money like that."

Kyra had to wait until he walked around and took a seat on the driver's side before she could tell him, "It wouldn't be a waste, Donovan. I owe you a lot."

"You don't owe me anything, Kyra. Stop saying that."

Grrrr. "You're so frustrating. But I don't care what you say, you're going to let me pay you back for some of the stuff you helped me with – the groceries and my car repairs for sure."

"Okay, whatever," Donovan said as he backed out of the driveway. "How's your car running? Do you want me to take it to the carwash?"

Kyra grinned. "I'm pretty sure I can handle that. Are you trying to tell me something?"

"No. Just wanted to help."

"What can I do for you?" Kyra asked. "Why don't you let me help you sometimes?"

Donovan shook his head. "I can't think of anything I need."

"There's got to be *something* I can do for you..."

Donovan stared into her eyes and then at her lips. Luckily he had to look away, so he could watch the road. "What did your aunt say to you before we left," he asked.

Kyra frowned, but she didn't try to keep it from him. Donovan was relentless when he knew she was upset about something. "She said that since I got a job now, I have to start paying her for babysitting. She said she'll keep track of how much I owe, and for me to let her know when I get my check."

"Hmmm."

Kyra waited a few seconds. "That's all you have to say?"

"She's definitely looking for a free ride."

"*I'm* her free ride."

"But you can't keep arguing with someone you live with," Donovan warned. "I think, like it or not, you have to pay her."

"What?"

"What would you do if you lived alone? You'd have to pay *somebody* to watch your kids when you go to work and stuff. Might as well be your aunt."

For a moment Kyra was upset because he didn't take her side, but she realized Donovan was right, as usual.

"When I grow up, I want to be just like you," Kyra said with a smile.

Donovan grinned. "You're fine just the way you are. Every day I'm more proud of you."

≈ ≈ ≈ ≈ ≈ ≈ ≈

Donovan took Kyra to Pappadeaux Seafood Kitchen where they dined on smoked salmon, fried calamari and crawfish etouffee. It was still light out when they arrived. The friends watched the sun set through the restaurant's windows as they ate.

Pappadeaux was filled nearly to capacity with more couples than large parties. Kyra hadn't been on a real "date" in a long time. She knew she wasn't on a date with Donovan, but the atmosphere almost made it feel like one. She wondered what it would be like if Donovan kissed her when he dropped her off. She laughed at herself. She'd been wondering about things like that since they were children. Clearly it wasn't meant to be.

"What are you thinking about?" Donovan asked after the waiter took their plates away. He had a knack for asking that whenever Kyra was thinking about the *wrong* things.

"Just how nice it is to go out like this," she said. She sipped a frozen margarita through a straw. "I can't remember the last time I was in a restaurant this nice."

"What about your last boyfriend in Arkansas?" Donovan asked. "Y'all never went out on dates?"

Kyra put her glass down. "You know I don't want to talk about that loser."

Donovan frowned. Kyra told him precious little about Kat's father. All he knew was the guy's name was Leonard, and he was in jail for "drugs." Donovan didn't know if Leonard was selling or using, but he assumed it was the latter. Kyra said her time with Leonard got really bad towards the end. Donovan wanted to know exactly what happened, but he didn't want to push her.

"How do you like your new job?" he asked.

Kyra's smile was immediate. "I like it. I never thought about working in a school, around kids, but it's really cool. The other ladies in the office are so funny. They have me cracking up."

"I'm glad you're fitting in," Donovan said. "That's a great school. They always have good pass rates on the state tests."

"I know. They have posters everywhere," Kyra said. "You can't turn a corner without seeing how good they did."

Donovan leaned forward with his elbows on the table. He stared into her eyes. "I'm happy for you."

"Thank you." Kyra beamed. "Next month I'm giving you half my check."

Donovan shook his head. "Not this again."

"Listen," Kyra said, "you're going to let me pay you back. You did too much for me."

"I don't need your money."

"It's not about that. And why don't you need it? I work in the district now, so I know teachers don't get paid that much."

Donovan chuckled. "We do if we've been teaching for almost ten years. And I get more because I coach, too. You need to keep your money for the other things on your to-do list, like saving up for furniture so you can move out."

"You can't tell me what to do with my money."

Donovan rubbed his bottom lip. "I like that feisty Kyra. I miss her."

Kyra's blood raced as she watched him gently squeeze his mouth. She really wanted to suck that lip! No doubt that was the liquor talking. She hadn't had a drink in months. She sucked her own bottom lip between her teeth and licked on it instead. It tasted pretty good, with the margarita salt lingering. But she knew Donovan's lips tasted better.

"What about your girlfriend?" she asked. "Brianna doesn't care if I pay you back?"

"Oh, we broke up." Donovan's brain caught up to his comment a second later. He looked down at his empty wine glass rather than meet Kyra's surprised eyes.

"What?"

"Yeah, I meant to tell you."

He looked up at her. She looked upset.

But Kyra was more confused than offended. Why would he not tell her about such an enormous change in his life? And didn't this say something about how he felt about Kyra? Maybe Donovan didn't know that she had a crush on him, but if he felt the same way, he would've told her he was single, wouldn't he? Had

Donovan never considered that he and Kyra could be more than friends?

"When?" she asked.

"Um, last week."

"Why didn't you tell me?"

"You were, um, you were busy with your new job and stuff. It wasn't that big a deal. Plus I didn't want you to think you had anything to do with it."

"Are you sure I didn't?"

"I'm positive," Donovan said. "Me and Brianna were having problems, for a long time."

"But you didn't break up until I got here."

"That's why I didn't want to tell you," Donovan said. "I knew you wouldn't understand. I didn't want to put that on your conscious."

Okay, that makes sense, Kyra thought. "I'm sorry y'all broke up. Are you sure you're not hurting. I can't believe you didn't tell me. Do you miss her? Do you want to talk about it?"

"It's fine," Donovan assured her. "I feel at peace right now. Seriously." He smiled. "We're both in a better place. Brianna wasn't good for me. That stuff happens."

So what about us? Kyra wondered. She knew it was selfish to want to claim Donovan right after his breakup, but she couldn't help it. They may never get an opportunity like this again. She wanted to ask him outright, but she couldn't bear it if he rejected her. Donovan was her only childhood fantasy that hadn't been dashed yet. A few awkward moments passed while Kyra waited for Donovan to broach the subject.

"What about you?" he said. "You haven't met anyone?"

"No." *Nope. I'm totally single!*

"I'm sure you will," Donovan said.

Okay.... Kyra frowned. Was he really not interested at all? Maybe it was because he was still hurting, from Brianna. Surely that was it.

"What's up?" Donovan asked. "I see that look..."

"Huh?"

"Somebody *has* hit on you!" he said. His eyes brightened. "Come on, break bread. Who was it?"

Wow. Kyra couldn't believe he totally misread her signals. She needed to work on her womanly vibes. "There's nobody," she said. "The only person who has asked me out since I been here is the UPS guy who comes to my school."

Donovan's heart sank to the pit of his stomach. *Oh shit! There is someone!*

"Did, did you get his number?" he muttered.

"Um..." Kyra's heart thudded. Did he really want to talk about this, like they were just friends? Were they just friends?

"Come on," Donovan said. He felt sweat on his forehead, but he was too embarrassed to wipe it away. "Obviously you did, Kyra. Why don't you want to tell me? We can talk about anything, right?"

She nodded. "Yes, of course we can. I took his number. But I wasn't going to go out with him, though."

"Why not?"

"Because, I..." Kyra realized she didn't have a reason. Roland, the UPS guy, was handsome and polite. Everyone in the office thought he was a dreamboat. Kyra was flattered when he asked her out. She told him she'd think about it. He insisted she take his number, just in case. The only reason Kyra had to reject Roland was Donovan. "I don't know," she said.

"I think you should go out with him," Donovan said. He swallowed. His throat was bone dry. He tried to clear it. "You should get out and have some fun. You deserve to have fun, and be happy."

Donovan didn't notice Kyra's smile crack and fade.

"I don't think so."

"Why? Is there something wrong with him?"

Again Kyra had to shake her head.

"Then go, Kyra. You deserve to have a good time. When do you get to enjoy yourself – outside of when you're with me?"

"I guess I don't." She sighed. "Okay. I'll go out with him. I mean, if you give your approval."

Donovan felt like he got kicked in the stomach. "Kyra, you don't need my approval for something like that."

"But I value your opinion," she stressed. "I wouldn't go out with anyone, if you don't think I should..."

Donovan didn't understand why she wanted him to make the decision. He couldn't have been more biased. But he loved her too much to interfere with her happiness. He fought to keep his voice steady as he said, "Go ahead. Seriously."

Well. Kyra's shoulders slumped. *I guess that settles that.*

"Hey," Donovan said, eager to change the subject. "Do you remember the time we were at the park, and that naked man was hiding in the tree?"

Damn you, Donovan! Kyra almost screamed at him: *Hey, do **you** remember the time we were at your mother's house, and I told you I liked you, and you said you liked me, too. And we kissed. You kissed me like I've never been kissed before, and your hand was under my shirt, and my heart was beating so fast, and I was in love with you. Do you remember that, Donovan? 'Cause it's fun to remember all of these other stories, but when are you going to ask me if I remember when we kissed? When are we going to talk about that??*

Kyra forced a smile. "Yeah, I remember that. That, that guy was wild."

CHAPTER TWELVE
ROLAND

Donovan dropped Kyra off at 9:45, like a proper gentleman. When she walked through the door, Aunt Ruth checked the clock and told her she would charge $10 per hour for babysitting when Kyra went out with Donovan or anyone else she might meet. Ruth said she'd only charge $150 a week for babysitting Kat while Kyra was at work, rather than use the hourly rate. After talking with Donovan, Kyra thought that sounded reasonable enough. She surprised her aunt by saying, "Okay," before retreating to her room to change into something comfortable.

By ten-fifteen Kyra was nearly bored out of her mind. She wished Donovan would've taken her to the movies after dinner or even to his house. It was clear they weren't going to get anything freaky going on, but she would've liked to spend more time with him. She wanted to call him now, but Kyra was a little upset about their conversation at the restaurant.

Why would Donovan tell her to go out with the UPS guy? Kyra found it hard to believe Donovan didn't have any feelings for her at all. Their one kiss was a long time ago, but it meant a lot to Kyra. She would've sworn it meant something to Donovan, too.

Guess not.

Kyra lounged on her aunt's sofa with her cellphone in hand. She could hear Quinell and Kat in the bedroom laughing at a DVD she brought them. Aunt Ruth was hidden away in her room, where she preferred to spend most of her time.

Kyra pulled up the contact list on her cellphone, in search of someone she could talk to about her man troubles. She couldn't talk to her best friend because Donovan was the person she wanted to talk about. Kyra had less than forty contacts. It only took a few seconds to realize she didn't have any other confidants. She paused at the newest contact she saved and stared at the name.

Roland.

He gave Kyra his number three days ago. She noticed he was awfully sweet to her whenever he delivered packages to the school, so his approach wasn't a big surprise. At the time Kyra told him, "I don't think that's a good idea."

He asked her, "Why?"

"This is where I work," Kyra had said. Roland didn't work for the school district, but his and Kyra's only interactions were at the school. She didn't want any drama there.

"I understand how you feel," the UPS guy had told her. He was a tall man, not as tall as Donovan, but almost. He wasn't as big as Donovan either, and his skin was dark where Donovan's was golden brown. But once Kyra was able to look at Roland objectively (without Donovan reigning supreme over all men who dared to walk on two legs), she had to admit that the delivery man was attractive.

He wore glasses, and he had a perfect baby-afro. He opted for shorts with his uniform. He had a nice build. He was speedy with all of his deliveries, no matter how many or how big the parcels. And he never broke out in a sweat. He was definitely fit.

"Trust me, I don't do this at every place I deliver to," Roland had told her. "I find you very attractive, Miss Reynolds. I would like to see you for more than two minutes a day. Take my number. If I get shuffled to a different route tomorrow, and I never see you again, I'll feel better knowing that at least I tried."

Roland had a great smile, with the cutest dimples. His eyes were dark and alluring. His job may have been blue collar, but he carried himself with an air of dignity and authority. Kyra found it hard to reject him. It wasn't possible at all while he was standing there, staring at her with those pretty brown eyes.

She told him, "I'll think about it," and she saved his number in her phone. She stared at it now wondering if it was time to give up on her dream.

*Going out with a handsome man with a good job is **not** giving up on your dreams*, she told herself. *But you are living a*

*dream if you're waiting for Donovan to profess his love to you.
He told you to go out with this man, for Chrissake. And he
didn't tell you he and his girlfriend broke up. Don't you think
that would've been something worth mentioning if he wanted to
be with you?*

Kyra pressed the call button, mainly to shut up the voice in
her head. And then she regretted it when she saw what time it
was. 10:17 pm. Was it too late to call? She'd been out of the
dating game for so long. She didn't know what the rules were
nowadays.

"Hello?" The voice that answered didn't sound sleepy.

"Hi. This is Kyra. Is, may I speak to Roland?"

"Hey, this is me."

His voice was not as deep as Donovan's – *Stop it*! Kyra told
herself. His voice was nice. It was just fine.

"Hi, this is Kyra, from J.T. Elder. Were you in bed?"

"No. Thanks for calling. I didn't think you would."

"Were you busy?"

"Nope. Watching TV. Relaxing. Had a rough day."

"You had to work?"

"Yeah. But it's cool. Stacking that overtime. Thanks for
calling. What made you change your mind?"

"I still don't know if I changed my mind."

"Oh. Is, do you want me to help convince you? 'Cause I
can put up a pretty strong argument."

Kyra giggled. "Okay. Go ahead."

"Well, you may not know this, but Roland is stand up guy,"
Roland said. "He's been working the same job for fourteen years,
so you know he's getting that paper. He got his own car and his
own apartment, and he's not living with his mom. They don't even
like each other.

"And he's been telling me how much he likes you. He
never stops talking about this woman named *Kyra* who started
working at J.T. Elder. He said you're not just beautiful, but you're
professional, too. He would love to take you out, treat you like a
lady."

Kyra was surprised and impressed with his self-promotion.
Her smile was ear to ear. "I don't care how much money you
have."

"Oh, that's cool," Roland said. "I was just saying, you know, I do got some."

"You make an impressive argument for yourself."

"Roland's the best man I know," he said. "Nobody does it better."

"Cocky?"

"No. But I'm confident."

"Why don't you like your mom?"

"She's on drugs."

"Mine, too."

"See, we already got something in common."

Hmmm. Honestly Kyra expected Roland to give her a reason not to go out with him, so she could tell Donovan, and he'd stop looking for someone to take his place. But Roland was witty and hard-working, and apparently he had money (which Kyra really didn't care about). But more importantly, Kyra knew that she couldn't be with the one she was saving herself for, so why was she saving herself?

"So, can I take you out?" Roland asked.

"Okay," she said.

"What are you doing now?"

She laughed. "It's a little late, don't you think?"

"Is tomorrow good?"

"I can do tomorrow afternoon."

"Okay. Do you go to church?"

"No," Kyra said. But she felt that was something she should do. Maybe with Donovan. He did invite her, after all.

"Me neither," Roland said. "I'll call you around eleven, and you can let me know where to pick you up at."

"Alright."

"Thanks for calling," Roland said. "I'll talk to you tomorrow."

≈ ≈ ≈ ≈ ≈ ≈ ≈

Roland called the next day at 11 am sharp. Kyra gave him her aunt's address, and he said he'd be there at 12:30. Kyra had butterflies in her stomach as she got dressed. She still wasn't sure if she should go out with someone she worked with – even if they only worked together for two minutes a day.

139

When Roland knocked on the door, Kyra ushered the kids into her room and told them to stay there until she left. She answered the door wearing a black skirt with a sleeveless blouse. She didn't think she looked all that special, but Roland's eyes widened as he admired her from head to toe. Kyra smiled. Donovan used to look at her like that, when she first got back to town. Not anymore, though.

"Kyra, you look amazing."

Roland reached for her hand. Kyra was confused, but she offered it. Roland brought it to his mouth and kissed it softly. Kyra blushed. She didn't think anyone had ever done that to her.

"What a gentleman," she exclaimed.

Roland had a nice build, not particularly muscular, but he wasn't fat at all. He wore a collar shirt with black Dockers. His shirt was rather tight. He had it tucked in with the top three buttons open. Kyra had a good view of his chest, which was strong and smooth, but she thought his style was a little flashy.

Roland's skin was dark and beautiful. His baby 'fro was perfect, as usual. He wore a moustache with another tuft of hair on his chin, but not a full goatee. He sported aviator style sunglasses. He sleeves were rolled up, revealing an expensive watch on one wrist and an equally expensive bracelet on the other.

Kyra couldn't help but tell him, "You look a lot different than you do at school."

Roland smiled. "Different good, or different bad?"

"I... don't know yet," Kyra said. She was a simple girl. Most of the men from her past who dressed like this were pimps or drug dealers. But Roland's income was legit. He worked his ass off, five to six days every week. Kyra wondered if she was on a fault finding mission. "Different good," she decided.

Roland was still holding her hand. He led her down the two porch steps.

"You look just as good as you do in school," he said. "Have I told you how beautiful you are?"

Kyra smiled and looked away coyly. "A couple of times."

"Well you are," Roland said. He walked her to a new Chrysler 300 and opened the passenger door.

Kyra's jaw dropped. Now this was too much. "I'm sorry, but what do you do for a living?"

Roland laughed. "You know what I do for a living. I met you while I was working, as a matter of fact."

"But this car, your jewelry. Do you have a side job? Something *illegal*?"

"Nope." Roland shook his head. He looked surprised that she would ask. "I work hard, and I don't have a wife or any kids. I grew up with nothing, so now I like to have nice things. There's nothing wrong with that. I told you, I got paper."

"And I told you, I don't care about your money."

"Loosen up, please," Roland said. He spoke softly. "You wanted to know if I do anything illegal. I'm telling you I don't. I won't say anything else about money, if you'll get in this car and let me treat you like a queen."

After a noticeable pause, Kyra said, "Okay." She tried to let go of her hang-ups. She took a seat in the Chrysler and admired the style and elegance. Donovan's truck was nice, but this automobile was sleek and beautiful, with so many lights and dials on the dashboard, it could've been a cockpit. Definitely built to impress. And that wasn't counting all of the after-market bling Roland added to his whip. Exactly how much did he spend on this car?

Would you stop that? Kyra shook her head. Not only was she comparing Roland to Donovan at every turn, but she had him on the defensive for the way he chose to spend his money. She agreed to go out with him, so the least she could do was give him a fair shake.

Roland entered the vehicle and took a seat next to her. Kyra reached and touched his arm.

"I'm sorry."

"It's cool," Roland said, his smile bright and genuine. "Wanna see one of my money clips?" He laughed and said, "Gotcha," when Kyra's mouth fell open. After a moment she laughed, too.

≈ ≈ ≈ ≈ ≈ ≈

He took her to Cattleman's steakhouse in the historic stockyards section of the city. The restaurant was top notch all the way. Kyra couldn't believe she was being wined and dined by two handsome men in two consecutive days. Roland ordered a two

141

pound T-bone steak called The Cowboy. He suggested Kyra try *The Cowgirl*, but she opted for filet mignon with corn on the cob.

Roland asked her an assortment of getting-to-know-you questions, but Kyra didn't tell him much about her past. From her queries, Kyra learned that Roland was from Waxahachie, and he was the oldest of twelve kids. His mother and father were still together, and all of his brothers and sisters graduated high school. Some went to college. Kyra was thoroughly impressed.

The more Kyra got to know him, the less she thought of Roland as a showboat. He was sure of himself, and he was proud of the things he'd accomplished. But he was down to earth. His modest upbringing gave him an appreciation for the finer things in life. He liked to eat good foods and drink exotic wines and take vacations to locales his parents never even dreamed of.

But as interesting as Roland was, Kyra found herself thinking about Donovan again. She remembered what he said about Kyra taking him to an upscale steakhouse. Cattleman's might have been the best one in the area. Kyra was a little chagrined that she wasn't sharing the experience with her best friend.

When she realized her thoughts had wandered to Donovan again, Kyra pushed him out of her mind and looked into her date's brown eyes. Roland really was handsome. His confidence pushed his attractiveness up another couple of notches.

"Do you like working at the school?" he asked.

Kyra nodded. "Yeah. I've only been there a couple of weeks, but I can already tell I want to stay there for a while. What about you? Do you like your job?"

"It's alright," Roland said. "The pay is good, and I get to meet interesting people, like you." He gave her a warm smile.

Kyra returned his smile, but she wondered how many *interesting people* Roland met on his route. He told her it was rare that he was attracted to the women who signed for his packages, but Kyra would be a fool to think she was the only one.

"I want to open a business," Roland said. "That's my dream."

Kyra raised an eyebrow. "What kind of business?"

"A restaurant. I love food. And I love making money. I'm going to combine the two. I've been taking classes at the community college. Once I finish my business degree, I'll give it a shot."

"How do you have time for school?" Kyra wondered. "I thought you were always working overtime."

"I am," Roland said. "I can only take two classes a semester, sometimes just one."

"What kind of restaurant do you want to open? Soul food?"

"No. Why does it have to be soul food? Because I'm black?"

Kyra giggled. "Yeah, I guess so."

"That's the problem with young brothers and sisters today," Roland replied. "Everybody's scared to think outside the box. For your information, I want to open a pizza joint."

"Really?"

"Yeah. That's the one style of food black people haven't perfected yet. I want to put my stamp on the industry. I already have a lot of great ideas nobody's ever heard of, like pig's feet pizza with hot sauce and my world famous chitlin loaf."

Kyra couldn't help but frown. *Ewww. Gross.*

"Nah, I'm just kidding," Roland said. "It is gonna be a soul food restaurant. I didn't wanna tell you, after you guessed it."

Kyra cracked up. "You need to stop."

"I love seeing you smile," Roland said. He put his forearms on the table and leaned forward. "Miss Reynolds, I had a real nice time this afternoon. I would love to spend more time with you. I find you very attractive, and intriguing. I know it's only our first date, but I sense a connection here."

The intensity of his gaze made Kyra's heart flutter. Roland looked like he wanted to climb over the table and devour her. Kyra thought she might want to let him.

"Okay," she said. "I would like to see you again, too."

≈ ≈ ≈ ≈ ≈ ≈ ≈

Roland pulled into Aunt Ruth's driveway forty minutes later and put his car in park. It was bright and sunny outside. Kyra had a wonderful time, but she wasn't ready when Roland leaned in for an unexpected kiss. She turned at the last moment, and his lips encountered the back of her jaw.

"Oh, I'm sorry," he said. "I thought, never mind. I was wrong, and I apologize."

He didn't look too apologetic, but Roland had his sunglasses on again, and Kyra couldn't see his eyes.

"It's alright," she said. "I didn't..." She looked down at her hands.

"You don't kiss on the first date," Roland deduced. "I can dig it. Pardon my manners."

"It's okay," Kyra said. She looked up at him. "Maybe next time."

"As long as I have a next time to look forward to, I'm good," Roland said.

He hopped out of the car and went around to open Kyra's door for her. She felt like a princess as he took her hand and helped her out. If there was one thing she could say about Roland, it was that he was a certified gentleman – which is why his next move was so startling.

Kyra was willing when Roland reached to give her a hug in lieu of his thwarted kiss, but she pushed him away abruptly when his hands began to slide down her sides, towards her butt.

"Whoa." Kyra wore a half frown, half smile, still trying to keep it lighthearted. "Slow down there, boss."

"I'm sorry," Roland said. He stuffed his over-eager hands into his pockets. "Kyra, your body is amazing." He devoured her with his eyes while shaking his head. "I swear I didn't mean to do that. I wasn't going to touch – okay, yeah I was, but that wasn't my intention. My hands were literally drawn to your cakes. I am so sorry."

Kyra wasn't impressed by his flattery, and she was confused by his boldness. What kind of man gets rejected when he goes for the kiss, but he still tries for a little grab ass? Interestingly, a part of Kyra was attracted to his daring. Roland saw what he wanted, and he went for it, even after he'd just been told that he couldn't have it.

She chuckled. "Alright, I'll let that slide. Goodbye, Roland."

"Good day, Miss Reynolds."

Kyra knew he was watching her ass as she walked to the door. She looked back anyway. Sure enough Roland hadn't moved an inch. Kyra shook her head, but she couldn't wipe the grin off her face. This man wanted her, *badly*. But Kyra sensed Roland might be one of those love 'em and leave 'em type of guys.

≈ ≈ ≈ ≈ ≈ ≈

She debated whether she should tell Donovan about her date or not. Kyra was eager to talk to someone. Donovan was the most likely candidate, but she worried he might get upset. But Kyra didn't know why that would be the case. It wasn't like Donovan wanted to be with her. In fact, Kyra wouldn't even have gone out with Roland if Donovan hadn't insisted.

She called him at 7:30 while she was washing dishes from Sunday dinner. When Donovan answered, Kyra heard dogs barking in the backyard.

"Hey."

"Hey," she said. "You walking the dogs?"

"Yeah. What's up? Did you have a nice day?"

"I did," Kyra said. "I... I went out with Roland." Kyra felt her heart thudding. She felt like she was confessing to an illicit affair.

Donovan stopped dead in his tracks, not sure he heard her right. His dogs were trying to go after a wily squirrel. Donovan yanked the leashes a little harder than he meant to, and Doc and Wyatt came to an immediate halt. They looked back at him with confused expressions.

Donovan's breathing was ragged. He hoped Kyra would think it was from his run. "You did what?"

Kyra's heart shot up her throat. Now she *really* felt like she was telling her boyfriend she cheated on him. Donovan said, *You did what?* but Kyra heard, *YOU DID WHAT?!*

"I, uh, you said it was alright if I went out with Roland, right? The UPS guy from school..." Kyra's eyes were wide. She stopped washing dishes and stood stiffly with her hands submerged in the water.

"Oh, uh, yeah," Donovan said. His tone softened considerably. "Yeah, I did. You, you didn't have to ask me, though. You can go out with whoever you want."

Why did I tell her to go? Donovan's face was twisted in despair. He gripped his leashes so hard the pink in his fingernails

turned white. He was glad she didn't deliver this news in person.
He wouldn't have been able to hide his reaction.

"Did, did you have a good time?" he asked.

"Um, yeah, I did," Kyra said. She was near panic, too.
They never had a conversation this awkward before.

"Where'd you go?"

"Cattleman's Steakhouse." Kyra felt another stab of guilt,
like she violated a locale that was special to her and Donovan. But
how ridiculous was that? The closest she and Donovan ever came
to the restaurant was him saying he wanted to go somewhere
fancy.

"I thought you were going to take me there."

Kyra's mouth fell open. *Oh my God!*

"I'm just kidding," Donovan said. "How was Roland? Did
he mind his manners?"

This conversation had Kyra's head spinning. Was Donovan
mad or wasn't he? She wiped her hands on a towel and took a seat
at the kitchen table. "He was really nice." She cleared her throat.
"Except for when he dropped me off. He tried to kiss me."

Donovan had to take the phone away from his face so she
wouldn't hear him panting and growling. The contents of his
stomach flipped. He felt like he might throw up. Of course Roland
tried to kiss her! Kyra was beautiful and vivacious. What did he
think was going to happen? Again Donovan regretted giving his
approval for their date. But who the hell was he to interfere with
Kyra's love life?

"I didn't let him," she said.

"Wh, why not?"

"I don't kiss on the first date."

"I didn't know that."

"You never asked me out on a date," she hinted.

"True," Donovan said.

"Are you sure you're okay talking about this?" Kyra asked.

"Yuh, yeah. Why'd, why do you ask?"

"I know we talk about everything," she said. "But we never
really talked about people we were dating."

Dating? Was she *dating* him now? Donovan thought it
was *one goddamned date!*

"You can talk to me about anything," he said. "So how did
this almost-kiss go? Did he come at you with his eyes already

closed?" *What the hell are you doing? You know you don't want to know!* But Donovan did want to know. He hated what he was hearing, but he needed to know everything. If she didn't tell him, he'd go crazy imagining all types of erotic scenarios.

"He leaned in with his eyes closed," Kyra said with a giggle. Maybe she and Donovan could talk about this kind of stuff after all. It would close the book on her fairy tale love affair with him, but having Donovan as her best friend was just as special.

"Did you scream?"

"No, I didn't scream. I told him to back off."

"That's cool. You weren't mad?"

"No. But I got a little upset when we got out of his car, and he tried to grab my ass."

Donovan saw fire. Red, hot molten lava. "What, what'd you do?" he managed.

"I pushed him off me. He asked for a hug at first, but his hands started moving. You know how y'all do."

"Huh huh." Donovan wasn't so much chuckling as he was struggling for breath. "So, are you going to see him again?"

"I don't know. Everything was going good on our date, all the way till the end. He was moving too fast, and I didn't like that. But if he would slow it down some, he might be a good dude. What do you think?"

I think I lied about being able to handle this conversation. "I think if you feel pressured, you need to make sure he knows where you draw the line. If he can't accept that, then he has to go."

"That's great advice," Kyra said.

Donovan thought so, too. But he wasn't sure how he came up with it under the current circumstances. He felt like he was having a stroke. He wanted to destroy something. A UPS truck would be a great start.

"Finish your run," Kyra said. "I'll call you later and tell you more about him."

Oh happy days! "Alright."

"Don't run too hard."

"I won't," Donovan said, but he was so wound up, he felt like he could run all the way to the freaking moon! "Talk to you later."

CHAPTER THIRTEEN
THE OCTOPUS

Kyra talked to Roland a few more times throughout the following week. And of course she saw him each day when he delivered parcels to J.T. Elder. Kyra didn't feel good about that, not at first. She was the new girl in the office, and she was also the youngest. So far everyone liked her. She didn't want them to know she was already dating the UPS guy after only three weeks on the job.

She told Roland how she felt, and he promised not to show her any special attention at work. He kept his word. So far none of Kyra's co-workers had caught on, even though Kyra's arms broke out in goose bumps at exactly 10:45 every morning, around the time Roland was expected to grace their presence.

Kyra didn't sign for his packages every time, but whenever she did Roland would smirk at her while she scribbled on his digital signature pad. Kyra would smirk at him, too, and then she'd return to her desk and carry on as usual.

Roland was a totally different animal when they talked on the phone. He kept Kyra smiling with his humor and his constant flattery. He kept her astonished with the long hours he put in at UPS, sometimes up to 16 hours in one shift. He kept her heart racing with his smooth talk and eagerness to see her again.

Kyra was nowhere near ready to have sexual relations with him, but Roland made it clear that he would worship her body and satisfy every single inch of it to the best of his abilities. He didn't tell her this directly, but there were innuendos aplenty.

Kyra didn't tell her best friend *everything*, even though Donovan wanted to know as much about Roland as possible. Kyra didn't know what to make of it. Donovan even offered to babysit for her when Kyra told him she was seeing Roland again on Saturday night.

"That would be great," Kyra said. "But why would you want to do that?"

"I'm not doing anything this Saturday," Donovan told her. "It'll save you some money on babysitting. How much do you owe your aunt by now? A few hundred?"

"A lot," Kyra said. "One-fifty a week when I'm at work."

"See, you don't need to keep adding to that bill. And I want to see Q anyway. He asked if he could get online on my Xbox."

"What about Kat," Kyra said.

"I love Kat!" Donovan replied. "She likes me, too – she just doesn't know it yet. The best way to make her comfortable around me is to leave her here, and let me take care of her. She's potty-trained, right?"

"Yes."

"Then I'm good," Donovan said. "I've never seen her crying."

"She doesn't cry much," Kyra confirmed. "I'm sure she'll be okay. It's you I'm worried about. No man has ever volunteered to watch my kids before. I'm worried you won't like it."

"I'm not just any man," Donovan said with a chuckle. "Didn't you say you wanted me to be their godfather?"

"Yes." Kyra's heart swelled. She threw that at him during one of their late night phone calls. She didn't think he was actually interested.

"Then bring my godchildren over here when you go out on your–" Donovan had to clear his throat. It was trying to close up on him. "– date. Your date."

"Alright," Kyra said. "I'll call Roland and tell him I'll meet him at the restaurant, so I can drop the kids off on my way."

"Okay," Donovan said. "I'll be here."

"You're the best," Kyra said. "Thanks."

"You're welcome." Donovan disconnected, and then he hung his head in shame. "I'm a fool," he said with a slump of his massive shoulders. There was no one in the house to argue against that.

≈≈≈≈≈≈≈

Four hours later Donovan's home was filled with something he'd never heard there before: The pitter patter of children's feet. Well, one child, to be exact. Kat was a lot less nervous about spending time with Mr. Mitchell than either he or Kyra imagined. For the first five minutes after Kyra dropped off her kids, Kat sat on the couch and watched Donovan who sat on his recliner.

Quinell was already in the den checking out Donovan's gaming systems. Donovan feared Kat was going to sit and stare at him the whole evening, but the toddler abruptly climbed off the sofa and walked to Donovan's recliner. She looked up at him. He smiled and raised an eyebrow, wondering what she would say. Kat looked around, and then she turned towards the coffee table and fingered one of the magazines that was stacked there. She flipped through a few pages and then looked around the room again for something more interesting.

She found it in a collection of whatnots Donovan had on his entertainment center. Donovan rushed to stop her when Kat wrapped her stubby fingers around a tiny, bronze elephant.

"Whoa, what are you doing?"

Kat looked up at him indignantly and said, "*Mine.*"

Donovan took the elephant from her and said, "No, that is not yours. This is mine."

Kat stuck out her hand, palm up. "Lemme see it."

Donovan's smile was big and toothy. Kat never spoke to him at all, but now they were having a legitimate conversation.

"Do you want to *see it* or *have* it?" he asked.

"See it!" Katavia said. She was irresistible.

"Okay. Here you go." He placed the elephant in her hand.

Kat's eyes lit up, and she giggled. "Mine!" she declared and took off running, laughing the whole time. Donovan's jaw dropped. He couldn't believe he'd been duped.

"Oh, no you don't!" He took off after her, surprised by how nimble she was on those chubby, little legs.

≈ ≈ ≈ ≈ ≈ ≈

An hour and a half later Donovan's Saturday night was filled with much of the same. Kat continued to explore and claim the many treasures she found as her very own. Donovan stopped chasing her after the second one. He even told her, "Yes, you can have that," to a few of the items she wanted. But Kat never played with anything for more than twenty minutes before she lost interest and continued her expedition.

Quinell was fully enthralled in Donovan's video games. Donovan played with him for nearly an hour, but he had to stop when a visitor rang his doorbell. Ten minutes later, Donovan had to answer his door for a second visitor. This one was unexpected.

Rodney had been Donovan's best *male* friend since high school. Rodney never left Overbrook Meadows, but he graduated from a local university and secured great position at the Channel 9 newsroom in Dallas.

Jonathan was a former student of Donovan's. He graduated two years ago and was currently a sophomore at Texas Lutheran. Donovan spent a good deal of time mentoring Jonathan at Western Hills. Because of turbulent conditions at home, Jonathan lived with Donovan for a couple of months after graduation. Donovan loved him like a son.

Rodney was one of few people in Donovan's life who knew Kyra when they were in high school. He had never seen Donovan babysit anyone's kids before, and he thought it was hilarious. When Donovan revealed that he actually had feelings for Kyra, Rodney's jaw dropped.

"Wha, what'd you just say?"

"I said I like her, man. I think I might, you know, I probably do..." Donovan shrugged. He rubbed his large hands together in his lap. He was sure he looked as pitiful as he felt. Donovan didn't have a problem discussing this with either of his friends, but the look on Rodney's face let him know he was in for more heckling.

"You like Kyra?"

"Yeah," Donovan said. He looked around uneasily. "Keep you voice down. I told you her son's in the den."

Kat was in the living room with the men, playing with oversized Legos her mother left with her. She was paying them no mind.

"He can't hear us," Rodney said. "I'm not even talking loud." Rodney was dark-skinned and slightly overweight. He was married with one child.

"Keep it down anyway," Donovan told him. "You never know."

"Alright, alright," Rodney said. He leaned forward with his forearms on his knees. His expression was comical. "You're talking about the woman who's out on a date with another man? You like this woman?"

Donovan sighed and rolled his eyes. Jonathan sat on the couch with Rodney, on the opposite end. He shook his head slowly as he stared at his former coach.

"Yes," Donovan told Rodney.

"And you're *babysitting* for her, so she can go on a date with another man?" Rodney clarified.

Donovan's chest rose and fell. He hated being the butt of Rodney's jokes. "Yes."

"Well," Rodney said, leaning back in his seat. "There's only one thing to say about that."

"And what might that be?" Donovan asked.

"*Nigga, is you crazy*?" Rodney burst into laughter.

Jonathan thought that was hilarious as well.

"Say, watch your language," Donovan said. He rubbed his forehead. "I think I'm losing it, y'all."

"Yeah, I think so, too," Rodney said. "And I knew you liked Kyra! I knew it when we were in high school!"

"Alright," Donovan said. "Alright. So I like her."

"Why didn't you tell her when she came back?" Rodney wondered. "Y'all could've been together this whole time."

"Because I was with Brianna," Donovan explained.

"And by the time you broke up with Brianna, Kyra was already going with this other guy?" Jonathan surmised.

"No, not exactly," Donovan said. "I broke up with Brianna *before* Kyra met this other cat. But..." He hesitated, knowing what they would say. "I told her to go out with him anyway." Donovan hung his head in shame. The room was silent.

"*Nigga, is you crazy*?"

"Man, I told you to watch your language!"

"Alright, alright," Rodney said. He tried to wipe the smile off his face, but it was impossible. "Okay, D. Please tell me; why did you tell Kyra to go out with another man?"

"Because I didn't want to mess up our friendship," Donovan said. "We always been better as friends."

"I feel you on that," Rodney said. "So why don't you and Kyra just stay friends?"

"Because I want her," Donovan said. "I don't want her to be with nobody else."

"You can't have both," Jonathan said.

"What do you know?" Donovan replied. "You're still wet behind the ears."

"I had a good friend who was a female," Jonathan said. "Then we started having sex. We broke up, and now we don't talk anymore. Like, not at all. We were really close before that. I miss her."

"That's what I'm talking about," Donovan said, his eyes brightening. "I don't want to mess up my friendship with Kyra."

"Then quit tripping," Rodney said. "Be happy that she's your friend, and leave it at that. As far as you liking Kyra, you'll be alright when you find another girlfriend."

"Yeah, you're right," Donovan said. That was good advice. He didn't need to be with Kyra. He could transfer his feelings for Kyra to another woman. Wait. Was that even possible? Something about it didn't sound right.

≈≈≈≈≈≈

Donovan's friends were gone by the time Kyra returned for her babies. He answered the door and welcomed her inside at 10:52 pm. Kyra looked happy and as lovely as ever. Her brother Duke sent her $500 when she got the job at the school. Kyra used the money for new outfits for herself and the kids. Most of the clothes she got herself were for work, but she got a few dresses for after work, too. Donovan thought she looked awesome in everything he'd seen her in.

Tonight she wore a red skirt with a black top. The skirt was form-fitting. Kyra's hips were mesmerizing. Donovan didn't understand how it was possible from them to protrude from her body at such a degree and then quickly shrink towards her waist and thighs. Those hips were the perfect size for Donovan's hands. Kyra's blouse showed off quite a bit of cleavage. Donovan was both attracted to her and jealous because she dressed this way for another man. He didn't like to think of Roland's eyes rolling over her throat and chest and her soft, succulent breasts.

Even worse, Donovan knew he'd hear about Kyra's whole date, from start to finish. She'd tell him how Roland looked and what he said and how she felt about it. Kyra would tell him if Roland tried to kiss her again and if she liked it and if she was starting to like him. Sadly, Donovan would be the one to pry all of these details from her. He didn't want to, but at the same time he had to know.

"How was everything?" Kyra asked. "Did they give you any trouble?" She wore her hair down and layered. Her makeup was faint but perfect. Donovan's heart skipped a beat as he watched her. He didn't think she'd ever looked more beautiful.

"Everything was fine. Kat's quite a character. She had me fooled."

"What do you mean?"

Kat rushed into the room at the sound of her mother's voice. This time she had two neckties in her hands. Donovan closed his bedroom door, so he had no idea where she found those.

"There's my precious baby!" Kyra knelt to give her a hug and a kiss. "Where'd you get these?" She took Donovan's ties away from her and placed them on the coffee table. Kat went after them immediately.

"Mine!"

"No those are not yours," Kyra said. She picked her daughter up to keep her away from them. "Where's Q?"

"He's in the den. Q!" Donovan shouted down the hallway. "Your mom's here!"

They heard Quinell's "*Aww, man!*" all the way in the living room.

"Thanks for watching them," Kyra said.

"No problem. How was your date?"

"It was great." Kyra's eyes were twinkling. "But I think Roland might be part octopus."

Donovan's smile fell. "Why you say that? He tried something else?"

"Yep," Kyra said. "An exact repeat of last time."

Hot coals began to burn behind Donovan's eyes. Kyra didn't notice because Q walked into the room at that moment. She looked down at him.

"Hey, did you have a good time?"

"Yes. Mr. Mitchell said I can have his PS3. Can I get it?"

Kyra frowned. "No, boy. You're not taking anything out of this house."

Q's whole face drooped.

"It's okay," Donovan said. "I told him he could have it. I don't play with it anymore, since I got my Xbox."

"No, Donovan," Kyra said. "I don't like that. I'll buy him one when I get my check."

"You can't pay for *everything* with your first check," Donovan said good-naturedly. "Go put your kids in the car, and I'll unhook the system for him. I wanna talk to you about your date, when you get back."

Kyra continued to frown, but she left the house and did as he asked her. She strapped Kat into her car seat and turned the engine on so the air-conditioner would blow. Before she went to retrieve the PlayStation, she gave Quinell a hard look.

"Did you ask him for that thing?"

"No." He shook his head fiercely.

"Don't be going to people's house asking for stuff."

"I didn't, Mama. I swear."

Kyra narrowed her eyes and stared at him for a few more seconds before she closed the door. When she reentered Donovan's home, he had what looked like a very expensive electronic unplugged and waiting for her. Kyra started shaking her head before she spoke.

"Donovan, that's nice of you, really. But we can't take that. That's too much."

Donovan stood next to his recliner wearing camouflage shorts with a black tee shirt. His expression was dark. He told her, "Yes you are taking it, and I'm not going to argue about it. I told Q he can have it. That's the end of it."

Kyra was startled by his demeanor. "Okay. I, I didn't know it meant that much to you."

"I don't care about this game," he said. "I want to know about your date. What do you mean he was part octopus?"

Kyra's heart began to race. She hadn't felt this way since the first time she told Donovan about Roland. They talked about him plenty of times since then. Donovan never reacted like this.

"It, it was nothing," she said. "He was just being silly."

"Tell me what happened."

155

Kyra swallowed hard. "I, I, we went out. He took me to Maggiano's. We had a good time. When he walked me to my car, he tried to kiss me again. I kissed him." Kyra had to lower her gaze. She never felt this nervous around Donovan. "Before I got in my car, he said he wanted a hug, too. I told him not to try anything like last time. He said he wouldn't, but his hands started moving. I pushed him off."

She looked up at him. Donovan was clearly upset. And he was huge. His anger seemed to add ten feet to his height. The last time Kyra saw that look in his eyes, they were children and she told him her mother's boyfriend tried to pull her sheets away while she was sleeping.

"Do you like him," Donovan asked.

"I, I, I don't know," Kyra said. "I wouldn't have kissed him, if I didn't like him. But I don't like how fast he wants to move. I can tell he wants to go way too fast."

"I don't want you to see him anymore," Donovan said. He didn't mean to, it just came out. Once it was out there, Donovan felt like a fool. What the hell was he doing? Kyra said she liked her new friend. Donovan should've given his advice and left it at that. Instead he practically commanded Kyra to stop seeing Roland. What would she think of him?

But without skipping a beat, Kyra said, "Okay." She looked him dead in the eyes. Her heart was hammering. Her chest rose and fell so quickly, she knew Donovan saw it.

A cool rain washed over Donovan. His red, hot anger was immediately doused. But he didn't feel good about what he just did.

"I'm sorry. I shouldn't have said that. You can keep seeing him if–"

"I'm not going to see him again," Kyra stated. She was staring deeply into his eyes. Donovan didn't think she'd blinked at all in the past minute.

Without warning she approached him and wrapped her arms around him. Donovan immediately grabbed her and held tightly. Kyra laid her face against his chest. She said, "Thank you, for everything."

Donovan lowered his head until his nose and mouth brushed the top of her head. He inhaled her wonderful scents. His arms moved slowly across her back as his hands touched and clutched her flesh. Kyra's body was on fire. The best friends hugged plenty of times since she returned, but never like this.

Donovan felt light headed. He didn't realize what was happening until there was a mass of hard muscle between his legs. His manhood pushed against his shorts and then against Kyra.

Embarrassed, Donovan broke away from the embrace. He took a step back. "I'm sorry."

"Sorry for what?" Kyra asked. She didn't look down at what she had felt on her stomach. She wanted to. She wanted to look so badly her heart ached. But she kept her eyes glued on Donovan's. Her expression was daring and alluring and knowing.

"Nothing," Donovan said.

"Then don't apologize. You didn't do anything wrong," Kyra said. She took a few steps back. She felt pressure in her lower belly as she moved. She felt her muscles clench a little lower down. Her legs threatened to give out on her, but Kyra managed to turn and exit the house.

Donovan was enchanted by the sway of her hips as she moved. For the first time in his entire life he watched Kyra's ass like he wanted it, and he didn't feel one bit guilty about it. Kyra's words were still ringing in his ears.

You didn't do anything wrong.

Kyra didn't realize she left the gaming system until she got behind the wheel of her car and Quinell started whining about it.

"I'm sorry. Go, go get it," she told him. She would've gone herself, but her eyes were still wide, her blood racing. She sensed that if she went back inside Donovan's house, she wouldn't be leaving anytime soon.

CHAPTER FOURTEEN
HOMECOMING

The following Friday Donovan's Mad Stallions faced the North Side Steers for their homecoming game. Donovan's team was on a surprising three game win streak, bringing their record to 3-3. There was magic in the air that night. Many of the fans who were praying to end the season with an even record were now wondering if Western Hills could pull off a *winning* season.

Unfortunately, it was not meant to be. North Side's blitz package completely overwhelmed Donovan's offense on a few crucial plays that led to two interceptions and a fumble. Donovan's team lost 26-17. It was a bitter defeat, but the festivities of the homecoming celebration took a little of the sting out of it.

Donovan called Kyra later that night, a little before midnight. She was still awake, eager to hear about tonight's game. She would've gone herself, but Kat was under the weather.

"Hey," she said. She went to the living room and got comfortable on the sofa. "Sorry about the loss."

"Oh, you heard already?" Donovan sighed. He sounded exhausted.

"Yeah. I was keeping up with it on the radio. It was close, for a minute there."

Donovan smiled. "You listened to my game on the radio?"

"Yeah, I'm surprised, too," Kyra said. "That announcer was boring as hell."

Donovan laughed. "How's Kat?"

"She's actually better now," Kyra said with a trace of irritation. "She's eating and everything. I hate that I missed your game."

"It's cool," Donovan said. He yawned. "It's been a long night."

"Are you tired? Want me to let you go?"

"No, I'm alright." Donovan stretched out on his bed. "I'm laying down now. I'm cool."

Kyra nibbled her thumbnail. She longed to crawl into bed with him.

"So what's up with your defense there, coach?"

Donovan chuckled. "You realize it wasn't me out there playing, right?"

"That's no excuse," Kyra said. Her smile lit up the darkness. "Your offensive line was playing like they'd never seen a blitz before."

"Whoa," Donovan said. "That's a little harsh."

"I'm just kidding. That's what the man on the radio said."

"The boring guy?"

"Yeah, him."

"It was still a great night," Donovan said, closing his eyes. "Everybody was all dressed up. They had the halftime presentations, the homecoming king and queen."

"I know," Kyra said. "That's the main reason I wanted to go. I never went to a homecoming game before."

"If I wasn't coaching, I would've loved to take you," Donovan said.

Kyra's heart danced at the thought of it. Homecoming games had a romantic feel to them – well, that's what she gathered from the pictures they put in her senior yearbook in Little Rock. The boys and girls got dressed up, and the boys bought their sweetheart a mum with both their names on it. During the game, students would disappear under the bleachers for flirting and smooching and sometimes a little more.

"How have things been going at work?" Donovan asked. "I still feel bad about interfering with your, um, relationship."

Kyra giggled. "*Relationship*? Donovan, I was not in a relationship."

"That was your boyfriend," he insisted.

"No it wasn't."

"You kissed him."

Kyra's grin was devilish. "Jealous?"

Donovan felt the heat rising between his legs again. "Yeah. Kinda."

Kyra sat up straight. Her pulse began to race. He was jealous? Really? What did that mean? They never got this close to talking about how they felt about each other.

"How is it at work with Roland," Donovan asked. "Does he treat you any different?"

No, don't change the subject! "He treats me fine," Kyra said. "I don't be thinking about him. Um, you were jealous?"

Donovan grinned. "What do you want me to say?"

"I don't know. But I do think that's worth talking about, don't you?"

"Do you think I got mad when you told me about that jerk, because I want you all to myself?"

Kyra's mouth went dry. Her eyes were wide and anxious. "Did, do, do you?"

"I think we should talk about it," Donovan said. "But I'd rather do it in person. Hey, I just had a great idea!"

Kyra didn't think things could get any better. She was on the edge of her seat. "What?"

"Guess who's having their homecoming game tomorrow night?"

Kyra had no idea. Her brain was still stuck on *I think we should talk about it.* "Who?"

"Finley High!" Donovan said. "Do you want to go?"

Kyra thought she might pass out from an awesomeness-overload. A homecoming game at Finley High School *with* Donovan *and* he wanted to talk about whether he was jealous and wanted her all to himself or not? She couldn't get her answer out fast enough. "Yes, I want to go! Hell yes!"

"Great. I'll pick you up at seven-thirty. Can you get your aunt to watch the kids?"

"Will this be like, a real date?" Kyra dared to ask.

"I reckon so," Donovan said. "Wouldn't be right if I ran your boyfriend off and didn't offer to take you out myself."

≈≈≈≈≈≈

Donovan showed up the next evening wearing dark pants with a royal blue button down that matched his Finley High School baseball cap. His shirt was short-sleeved, and it was tucked in, showing off his remarkable upper body and slim waist.

Kyra wore a fuchsia dress that dipped low in the back and in the front. The dress wasn't form fitting, but Kyra's curves shined through anyway. Her breasts were nice and perky. Her lipstick matched her dress. She grinned at Donovan and blushed when he smiled at her. She felt like a school girl.

"Here, this is for you," Donovan said, and it was only then that Kyra noticed he had one arm behind his back. He produced a blue and white mum with four-foot streamers that were decorated with little footballs and bells and school specific lettering.

Kyra squealed as she took it from him. This was her very first mum! It was fifteen years late, but she was happier now than she would've been if she received it in high school. One of the streamers read, "GO GRIZZLIES!" Another said, "FINLEY HIGH SCHOOL 2013." The *best* one read, "KYRA + DONOVAN." Kyra's eyes were glossy as she looked up at him.

"They, um, they asked if it was for a girl, and I told them you were my date."

Yeah, whatever, Kyra thought. She knew that whoever designed the mum would only put their names together like that if Donovan told them it was for his *girlfriend*. He didn't have to admit it, if he didn't want to.

"Put it on me," she said. She gave Donovan the mum and thrust her chest in his direction.

Wow. He tried to keep his eyes on the work at hand rather than get lost in Kyra's cleavage. "I'm not sure if I know how to do this..."

He reached and fumbled with her dress. Kyra giggled at him as he tried to attach the mum without touching her skin.

"Try a little harder," she teased. "Don't be afraid to get up in there."

A few beads of sweat blossomed on Donovan's forehead. "I haven't had my hands near these babies in fifteen years," he muttered.

Kyra's heart stopped. She looked into his eyes. Donovan winked at her and smiled.

He did remember!

"Got it." Donovan withdrew his hands, and the mum remained firmly attached. He reached for Kyra's hand. "Shall we go?"

Kyra bypassed his hand and gave him a quick hug and a kiss on the cheek. "I'd be delighted," she said and led the way outside.

≈ ≈ ≈ ≈ ≈ ≈

Donovan drove her to Milton Stadium, the host of Finley High's homecoming game. It was an impressive structure, built in the late seventies. Nostalgia was in the air from the moment they entered the parking lot and saw the school buses lined up. Nearly every car and truck had Finley High's colors and fight slogans painted on the windshield.

The parking lot was filled with teenagers who were dressed to impress. The boys wore their shiny shoes. All of the girls had beautiful mums, the bigger the better. There were also a good number of older fans who had been coming to Finley's homecoming games since their graduation.

Kyra heard the band warming up when Donovan helped her out of his truck. Her heart knocked at the same pace as the bass drums. She hadn't heard Finley High's class song in so long, she had forgotten the words. But she never forgot the melody.

The game started with a kickoff that was returned all the way for a touchdown by the opposing team. But Kyra couldn't have been happier. Sitting on the bleachers with Donovan with Finley High students and banners all around them made her feel like she was in a time portal. Her mind was flooded with memories; bells ringing, fights after school, science projects gone horribly wrong. Donovan was there through all of it.

The BFF's watched the sun set as the home team miraculously tied the score at 20 to 20 by the end of the second quarter. The stadium went crazy at halftime with the battle of the bands and the presentation of the Homecoming Court. Everyone hustled to get snacks and refreshments after that. Donovan wanted to get some popcorn and candy, too, but he suggested they wait until the beginning of the third quarter, when the lines wouldn't be long.

"I can't thank you enough for tonight," Kyra told him. She half turned on the bleacher so she could look him in the eyes. "I used to dream about things like this; a homecoming game, my mum." She couldn't stop smiling. "You make me so happy."

"It's the least I could do," Donovan said. He took his cap off and brushed his hair forward with his hand. Kyra loved his haircut. The waves on top were a work of art.

"Why do you say that?" she asked.

"Because I told you to break up with your boyfriend." Donovan shook his head. "I still don't think that was right."

"Stop saying that," Kyra said. "He wasn't my boyfriend, for one."

"Were you gonna go out with him again?" Donovan asked. "Tell me that."

"I don't know," Kyra said. "Probably not. The bottom line is he's gone now, and you don't have to be jealous anymore." She smirked at him.

Donovan grinned. "Who said I was jealous?"

"You did."

"You really want to talk about that, huh?"

"It's the closet you ever came to saying you like me," Kyra noted. "So, yeah, I think it's kinda important."

Donovan looked up at the sky. He stared up there for so long, Kyra looked, too, wondering what she was missing.

"Do you remember when we kissed?" he asked abruptly.

Kyra's heart jumped all the way to the back of her throat. *Oh my God! Finally!* She swallowed and exhaled slowly. "Yes."

Donovan wasn't smiling now. There were a lot of people moving around them, but Kyra had tunnel vision. She only saw one person.

"Do you remember the song?" he asked.

Kyra nodded. "We Can't be Friends, by R.L. and Deborah Cox."

Donovan grinned slightly. It was a cheerless smile. "I remember, too. I'll never forget that song."

"Me neither," Kyra said. She hung on each one of his words, as if Donovan was about to reveal the secret of life.

"I cry every time I hear that song," he said.

Kyra gasped. "I do, too."

163

"I used to try to avoid it," Donovan said. "I'd change the station and listen to something else. But once I heard even a little piece of that song, I couldn't help but think about that day. I end up changing to the station back, so I can hear the rest of it. After a while, I stopped trying to avoid it. That song always reminds me of you, and I liked thinking about you, even though it hurt."

Kyra's eyes filled with tears. She wiped them quickly so she could maintain focus on Donovan's eyes.

"That song scares me," he said. "That's why I've been acting the way I have. That's why I didn't want to tell you how I feel."

"How, how do you feel?"

Donovan looked puzzled. "I love you, Kyra. I always have. You know that."

If Kyra discovered a drug that could give her the surge of euphoria she felt at that moment, she would destroy it. It was too powerful. All of her anxiety and pent up frustration and longing spun together like a tornado in her chest. There was a great explosion, leaving the purest form of joy and love and peace in its wake. It was so wonderful, Kyra thought she might pass out.

Again her eyes squirted tears. Donovan reached to wipe them this time. His touch was soft yet electrifying. Kyra was unaware that she leaned her face into his strong hand.

"I love you, too," she whispered.

Donovan smiled and nodded. "I know."

So where do we go from here? Kyra's heart yearned for an answer, but she didn't ask. She knew Donovan was about to tell her. He had always been the rock in her life, ever since she was a child. She trusted him 100%, knowing he would never do anything to harm her.

"I did get jealous when you went out with Roland."

"I didn't want to make you jealous," Kyra said.

"I know. I told you to go out with him, even though I knew you wanted to go out with me instead."

Kyra grinned. *So you could tell?*

"The reason for that goes back to that song and our kiss," Donovan stated. "I lost you for fifteen years, and I never want to lose you again. I'm afraid that if we have a relationship, and something goes wrong, we won't be friends anymore, like last time."

The mere thought of it brought Donovan a fresh wave of the heartache he felt when his mother kicked Kyra out of their home. His eyes glistened. He brushed the moisture away with his shoulder.

Kyra's heart bled for him. No one had ever loved her as much as Donovan did. It was the most amazing feeling in the world.

"That's why I feel bad about telling you not to see Roland," he said. "Because I still don't know if you and I should get in a relationship like that. I shouldn't have interfered with your love life unless I was sure."

Kyra felt a tinge of disappointment. He wasn't sure. She was ready to give herself to him in all capacities, but Donovan wasn't sure. Maybe he was right. Was their fairytale love affair meant to be, or was it their eternal friendship that was destined. There was no way to know for sure. Kyra knew Donovan would complete her life in either scenario. She smiled.

"I'm ready for whatever you decide. You don't have to make a decision right now. I'm not going anywhere."

Donovan returned her smile, though he knew it was wrong to hold Kyra's heart hostage indefinitely. She was a beautiful woman, and she deserved to fly. Donovan let her go two weeks ago, but he pulled the string tied to her leg when she flew too far away from him. That was something he could never do again, regardless of what their future held.

The referee blew his whistle, signaling the beginning of the third quarter. Donovan noticed the seats around them were filled again.

"You wanna get some snacks?" he asked Kyra.

She nodded. Donovan stood and took her hand and helped her up. He looked her up and down, the bright stadium lights twinkling in his eyes.

"You know you're wearing the hell out of that dress, don't you?"

"Thank you, Mr. Mitchell. You are one handsome devil yourself."

≈≈≈≈≈≈≈

165

Donovan got popcorn and soft drinks for both of them. Kyra got a pack of cherry Now & Later's and a pickle, or as Donovan called it, *The Hood Chick Special*. They took a leisurely stroll around the stadium on the way back to their seats, and Donovan was delighted to run into his former football coach.

Coach Jackson was no longer molding bright minds and strong bodies at Finley High, but he never missed their games. He congratulated Donovan for everything from his game winning sack against Rosemont in 1997 to his current coaching success at Western Hills. It took Donovan nearly ten minutes to end the conversation.

"Sorry about that," he said, chuckling, as he and Kyra continued their moonlit promenade.

"That man loves you to death," she said. She was just as proud of him. Donovan was proof that you don't have to make a million dollars or invent the next iPhone to have an impact on people's lives. He was a hometown hero.

"It was hard for me to keep my mind on what Coach Jackson was saying, with you over there popping those Now & Later's," he told her.

Kyra gave him a curious look. Donovan grinned at her as he sipped his soda.

"What do you mean?"

"What do you mean *what do I mean*. You know good and well what I mean."

Kyra laughed. "Boy, you're talking in riddles. I have no idea what you're talking about."

"You don't remember the cherry Now & Later's?"

Kyra shook her head. "I always used to eat these. They're my favorite. I haven't had any in over a year."

"I'm talking about that day," Donovan said. "*Our kiss.* You were eating cherry Now & Later's."

Kyra thought she remembered every second of *that day*, but she didn't remember that. "I used to eat them all the time," she said. "What about it?"

"I tasted it," Donovan said. "When I kissed you."

Kyra grinned mischievously as she realized what he was saying. *Oh.* "You remember what my tongue tastes like?"

Donovan stared at her beautiful lips as she spoke. Her tongue was completely red because of the candy.

"Kyra, I've dreamt of that taste, of your mouth, those red lips. You shouldn't have ate that candy. I'm having all kinds of flashbacks. You don't know what it's doing to me."

Damn. And Donovan didn't know what he was doing to Kyra! The look in his eyes had her heart racing again. But they already talked about this. Donovan said he didn't want to cross the threshold. She didn't think a pack of candy could change that.

"Come on," he said. Donovan dropped one of the sodas he was carrying and grabbed her hand. He began to move so fast Kyra lost hold of her pickle. She looked back at it as it rolled into the ice from Donovan's spilled soda.

"What's wrong? Where are we going?"

"You'll see."

Donovan's pace increased as he moved deftly around the pillars and concession stands at the stadium. Kyra thought he was in a rush to get back to their seats, but Donovan hurried past the corridor that led to the stairway. He stopped when they reached a locked gate. But it wasn't locked. The chains were draped through both sides to make it appear impassable, but Donovan pulled the chains free, and the gate swung open.

Kyra couldn't have been more perplexed. "What are you doing?"

"Come on," he urged. He tossed his other soda and their popcorn in a nearby receptacle before he slipped inside the gate.

Kyra followed with butterflies flittering in her stomach. *What in the world?*

Once inside, Donovan draped the chains over the lock, like it was when they found it. He took Kyra's hand again and led her deeper into the underbelly of the stadium.

Kyra noticed the bright lights above didn't fully permeate this secluded area. But the noise from the crowd was just as loud. In fact, it sounded like they were right in the midst of it. Soon there was grass and gravel beneath their feet rather than concrete. There were discarded cups and food wrappers almost everywhere. Kyra looked up and saw slits of light shining through long metal planks. She looked closer and saw an assortment of shoes that still had legs attached to them. A lot of the feet were moving.

Oh my God, he took me under the bleachers!

Donovan finally came to a stop when he reached a large pillar. He turned and faced Kyra. He took her by the shoulders and turned her around. He backed her against the pillar and let her go. The bells on Kyra's mum jingled in the darkness. Her breaths were hurried.

"What are we doing here?"

"Are you scared?" Donovan asked.

"No. Not with you." Kyra's eyes were wide. Her breasts rose and fell. It was hypnotizing, that lush caramel colored cleavage. Donovan took a step towards her.

"What do kids do under the bleachers?" he asked. Kyra saw the glimpse of a smile teasing his lips.

"They, they make out?"

Donovan nodded. "That's how I know how to get in here. I found quite a few students under these bleachers over the years."

"Okay," Kyra managed. "But why are *we* here, together?"

"Because of you and your Now & Later's," Donovan said. "You have no idea how bad I want to taste you." He took another step.

Kyra was nearly trembling. "But, but I thought you said—"

"I know what I said. And I decided what I want. I want you. I want those red lips. Right now."

Kyra nearly swallowed the candy in her mouth as Donovan closed the distance between them. He put his hands on her hips, and Kyra's whole body was electrified.

Oh yes. Oh my God!

Donovan closed his eyes a moment before his lips met hers. Kyra shuddered and moaned involuntarily. Donovan sucked her bottom lip. She was so sweet! Kyra kissed him back. Her heart was like a locomotive. Cymbals clashed overhead as the band celebrated a Finley High touchdown. And then came the drums. It was so loud!

The crowd cheered. They stomped their feet. Donovan was a demanding lover. He gripped her tightly. His tongue slipped inside her mouth, and he quickly claimed the space as his own.

"Oh, Kyra!" He pulled her hips, hard, until she could feel his wanting. His hands slipped to the back of her dress, and he squeezed her ass. The material was so thin. And Kyra felt so good. Donovan was blind with passion. Kyra felt the muscles between her legs clenching, over and over again. The sliver of candy in her mouth slipped into Donovan's. He quickly swallowed it and sucked Kyra's tongue in search of more.

The throbbing in his boxers was as fierce as it was fifteen years ago, but there was no hesitance this time. No fear that they would be found. No fear that they would have to stop before this kiss reached its conclusion. His hands skated up and down Kyra's frame. His chest thundered. He knew it would be like this! He always knew.

Kyra gasped for air when Donovan left her mouth and sucked the flesh beneath her ear. She threw her head back and moaned her approval. Donovan greedily licked the hot skin she exposed to him. His tongue was on fire. And Kyra was, too. She felt the slickness in her panties. She wanted Donovan to touch her there. She grinded against his body. The friction against her clitoris made her shout out in ecstasy.

"*Oh!*" She was so loud. She couldn't help it.

Donovan had her backed up against the pillar. He grinded his hips between her legs. He was rock hard. Kyra could feel every inch of it.

"I want you so bad!" he moaned.

"I want you, too," she panted. "I love you."

Donovan pulled back so he could look into her eyes. "I love you, too. I always have."

He kissed her again. Kyra ran her hands up his sides. Donovan was ripped! She raked her hands over his abs, up to his chest. She squeezed his pectorals. *Oh wow.*

"Come home with me," Donovan said.

Kyra couldn't hear much beyond the blood rushing past her ears. "I love you," she muttered. "I love you, Donovan."

"I want to take you home," he said. "Can you stay with me?"

"Yes," Kyra whispered. "Forever."

CHAPTER FIFTEEN
ETERNALLY YOURS

Kyra ended the call with her aunt and returned her cellphone to her purse. She looked up at Donovan who was watching her instead of the freeway.

"What'd she say?"

Kyra blushed. "She said yes."

Donovan's smile brightened. "That's awesome."

Kyra nodded. She was still stunned from Donovan's stunt under the bleachers. "That was some kiss."

"It was," Donovan agreed. "It was the best ever."

"Really?"

He looked over at her. Kyra's eyes were dark and beautiful.

"The first time we kissed was the reigning champ," he said. "But tonight was better."

Kyra's heart nearly floated out of her chest. Donovan was a gorgeous man and a popular football player. She couldn't believe his two best kisses were the ones he shared with her.

"Me, too," she said. "They were my best."

"Which one was better?"

Kyra giggled. "That's a hard one. That first kiss... I dreamt about it for years. It was special for a whole lot of reasons. But tonight..." She shook her head slowly. "You blew my mind, Donovan. I've been waiting so long. I thought it wasn't going to happen. It was monumental. But the first one was, too."

"Dang," Donovan kidded. "I would've hoped I improved a little over the years."

Kyra placed a hand on his thigh. "Oh, you have."

"Nah, I don't think I impressed you enough," Donovan stated. "I have to try a little bit harder, when we get to my place."

Kyra grinned. *Wow. I'm going to spend the night with Donovan Mitchell.* Even as she said it aloud in her mind, and Donovan piloted his F-150 towards their destiny, Kyra didn't fully believe it.

He placed his hand over hers and caressed it tenderly. Kyra looked into his eyes and smiled. She turned her hand over so they could interlock fingers. They held hands the rest of the way.

≈≈≈≈≈≈

Minutes later, they arrived at Donovan's house. Kyra's heartbeats quickened as she walked through the doorway. Donovan closed and locked it behind her.

"Do you want something to drink?"

Kyra nodded. She followed him to the kitchen where Donovan pulled two bottled waters from the refrigerator. He handed her one and leaned on the counter watching while she unscrewed the top.

"Here, let me get that for you."

Donovan approached and unfastened her mum. Kyra noticed his fingers were trembling slightly.

"Are you nervous?" she asked after he placed the mum on the counter.

Donovan nodded. "You can tell?"

"A little."

"Are you?"

Kyra nodded.

"Good." Donovan grinned. "We can be nervous together."

Kyra smiled, too.

"Come in here," Donovan said and led her back to the living room.

He took a seat on the sofa, and Kyra sat next to him. She took a sip of water before she placed the bottle on the coffee table.

Donovan watched her carefully. "Do you want to be here?" he asked.

"Of course."

"Do you want to spend the night with me?"

Kyra blushed. She looked down at her hands. She nodded.

171

Donovan reached and lifted her head with two fingers under her chin. "Are you sure?"

Kyra took a deep breath. "Yes."

"Are you worried about what it might be like, afterwards?"

"I don't ever want to lose you."

"I don't either," Donovan said. "We're going to be together forever."

"You promise?"

"I promise."

They sealed his pledge with a kiss. Kyra giggled. Her tongue was still blood red. Donovan leaned closer and kissed her again. He savored the flavor of her bottom lip. He leaned closer still, until he was nearly on top of her. Kyra had no choice but to recline on the soft cushions. Donovan placed a hand on her hip. He slipped his tongue inside her mouth as his fingers inched their way towards her breasts.

He left her mouth for a moment to plant hot kisses down her neck. Kyra threw her head back, enjoying the sweet sensations his mouth gave. She gasped when he sucked her exposed cleavage. Donovan's hand met his mouth there at the same time. He fondled her breast with his large hand while fingering her nipple with his thumb. Kyra felt electricity shoot through her chest. Her nipple hardened. Donovan squeezed it between his thumb and first finger until her whole body shuddered. She put her arms on either side of his neck and stroked his trapezius muscles, silently begging for more.

But Donovan backed away abruptly. He stared at her with his lips parted. His eyes were dark and eager, almost animalistic. Kyra's heart thundered. Donovan stood. The bulge in the front of his pants was as clear as day. He made no attempt to hide it, so Kyra stared at it unabashedly. Donovan reached for her, and she offered her hand. He pulled her to a standing position and led her down the hallway.

Kyra swallowed hard when she entered his bedroom. Donovan didn't turn on the lights. He released her hand when they reached his bed.

"Sit down."

Kyra did as she was told. Donovan's bed was high off the floor. Kyra's feet dangled as she scooted back on the mattress. Donovan faced her, with his back to the door. The light was on in the living room, but it wasn't enough to fully illuminate the hallway. Kyra saw little more than a silhouette as Donovan reached to unbutton his shirt – but what a silhouette it was! When he removed his shirt, Kyra saw how carefully defined his neck and shoulder muscles were. His back fanned out like a cobra; it was so sculpted, she could see it from the front.

Donovan tossed his shirt towards the closet and slowly unbuckled his belt. Kyra could barely see, but she couldn't look away. He pulled his belt free of the loops and dropped it in the general direction of his shirt. He unbuttoned and unzipped his pants in the same fluid motion. He pushed the slacks off his hips, and they fell the rest of the way down his legs. Kyra subconsciously held her breath. It was so dark, she couldn't tell what color his boxers were. She strained her eyes to no avail.

Donovan stepped to her and put his hands on her shoulders. Kyra looked up at him, but her eyes kept darting to his boxers. Donovan slid her dress straps off her shoulders and asked, "Does it zip in the back?" Kyra nodded. Donovan stepped closer so he could undo the zipper. His manhood pressed against her stomach, and Kyra's eyes widened. *Oh my God, he's huge!*

Donovan unzipped her and asked her to, "Stand up, so I can get this dress off."

He helped her off the bed and then pealed the dress off slowly. When Kyra was down to her undies, Donovan placed his hands under her arms and ran them down her sides, creating ripples of energy that made Kyra tremble.

"You have an awesome body," he said. "Do you mind if I turn on the lights?"

Mind? Kyra was sure she wanted that more than he did. "No. Please, turn them on."

He reached back, and Kyra was momentarily blinded by the brightness. As her pupils constricted, she was treated with a vision more breathtaking than any of the world's natural wonders.

This is not real.

Donovan's skin was smooth and chocolaty from head to toe. His chest was like nothing she'd ever seen in real life. There was a definite crease between his pectorals. His nipples were dark and enticing. His chest protruded from his body at least an inch. Donovan's arms and shoulders were just as delectable, but it was his chest that captivated Kyra.

And then there was his package. Kyra looked down, and
her mouth watered and fell open at the same time. *Oh my damn.*
Donovan was so hard, the fabric in his boxers was stretched nearly
to the breaking point. The fat head she felt poking her when
Donovan took her under the bleachers looked to be plumb-sized.
Kyra's kitty shuddered pleasantly in anticipation.

"Do, does it hurt?" she asked, her eyes trained on one
button at the front of his boxers that was sure to pop off at any
moment.

"A little," Donovan admitted.

Kyra reached down tentatively and pulled the front of his
boxers down. Donovan's erection jumped up to greet her. Kyra
inhaled sharply. She wrapped one hand around it, and then the
other. She actually had room for both. His flesh was incredibly
warm. She felt his blood racing beneath her fingers. She squeezed
him slightly, and his manhood pulsated in response. Kyra lightly
bit her bottom lip.

Donovan groaned as he reached around with both hands to
undo her bra. Kyra regretted that she had to let go of him for a
moment so he could slide the undergarment off her arms. Her
hands went right back to her new friend. She squeezed him a little
harder, and Donovan's stomach tightened. She looked up at him.
He was breathing deeply, staring into her eyes. He leaned down
and kissed her. Kyra felt him jump in her hands again. She
stroked him slowly as their tongues danced.

Donovan grabbed her ass with both hands and was
delighted to find that Kyra wore a thong. The feel of her bare flesh
beneath his palms and the way Kyra stroked him with her soft,
smooth hands made pre-cum seep to the tip of his penis. He
fondled her with increased vigor. Kyra's ass was plump and
round. She looked down at his manhood and hummed with
pleasure.

"Kyra you feel so good to me."

"You do, too, baby."

Donovan sucked her lips, and then his head dipped, in
search of the nipple he met earlier. Kyra's breasts were
ridiculously perky. Donovan let go of her ass so he could caress
them fully for the first time. They were soft and warm. Donovan
brought the right one to his mouth and devoured her nipple.

"Oh!" Kyra's eyelids fluttered while Donovan's lips and tongue worked hard to please her. She grabbed the back of his head with both hands. Donovan tweaked one nipple with his fingers while he sucked and nibbled the other. When the opposite one was as hard as a pebble, he switched sides, showing them equal affection.

Kyra's chest had never been stimulated so thoroughly. Donovan didn't have any timing she could pin down. Sometimes he sucked softly, sometimes hard. He licked one nipple tenderly, like he was enjoying ice cream, while at the same time squeezing her other nipple so hard she felt a lightning bolt shoot through her chest and down to her toes.

Just when she thought she knew what was coming, Donovan stopped suddenly and reached for her panties. He pulled them past her ass and down her thighs. They fell the rest of the way to the floor. Donovan placed both hands on her hips as he kissed her again. They were both completely nude now. Kyra had never been more eager to make love. Donovan's patience was driving her crazy.

"Get on the bed," he said.

Kyra reached back to pull herself up. Donovan hoisted her at the same time. Kyra sat back on the mattress, astonished by his strength. She barely had to help at all.

Donovan had a smile on his face. "Kyra, you've grown into a very beautiful woman. You were fine back in high school. Now your body's straight up crazy."

Her face reddened as she grinned at him. Donovan turned to retrieve a condom from his dresser. Kyra brought a hand to her mouth as she checked out his backside. *That is one nice ass!*

Donovan turned back to her. His eyes narrowed. "Were you checking out my ass?"

"No," Kyra said with a giggle. She was biting her fingernail.

"Whatever," Donovan said. He maintained eye contact as he tore the condom open and rolled it the length of his penis, inch by inch. Kyra couldn't take her eyes off his hands and his dick.

"Light's off, or on?" Donovan asked. "Hey, I'm up here."

Kyra looked up at him. She chuckled nervously, her hand still covering her mouth. She really wanted to watch every bit of

Donovan the first time they made love, but the darkness had even more allure. "Off," she replied.

Donovan turned slightly to flip the switch. Kyra got another glimpse of his bubble butt before Donovan was once again a silhouette. He approached the bed and told her, "Scoot back."

Kyra pushed herself to the middle of the mattress. Her legs were really trembling now. She nearly cried out when she felt Donovan's hands on her feet. He ran his fingers the length of her calves and up to her knees, enjoying the feel of her smooth skin. Donovan climbed onto the bed slowly, as if he was stalking her. Kyra could barely see, but she felt his hands push into the mattress. She opened her legs for him. Donovan quickly occupied the space. He kissed her breasts and her neck on his way up, and then he braced himself on his powerful arms and stared down at her.

Kyra's heart thumped like a bass drum. She swallowed and tried to relax her body for what she feared might be a painful insertion.

"I'm sorry," Donovan said. "I feel like I've been hard for over an hour. I don't think I'll last too long, this first time."

This first time? Did that mean she was guaranteed seconds? Kyra nearly squealed in delight.

"Me, too," she said. "I think all you–" There was another powerful shudder between her legs. She was beyond ready. "All you, all you have to do is touch me," she finished.

Donovan lowered himself so he could kiss her. She still tasted like cherry candy. He sucked on her bottom lip and lightly nibbled it. "Are you ready?"

Kyra nodded. But then she remembered he couldn't see her. "Ye – *aahhh*!"

Donovan did see her nod. He had only pushed the head in. Kyra was so wonderfully moist, he thought it was smooth sailing. But her walls were tight.

"Are you okay?"

"Uh, yes," Kyra breathed. She gripped the sheets as tightly as she could. It had been a while since she last had sex, and the pain was nearly searing.

"Relax," Donovan told her. "Relax your whole body."

Kyra took his advice. She sucked in a few breaths, and her muscles loosened considerably. Donovan pushed again. Kyra felt him slide inside her. Every inch of him brushed her clitoris along the way.

"*Oh, Donovan.*"

When she thought he'd filled her up completely, he kept going. Kyra didn't know there was more; no one had ever been that far.

When he finally stopped, Kyra's eyes were wide and fully dilated. Her hands were sweating from gripping the sheets. Donovan told her, "Relax, baby. I love you," and Kyra's heart melted. A tear rolled from her left eye towards her ear. It itched, but she didn't reach to wipe it. Donovan backed out halfway and entered her again slowly. He developed a rhythm, each time backing out a little more until he was able to pull out completely and start all over again.

He seemed so calm, while Kyra was having a fit of conniptions. The muscles below her waist had been contracting since their kiss under the bleachers. Now they were clenching around Donovan! Her climax was already starting to build.

Donovan increased the speed and the force of his strokes until he punched the back wall with each one. Kyra cried out every time his balls smacked her ass. It was involuntary, but her moans of pleasure turned Donovan on even more.

"*Oh, baby!*"

Kyra felt her clitoris throbbing with each stroke. The pressure reached a boiling point. She abandoned the sheets and grabbed hold of Donovan instead. Her nails dug into his back as he pumped faster and faster. She heard their thighs slapping over the sound of her own wails. He was digging for China now. Deeper than deep.

"*Kyra!*"

She reached her climax a few seconds before he did. The feel of her walls squeezing him mercilessly pushed Donovan over the edge. He slammed in hard and stayed there. Kyra felt him grow *even harder* as he pulsated inside of her. Her mouth fell open. Her heart nearly jumped out of it. She saw bright splashes of white and pink that illuminated the darkness. Fifteen years of longing and wanting flowed from her body in a sweet nectar that coated Donovan's penis as he slowly lowered his body onto hers.

Kyra was still in the midst of the most delicious orgasm. Every move Donovan made caused her kitty to quiver, made her release last even longer. Finally he pulled out completely and lay beside her. Kyra was exhausted. She didn't know if she was falling asleep or passing out. With her last bit of energy, she managed to roll onto her side. Even this movement created enough friction between her legs to give her another after shock.

Donovan put his arms around her and kissed softly behind the ear. Kyra wasn't sure if her eruption was fully over before she gratefully succumbed to sleep.

≈ ≈ ≈ ≈ ≈ ≈

She woke up some time later. Kyra was surprised and disappointed to find herself alone in Donovan's king size bed. It was still pitch-black outside. Kyra rolled over groggily, looking for Donovan's alarm clock. She found it glowing brightly on the dresser. It was 1:45 am.

He must be in the bathroom.

But then Kyra caught the scent of something tantalizing. She listened, and she could now hear someone in the kitchen. Kyra's stomach growled. *Mmmm.* The more she sniffed the air, the better the aroma smelled. She was suddenly ravenous. She wrapped the sheets around her nude body as she climbed off Donovan's bed. *Why was it so tall?* Of course that was because Donovan was tall; six feet, four inches to be exact.

And he was big, too. And they made love. Kyra smiled in the darkness. She and Donovan made love. And it was awesome. Kyra straightened her hair as best she could with her fingers as she walked down the hallway. Donovan's carpet was soft. She couldn't think of one thing about him that wasn't absolutely perfect.

She found him in the kitchen cutting vegetables while cubed chunks of chicken breast sizzled on the stovetop. Donovan wore a clean tee shirt with baggy shorts. He looked exceptionally tall as he leaned over the counter with an onion in hand. Kyra loved the shape of his powerful back. She admired his butt until he became aware of her presence and turned around.

"Morning, sunshine."

"Morning," Kyra said. She leaned on the doorframe and yawned. "So you're a master chef, too?" She was no longer surprised by anything Donovan could do.

"No," he said. "Anybody can make quesadillas. You hungry?"

"Yes. Very."

"Me, too," Donovan said. "That's why I woke up. I planned to take you to dinner after the game. We didn't get to do that," he said with a grin. "And I dropped the only food I had – my popcorn and soda – when you dragged me under the bleachers, like some wild woman."

Kyra laughed. "Yeah, right."

"Do you want to take a shower?" Donovan asked.

"Yes, but I don't have anything to wear."

"I pulled some stuff out for you. It's on the coffee table."

He nodded in that direction. Kyra went to check out what he had for her while Donovan tended to his meal. She didn't want to be angry with him, but she couldn't believe Donovan was offering her another woman's clothing – after their first night together! That hurt.

But Kyra's frown turned upside down when she reached the coffee table. Donovan had a pair of sweat pants that he cut the legs off and converted to shorts. There was a pair of men's boxers, size medium and a large Western Hills tee shirt. All of the clothing was a little too big for Kyra, but she wouldn't look ridiculous when she put it on.

She scooped up her outfit and went back to the kitchen. "Where did you get this? I know it's too small for you."

"I had a former student living with me for a while," Donovan said. "I'm sorry, that's all I have that might fit you. I know the shorts are too big, but they have a drawstring."

"No, it's perfect," Kyra said.

"You look good in anything," Donovan assured her. "Like right now, I want to yank that sheet away and make love to you right here in the kitchen. But I'm practicing restraint."

Kyra's eyes widened. She grinned. "In the kitchen?"

"Yeah," Donovan said, nodding. "Up against the refrigerator."

Oh wow.

"How, how would that work?"

"I'd have to pick you up," Donovan explained. "...lean your back against the fridge for support. I never did it before, but you got me thinking about it."

Oh double wow!

Kyra almost dropped the sheet herself and made him put his money where his mouth was, but she really wanted to get cleaned up first.

"Let me... go ahead and get in the shower," she said.

"Alright, scary. I'll have your food ready when you get out."

"I'm not scary," Kyra said as she walked away.

"So you say. You're gonna have to face me in this kitchen sooner or later."

Sweet! Kyra kept walking. She hoped it would be sooner rather than later.

≈ ≈ ≈ ≈ ≈ ≈

The bathroom was still a little steamy from Donovan's shower, so Kyra knew he hadn't been up that long. She'd never been in Donovan's bathroom at all, but now she was about to bathe in it! She was super excited. She didn't even feel sleepy anymore.

Donovan's washroom was clean and neat. The tub was huge, nearly twice the size of either of the ones at Aunt Ruth's house. He didn't have big variety of bathing supplies, just the essentials; body wash, shampoo a back scrubber and a bath sponge. Kyra checked her appearance in the mirror. She didn't look too bad at all, all things considered. She dropped her sheet and stepped into the tub and was soon having one hell of a Calgon moment.

The water felt great. It was hot and relaxing. Kyra didn't want to leave the tub after she finished bathing, but she knew there was something even better waiting for her in the living room – or maybe in the kitchen, somewhere near the refrigerator.

She left the shower and dressed in the clothes Donovan provided for her. The boxers fit surprisingly well, but the drawstring on the shorts was essential. She put on the tee-shirt and thought she looked a little tom-boyish. But Kyra felt fresh and comfortable when she rejoined Donovan in the kitchen. He had a plate waiting for her. His quesadillas looked scrumptious.

"You look great," Donovan said when he caught sight of her. "You ready to eat?" He pulled a chair out for her.

"Yes, I am. Thanks for the clothes, and the food!" Kyra took a seat and inhaled the rich scents wafting from her plate. Donovan even provided a small bowl of salsa for dipping. "This is perfect," she said. "Your mama taught you how to make these?"

"No, Miss-Know-It-All. I learned from TV, one of those cooking shows."

"Donovan watches cooking shows?" Kyra said as she took her first bite. *Mmmm.* Melted cheese, juicy chicken, green onions and tomatoes. It was perfect without the salsa.

"I have a lot more surprises," Donovan said as he sat across from her. His plate was still full. He waited on her rather than chow down while she was in the shower. It was a little thing, but it made Kyra feel special.

"I bet you do," she said. She giggled and then quickly devoured her late night snack.

≈ ≈ ≈ ≈ ≈ ≈

"I'm glad you changed your mind about kissing on the first date," Donovan said. The dishes were put away, Kyra's belly was nicely full, and Donovan surprised her with a chilled bottle of Moscato. They sat together on the living room couch sipping and talking. It was three a.m.

Kyra covered her mouth as she laughed. "Whatever. You know that rule didn't apply to you."

"Really?" Donovan said. "I feel special."

"You are," Kyra said. "You know that. I don't even feel like we went on a *first date*. It was more like we were starting a new phase of our friendship. It was exciting, so we *celebrated*." She grinned. Her face reddened.

"I like that," Donovan said. "*A new phase.*"

"But our friendship will always come first," Kyra said. "If you're mad at me because of something I did as your girlfriend, you still have to be my best friend."

"No doubt," Donovan said. "But you're more than my girlfriend, Kyra. Girlfriends come and go. You're not going anywhere. You'll be with me forever, right?"

Kyra's heart sighed. "Yes, Donovan. You know I'm not going anywhere."

"Good. So I was thinking you and Kat and Quinell should come and live with me."

Kyra's jaw dropped. "When were you thinking that?"

"For a while now. I don't like the idea of all three of y'all in one bedroom. That's not cool."

"But you know I'm getting my own place."

"You said you'd be with me forever, so why do you want to get your own place? You do plan to marry me and live with me at some point, right?"

Kyra thought she might have a heart attack. Was that a proposal? She couldn't get a response out.

"I mean, it's my assumption we're going to get married," Donovan said.

Kyra's eyes filled with tears. "Yes, Donovan. That would be a dream come true."

"Alright. We're on the same page. I'm just saying you can move in with me whenever you're ready to leave your aunt's house. Today, tomorrow. Whenever. No pressure."

Today? Tomorrow? Kyra didn't know what to make of it. She would love to live with Donovan. And his argument made sense. But surely it was the wine talking. Living together would be a HUGE adjustment – for both of them. Donovan didn't know what he was saying.

"Are you alright?" he asked.

He reached to wipe her tears. This was the second time he did that tonight. Kyra realized she was an emotional wreck.

She chuckled. "Yeah, I'm alright."

"I know what will make you feel better," Donovan said.

"Oh? What's that?"

He reached into her lap and pulled the drawstring on her shorts, undoing the bow she tied. Kyra smiled. When she looked up at him, Donovan leaned closer and kissed her, softly. His lips were sweet from the wine. Kyra slipped her tongue into his mouth as Donovan reached and caressed her breasts.

"Come with me," he said between kisses. "To my bedroom. I want to make love to you. For real this time."

For real this time? "Okay," Kyra whispered.

Donovan rose from the couch. He took Kyra's wine glass and then helped her to her feet.

≈ ≈ ≈ ≈ ≈ ≈

Donovan took her to the bedroom *again* and asked Kyra to sit on the bed. He turned on the lights and stood before her. With Kyra sitting on his mattress, they were roughly the same height. Donovan kissed her softly and then helped her out of her shirt. Kyra didn't have a bra on. Donovan caressed both of her breasts with both hands. He fondled her nipples with his thumbs until they were both perky, and then he told her to lie back on the mattress. Kyra did so. Donovan helped slide her shorts and boxers off her legs. He looked down at her beautiful, nude body.

Kyra had her knees bent, her legs closed. Donovan pried her knees apart and ran his hands from her stomach to her chest. He caressed her hot flesh lovingly. His touch sent shivers up and down her spine. Kyra watched him in silence.

Donovan pulled his tee shirt over his head. He removed his shorts and underwear and placed his hands on Kyra's knees again. He was still standing on the side of the bed. He stepped closer, and Kyra felt his manhood brushing her pubic hair. Her breaths quickened. Donovan pushed his hips forward, and she felt his erection slide up to her belly button. The sensation made her gasp. She sat up on her elbows and looked between her legs.

Donovan stroked again, back and forth. His penis was on top of her rather than inside. It was hot and weighty. Donovan pushed all the way, until she felt his balls on her labia. Kyra's heart was thumping now. She realized he could make love to her in this position. Her kitty moistened and tightened in anticipation.

Donovan brought her knees together until her thighs closed on his penis from both sides. Only the head was sticking out from Kyra's perspective. And what a plump and lovely head it was! Kyra wanted to suck it. She wanted to feel him in her mouth.

Donovan released her and walked to his dresser. Kyra's entire body immediately yearned for his return. Donovan found another condom. He went to a nightstand that had a stereo sitting on top of it. He turned it on and pressed a few buttons until a smooth R & B tune dripped from the speakers.

Donovan returned to the bed and stood before Kyra. He put his hands on her knees and spread them again. Kyra looked up at him anxiously. Donovan ran his hands from her knees to her inner thighs. Kyra shuddered involuntarily.

"Does it tickle?" Donovan asked.

Kyra nodded. "A little."

Donovan's hands met at her wet center. He stroked her labia with what felt like all ten fingers. Kyra lay back on the mattress, enjoying the pleasure he gave her. Donovan found her clitoris and stroked it slowly with his thumb.

"Ooh!" Kyra began to squirm on the bed.

While still toying with her hardening nub, Donovan inserted one of the fingers from his other hand, and then another. He stroked her slowly, loving how wet she was getting for him.

"Ah!" Kyra's head shot up. She panted, staring at Donovan. His body was ripped. He was staring between her legs, working his fingers expertly. Who would've thought a burly football player could be so surgical with his hands? Donovan didn't notice her watching him. He was totally lost in the feast his eyes beheld. The look on his face turned Kyra on just as much as his magical hands.

Finally he looked up at her. The muscles in Kyra's stomach tightened and loosened with each breath.

"You have such pretty lips," Donovan said.

Kyra closed her mouth. She licked her lips subconsciously.

"Those are nice, too," Donovan said. "But I meant these." He removed his fingers and caressed both sides of her labia as he spoke.

Kyra was already on the verge of an orgasm. She was speechless. Donovan stunned her further by dropping to his knees. Kyra immediately closed her legs. Donovan was now eye level the lips he was so fond of. She knew he wanted to kiss them. Patiently, he pried her knees apart. Kyra legs were quivering. Donovan maintained eye contact as he took the first lick. His tongue was like electric fire.

"Oh!"

Kyra's clitoris swelled and began to throb. Donovan closed his eyes as he licked her again, from bottom to top.

Oh my God. Kyra couldn't watch. She lowered her back on the mattress. She stared at the ceiling, and then she closed her eyes when Donovan's tongue got into a rhythm.

"Oh, Donovan."

His hands slid across her body as he lapped her juices. He caressed her inner thighs and her outer thighs. Both hands crawled up her stomach. He found her breasts and tweaked her nipples until they were perfectly erect. When Kyra's ass began to slide right and left on the sheets, Donovan grabbed her hips and held her still. When her cries of pleasure began to drown out the music, Donovan stopped abruptly and rose to his feet.

No!

Kyra's eyes flashed open. She looked between her legs and saw Donovan tearing a condom wrapper open. His lips were wet with her essence. Kyra eyes followed the condom as he brought it down his chest and past his flat stomach, where it met up with his throbbing erection.

Oh yes!

Kyra barely had time to lay back before Donovan entered her, all the way, balls deep on the first stroke.

"*Oh!*"

Her eyelids fluttered. Donovan was still standing on the side of the bed. Both of his hands gripped her thighs. He was staring at her, pumping hard and fast. Their hips met with an audible *Splack*! with each stroke.

Kyra's body was ready to explode, but Donovan slowed suddenly and stroked her long ways; all the way in, and nearly all the way out, each pump slow and sweet. He watched Kyra's face. She bit down on her bottom lip, and Donovan went all the way in and stayed there. When he started moving again, his strokes were short and quick, each time hitting the back end. Kyra began to pump her hips with the same timing. The room was completely bright. Everything was out in the open. Kyra never made love like this before.

Donovan went back to the hard and fast strokes, and Kyra felt her climax building again. She told him, "I'm cumming."

Donovan said, "I know. I feel it."

Kyra kept her eyes on his as her second release rolled down her body like a tidal wave. Donovan kept pumping rhythmically. Kyra watched him until her body twisted on the bed, and her eyes rolled to the back of her head. Donovan gripped her trembling thighs and slowed his pace. He loved the way Kyra's muscles clenched around his penis during her climax. He felt at home inside her. He loved to bring her pleasure.

He withdrew and slowly brought her knees closed. "Can you scoot back?"

Kyra didn't want to, but she pushed back until she could lay flat without her legs dangling off the mattress. Donovan got on the bed and lay next to her. Kyra rolled to her side, and Donovan did the same. He pressed his chest against her back, and placed his hand on her hip.

"You didn't..." Kyra took a breath. "You didn't cum."

"I'm about to," Donovan whispered into the back of her head. She felt his still hard penis pushing the back of her thighs.

Kyra grinned. She felt completely relaxed. "That's not gonna work."

"It will if you lift this leg a little," Donovan said. He stroked her thigh.

Kyra had never made love in this position, but she lifted her leg. Donovan shifted slightly, and his penis found her ridiculously wet opening. He slid inside. Kyra's love-lazy eyes flashed open. She moaned with pleasure.

"Ah..."

"Told ya," Donovan said. He still had his hand on her hip, his chest against her back. "Your ass feels so good in my lap," he breathed. He pumped slowly, filling her completely each time.

Kyra closed her eyes, enjoying the new angles he could hit from this position. After a while, she found that she could throw it back at him, while lying on her side. Donovan enjoyed that very much.

CHAPTER SIXTEEN
FOOL FOR LOVE

They didn't sleep again until five a.m. Donovan woke up at eight and sent his mother a text message, letting her know he wouldn't join her for church this Sunday morning. That was a rarity. He climbed back into bed with Kyra, and she immediately reached for him in her sleep.

Donovan woke up again at noon. He showered and dressed in his usual tee-shirt, shorts and sneakers. He woke Kyra up, and she showered again, too. She put on the outfit Donovan gave her last night, remembering that she only wore it for an hour before he undressed her again.

Kyra called home. Aunt Ruth said there were no problems, except she had an important message she needed to deliver. She sounded like it was bad news. Kyra didn't ask what it was. She didn't want anything negative to ruin her last moments with Donovan.

He dropped her off at 1:30 and kissed her lovingly in Aunt Ruth's driveway. Kyra held her dress and her mum in her lap. She felt a little self conscious, knowing her aunt would throw the sleepover in her face at some point, to try to make her feel low. Donovan told her she would never have that problem if she moved in with him. Kyra kissed him again, very slowly. She told him, "You don't know what you're saying. But, we can talk about it later."

≈ ≈ ≈ ≈ ≈ ≈ ≈

Donovan went straight to his mother's house after leaving Kyra. Beverly responded to the message he sent earlier. She asked if he could stop by for Sunday dinner, if he was feeling better. One thing Donovan would never turn down was his mama's home cooking, even if he'd have to explain why he missed church. He responded to her by text: I'm feeling great! I'll be there at 2.

When he arrived, Beverly had a three course meal prepared. Donovan grinned at the macaroni and cheese, baked potato and his mama's world famous meatloaf. He gave her a big hug and a kiss on the jaw.

"What's wrong with you, boy? Why you so excited?" Beverly struggled to get out of his bear hug, but she was smiling.

"I feel good, Mama. And you made my favorite dinner. What's not to be happy about?"

He took a seat at the kitchen table, and Beverly served him a plate. They made small talk while Donovan wolfed it down. He told his mom that he missed church this morning because he slept late, but he knew she would want a better explanation. Beverly waited until he was done eating before she brought it up again. By then Donovan was too full and lazy to be deceptive.

"How'd you sleep late if you were awake at eight o'clock to send me a text message?" Beverly asked.

"I was with Kyra," Donovan said. "She spent the night with me."

Beverly's eyes widened. She figured Kyra had something to do with it, but she thought it would take a billion questions before Donovan admitted it.

"I know I said we weren't going to have a relationship," he continued. "But I took her to Finley High's homecoming game yesterday, and there was a lot of nostalgia. I kissed her, and we decided to be more than friends from now on. Kyra's my woman now. I asked her to move in with me."

That was one hell of a mouthful. Donovan was rarely this forthcoming. Beverly couldn't process the information quickly enough. She sat quietly, staring and blinking for more than five seconds.

"Mama? Are you alright?"

Beverly nodded vaguely.

"You said you were going to stop hating on Kyra, right?"

She continued to nod.

"I know I asked you to accept her as my *friend*," Donovan went on. "But now I need you to accept her as my woman; soon to be my wife and your daughter-in-law. You can do that for me, cant you?"

Beverly was still nodding, but she shook her head when his words caught up to her. "Wait, wait, wait, wait..." She rubbed a pressure point between her eyebrows. "Slow down, Donovan. Just, slow down..."

He didn't mean to cause his mother any stress, but Donovan felt great. He didn't have any secrets. Everything was out in the open.

"I know this is a lot to digest," he said. "It'll probably take some time before–"

His mother held a hand up to stop him. "Hold on a second," she said. "Just wait a minute. I'm not as young as I used to be. I need a minute to think about all of this."

Donovan smiled.

Beverly gave him an irritated look. "Now you and Kyra getting together, that's not a surprise," she said. "I knew that was gon' happen from the second you told me she came back."

"But it wasn't planned."

"I know," she said. "You were with Brianna, and you didn't want to hurt her. I raised you good, and you're a good man."

Donovan's chest swelled.

"But if something's meant to be, nothing can stand in its way. I know you didn't break up with Brianna for Kyra, things just happened like that."

Donovan was glad she believed him.

"So you being with Kyra is fine with me," Beverly said.

"Really?"

"Yes, boy. I told you I would stop coming against her, and I have."

"Thanks, Mama."

"But what I want to know," Beverly said, "is why you feel the need to move so fast all of a sudden. You said you kissed the girl for the first time last night. You probably should've left it at the kiss, but whatever, I'm not in that."

Donovan looked down at the table bashfully.

189

"But why do you want her to move in with you? Why are you already talking about marriage? You and Kyra have only been together for one day, Donovan."

"I know, but it's not like I just met her. I've known Kyra all my life."

"But she's been your *woman*, as you call it, for one day, son. *One day.* Don't you think you should date her for at least a year, to see how it goes?"

Donovan shook his head. "No. We can't do that."

"Why not?"

"Because this isn't a *see how it goes* type of situation, Mama. We're going to be together forever. I don't have any doubts."

"Then why rush it?"

"Why not rush it?"

"Because it might not work," Beverly stressed. "I know you want the best for her, but you two might not be compatible as boyfriend and girlfriend. Maybe you were meant to be just friends."

"But we can't go back," Donovan said. "Not after what happened. I have to marry her, so we'll be together forever."

Beverly watched his eyes, and her heart melted. Donovan was in love. Big time. But she knew he was also afraid, and maybe irrational. "Listen to me," she said. "I think what you and Kyra did was major. You're right, it probably changed your relationship forever. But I think now you're scared that if y'all don't make it as boyfriend and girlfriend, you'll lose her as a friend, too.

"So you want to hurry up and move in with her and get married so you'll know for sure y'all will be together. But that's not the right way to do it, Donovan. If y'all have problems, you need to figure them out *before* you get married. *Before* you move her kids into your house. 'Cause it's not just you and Kyra that's gonna be affected by all of this. You got those two babies in the middle."

Donovan knew she was right, "But, Mama, there's no chance of me and Kyra breaking up."

"You don't know that," Beverly said. "And you're too scared to wait and make sure. But I'm telling you, it's better to find out before you make any major changes in that girl's life. You told me yourself; she's been through enough. You know I love you, baby. And I wish you and Kyra the best. But I think you're rushing into things. Have you talked to Kyra about this? Is this what she wants, too?"

Donovan sighed. "She said we need to talk about it."

"Then talk to her," Beverly said. "Listen to her – if you won't listen to me. Trust me, I'm not *hating on Kyra*, or whatever you called it."

Donovan chuckled.

"I'm not even complaining about you missing church this morning," Beverly continued.

Donovan had to lower his gaze again.

"I just want what's best for you," his mother said. She reached to hold his hand.

"I know," Donovan said. "And I love you." His eyes scanned the table. "...You and these leftovers. You don't need all of this food, do you?"

≈ ≈ ≈ ≈ ≈ ≈

Aunt Ruth tried to talk to Kyra when she got home, but she went straight to her room and changed clothes. She took her kids out for a late lunch and then went to get groceries with her very last food stamp card. Kyra would get her first check from the school district in five days. A month after that, she'd have a *steady income* for the first time in over a year. Kyra couldn't wait to move out of her aunt's house, but she still had to face her when she went home.

Aunt Ruth didn't help tote the groceries inside, but she helped Kyra put them away in the kitchen. While they worked, Ruth told her, "Girl, I got something to tell you."

Kyra told her kids, "Go to your room."

Ruth waited until they were gone before she said, "Leonard called."

Outwardly, Kyra didn't respond. She continued to put away the food. But inwardly Kyra's whole body suddenly felt cold and sick. If she was near a toilet, she was sure she'd vomit.

"Did you hear what I said?"

"He called from jail?" Kyra asked. She continued to work around her aunt who now stood by the stove with her arms crossed.

"No, he's not in jail," Aunt Ruth announced. "He say he's out of jail."

Kyra's knees buckled. She really was going to be ill. But she kept moving. She didn't want her aunt to know how much the news troubled her.

"How'd he get the number?"

"From one of them folks in Little Rock. I don't know who. Everybody know where you at, Kyra. Ain't no secret."

"What'd he want?"

"He want you to call him," Ruth said. "I took down his number for you." She went to the table and found a tablet. "Here it is."

Kyra continued what she was doing. She felt the beginning of a bad headache.

"You gon' call him, ain't you?" her aunt asked.

"I don't know," Kyra said.

"You got his baby," Ruth reminded. "You got to call him, if he wanna know about his baby."

Kyra finally went and stood in front of her. "He doesn't care about Kat. He never did."

"That's not what he told me. I talked to him for a long time. He pissed 'cause you took Kat out of state. He think that's illegal. And I *know* it is."

"Oh, you know it is?"

"Yes, and you know it too, Kyra. If that man wants to see his daughter, you have to let him. And if he go and get a lawyer and tell them you took his daughter out of state, they can take that baby from you. They'll give Kat to him."

Kyra's heart burned at the mention of someone taking either of her children away. That happened once before. Kyra would never let it happen again, especially not over a lowlife like Leonard.

"He's on drugs," she said. "Nobody's going to give my baby to a drugged out father."

"He said he's clean now."

"Whose side are you on?" Kyra wanted to know. "Why you taking up for him?"

"I'm not taking up for nobody," Aunt Ruth said. "I ain't doing nothing but telling the truth. I hope you do keep your kids, if it was up to me. I think you a good mother."

But Ruth's smug smile canceled out her positive words. Kyra knew that her aunt was tickled pink over this dilemma.

"I'm not calling him," Kyra decided. Her aunt had her so riled up, her heart was racing. "Since you like talking to him, you can tell him that. Tell him to try to get a lawyer to represent his dopefiend ass. Try to take me to court with his jail record and his needle marks. Tell him to bring all of that to court. I wish he would. You can tell him I said that."

Aunt Ruth was unfazed. "You ain't no saint yourself, Kyra."

Kyra's heart froze. She stared into her aunt's beady eyes. "Leonard told you something?"

"Kyra, everybody in Little Rock know what went on with you. And yeah, Leonard was mad. He told me a lot of stuff."

Kyra's nostrils flared. Her aunt was smiling, without smiling. Kyra had to assume Ruth knew everything. She looked away, remembering how bad it got in Arkansas. How bad *she* got. But Kyra wasn't like that anymore. There was no court in America that would take Kat away from her, not today, no matter how much Leonard cleaned himself up.

"I'm not calling him," Kyra stated. "And don't give him my cellphone number." She left the kitchen and went to check on her children.

≈ ≈ ≈ ≈ ≈ ≈

Kyra met Leonard four years ago. She wasn't a total party girl back then, but she did frequent the club scene on Friday and Saturday nights a little more than she should have. She usually left Quinell with her aunt when she went out, or with her grandmother. Leonard was a regular at a club called the Shark Tank. He was a high yellow dope boy with long corn rolls, flashy jewelry and a nice wardrobe.

Leonard didn't do too much dancing when he went out. He usually sat at a table with his partners and drank hard liquor while puffing on Newport 100s. Leonard wasn't a boss or even a mid-level dealer, but he made wise investments and saved more money than he spent. He was never broke, and he rarely went after women. Leonard had pretty boy looks; a baby face with light brown eyes. The girls loved him. They crowded his table every

Saturday night, which is why Kyra was surprised when he approached her as she exited the dance floor.

"What's up, lil mama. Who you here with?"

Kyra smiled as she looked him up and down. Back then she was completely stuck in the hood, mentally and physically. But Kyra had no idea that she lived in a bubble. There were no single doctors or carpenters or businessmen available, at least none that she ever came in contact with. Kyra was attracted to the same type of men her girlfriends were attracted to. And in those regards, Leonard was a ghetto star.

"What's your name?" she asked him.

"L Boogie. Or just Boogie. What's yours?" His eyes rolled down her frame and back up. Leonard liked what he saw. Kyra wore a short skirt with a sexy top. Four guys already approached her that night. She didn't give any of them the time of day. But Leonard had a certain appeal.

"Kyra," she said. "What's *L Boogie*? How you get that name?"

"I used to could dance," he said.

Kyra grinned. "I never seen you dance."

"That was a long time ago," he said. "When I became a man, I put away my childish ways."

Kyra didn't know that quote was from the bible. If she had recognized it, she would've been turned off by a thug spitting bible verses. "What's your real name?" she asked him.

"Leonard."

"Can I call you Leonard?"

"What's wrong with Boogie?"

Kyra thought his moniker was childish, but she didn't tell him that. "I just like to call people by their real names," she offered.

"That must mean you plan on saying my name a lot," Leonard said. "If that's the case, yeah. You can call me Leonard."

"Alright." Kyra beamed. She liked the way he talked. She liked the way he was looking at her, too. At that moment, Kyra had been single for more than four months. Her friends thought she was more than ready to get back in the saddle.

"You wanna come kick it with me at my table?" Leonard asked.

Kyra shook her head. "You got too many people over there. Plus I don't wanna be around all that smoke."

"You don't smoke?"

"Nope."

"You get high?"

"I smoked weed before."

"We can go get a table by ourselves, if you want."

"Alright." Kyra was still grinning. "Let me go tell my friends, so they won't be looking for me."

She and Leonard got a table and kicked it together for the rest of the night. After a few drinks, Kyra wanted to dance. Leonard didn't accompany her to the dance floor, but he watched her every move as she shook her tail feather under the disco lights. Leonard took her to Waffle House after the club closed, and he was respectful when Kyra told him she didn't mess around on the first date.

That was one thing Kyra found endearing about Leonard. He was as rough as they came, and he handled his business in the streets. But when it came to Kyra, he was always sweet and loving. He showered her with gifts, making sure she was always the best looking woman at every place he took her.

Kyra was a year into their relationship when she discovered Leonard used heroin. He snorted it from little capsules that he bought for five to ten dollars.

Kyra wasn't completely shocked when she caught him in the bathroom one day, because a lot guys in the neighborhood snorted *boy*, as it was called. Plus Leonard already drank heavily and smoked marijuana regularly. In fact, Leonard was high more times than not. Kyra was more upset because he kept his new drug of choice a secret.

"How long you been doing that?" she asked.

"About five months."

"Why?"

"Just something to do," Leonard said. He sat on the toilet with an empty capsule on the sink next to him. He wiped his nose. He was already starting to nod.

"Is that why you been looking so sleepy all the time?"

Leonard nodded lazily.

"You got to be careful with that stuff," Kyra warned. "I heard it'll take you fast."

"I know what I'm doing," Leonard said.

"Don't be leaving none of that mess where Quinell can find it," Kyra said, and that was the full extent of her drug intervention. By then Kyra loved Leonard more than she loved herself, so she never considered leaving him.

Leonard continued to snort his dope for the next year, and there were no problems. He continued to thrive in the drug game, and he always put Kyra first. Leonard was one of few dealers in the city who never cheated on his woman.

Not only did Kyra turn a blind eye to his drug abuse, but she found it beneficial in bed. Whenever Leonard snorted heroin, he developed what he called *dope dick*. The drug kept him hard and horny and unable to have an orgasm for hours at a time. Leonard was a sex machine, and Kyra was the only woman he had eyes for. She was so blinded by love, Kyra actually squealed with delight when she learned she was pregnant with Kat.

Unfortunately there's no such thing as a functional heroin addict. Leonard's drug use became more blatant because the only person he cared about pleasing had no problem with it. He began to lose money as his heroin habit jumped from $10 a day to $100. As he spiraled out of control, Leonard had no desire to leave the house to generate some type of income. By the time Kyra tried to intervene, Leonard was too far gone. He had taken to shooting his dope with a needle. Kyra watched him lose everything he had, his looks and health being the first to go.

She stayed because she loved him, and Kyra even put her family in jeopardy because of Leonard. But even today, she could not blame him fully. She understood that she made a man her whole world and allowed him to drag her all the way down with him, to the point where Kyra lost just as much as he did.

The worst part about it was Leonard wasn't even a good man. He was a drug dealer with no plans for the future past selling more crack rocks than he sold the day before. Kyra threw her life away for a complete loser.

She was mad at Leonard, but Kyra would always be more disgusted with herself.

CHAPTER SEVENTEEN
FAMILY MATTERS

The following week Donovan's Mad Stallions pulled off the shocker of the season with a win over the highly favored Seahawks from Langston Hughes High. The game was on Halloween, which added a surreal element to the bizarre night. Donovan's iffy punt returner even scored a touchdown with just twelve seconds remaining in the game, bringing the final score to 42-13.

The next day Donovan picked up his girlfriend and her two children for a Saturday outing that included the new Disney movie and an all-you-can-eat dinner at Don Pablo's. The date was November 1st. The brutal heat wave of summer had finally given way to the moderate temperatures of fall. It wasn't cool enough for a jacket, but it was nice to wake up in the morning and feel a cool breeze rather than the mid-eighty degree temperatures that usually greeted them at seven a.m.

Kyra received her first check from the school district on Friday. She wouldn't let Donovan pay for their movie, even though with tickets, popcorn and drinks for everyone, she ended up spending over fifty dollars.

"You should've let me pay," Donovan told her when they settled into their seats in the darkened theater.

"I'm alright," Kyra said. "I don't think we'll be going to the movies again for at least a *month*. But today I'm good. And I need to write you a check when you take us home. Don't let me forget."

"Sorry, I didn't catch that," Donovan said. He leaned closer and kissed under her ear.

Kyra giggled and reached for his hand. Kat sat on her right, and Quinell sat on Donovan's left. "Just because your kisses make me weak doesn't mean I'm gonna forget about what I owe you," she whispered.

She squeezed Donovan's hand, and he kissed the side of her neck again. His kisses were ticklish and electrifying at the same time. She and Donovan hadn't been intimate since the homecoming game last week. Kyra would never forget the feel of his mouth all over her body.

"If you write me a check, I won't cash it." Donovan spoke in a hushed tone.

"Then I'll give you cash," Kyra replied.

"I won't take it," Donovan insisted.

"I'll break into your house and leave it on the coffee table."

"If you break into my house, I have the right to do whatever I want with you," Donovan informed.

"What are you gonna do, shoot me?"

"No, but I might tie you to the bed," Donovan whispered, "teach you a good lesson."

Damn. Kyra felt a tingle roll from her chest to below her waist. "I'm *definitely* breaking in now," she said. "I never been tied up before."

"I never tied anyone up," Donovan said. "I was just kidding."

"I know," Kyra said. "But now you have to do it. And you can't let me go until you're completely satisfied." She gave him a wicked grin and kissed him on the lips.

Donovan had to return his attention to the silver screen. This bondage talk was turning him on, which wasn't so cool with Quinell sitting next to him. "We'll talk about this later," he told Kyra.

She laughed and then turned to offer Kat some popcorn.

≈ ≈ ≈ ≈ ≈ ≈

They went out to eat afterwards. This time Donovan gave the cashier his debit card before Kyra had a chance to open her purse. She started to complain when they got to their table, but Donovan nipped it in the bud, for good this time.

"Baby, can you come here for a second?" Donovan got up and walked away from the table.

Confused, Kyra went to see what he wanted.

"Listen," he said when they had some privacy. "All this talk about money needs to stop. I been telling you for a month that you don't have to pay me back–"

"Yeah, but–"

"There's no *but*, Kyra. I'm talking right now. You need to listen."

Stunned, she piped down.

"I love you, Kyra. I know you haven't said when you'll move in with me, but as far as I'm concerned, you're my girl for life. I don't do things for *you* anymore. I do it for *us*. So stop complaining about the money I spent. Let it go. There's a million things you need to spend your paycheck on, but paying me back ain't one of them. Understand?"

Donovan never used this authoritative tone with her. Kyra liked it. She stood on her tippy toes and kissed him unexpectedly.

Donovan frowned. "What does that mean?"

"It means I'm sorry, and you're right and what you say goes," Kyra replied.

"Really?"

She nodded. "Mmm hmm."

Donovan smiled. "That's great. Makes me feel better about the surprise I have for you."

"What surprise?"

"I'll show you when we leave here."

Kyra narrowed her eyes. She had no idea what it could be.

"You said whatever I say goes," Donovan reminded. "That means you can't complain about it. You have to shut up and take it, whatever I give you."

Kyra smiled. "I just had a bunch of dirty thoughts about that."

"About what?"

"About me shutting up and taking it."

Donovan chuckled. "That's not the surprise I'm talking about, but I got some of that in mind, too. Can you spend the night with me?"

"What about the kids?"

"Them, too," Donovan said. He walked off before Kyra could inquire about where they would sleep.

≈≈≈≈≈≈

Two hours later Donovan pulled into his driveway with three happy guests. Quinell was smiling ear to ear. He'd been to the movies before and out to eat a lot of times, but he never did both in one day. And the good times weren't over yet. Donovan had the best video games and consoles Q had ever seen. He hurried out of the truck and was the first one waiting at Donovan's door.

Donovan let everyone inside, and then he went to the den to show Q the Kinect he recently purchased for his Xbox. Kat was equally intrigued by the new device, so Donovan left her with her brother and returned to Kyra who was waiting in the living room. Donovan's chest grew warm as he rounded the coffee table and looked down at her. Kyra looked comfortable on his sofa. She had the remote in hand, and she kicked off her pumps already.

"That's what I'm talking about," Donovan said. "Got the kids playing in the den, my girl chillin' on the couch. You can't tell me this ain't a happy home."

"It is nice," Kyra said. She knew what he was getting at. "We need to talk about—"

"Wait," Donovan said. "Come here. I want to show you something."

He reached for her hand and helped her off the sofa. Kyra followed him down the hall. She thought he was taking her to his bedroom, but Donovan stopped at another door. Kyra knew he had a home gym in there. But when Donovan opened the door, she saw that all of his weight-lifting stuff was gone. It had been replaced with a queen-size bed. There were also two dressers that hadn't been there before.

Kyra looked at her man in confusion.

"For Quinell," Donovan said. "I was thinking that when y'all move in here, this could be his room. I got another bedroom I use mostly for storage. I'm going to clear that one out, too, so we'll have a place for Kat. As for tonight, I was thinking Q and Kat could share this bed, or he could sleep on the sofa in the den. I know it's three of y'all in one room at your aunt's house, so I think Q will be okay with sharing this room with Kat, just for tonight."

Kyra's heart quivered. No man ever treated her as good as Donovan did. She still hadn't confirmed that she would move in with him. She thought Donovan was being silly and spontaneous when he first asked her. But if he went through this much trouble, he had to be serious. Kyra took a seat on the bed. Donovan sat with her.

"What's wrong?" he asked. "I thought you'd be happy."

"I am," Kyra said. She looked into his eyes and smiled. It was a strange smile, because her eyes were filled with tears.

"Then why do you look like you're going to cry?" Donovan asked.

"Because I don't think you know what you're doing," Kyra said. "And believe me, this is a weird feeling, because I can always count on you to do the right thing."

"Why do you think I'm not doing the right thing now?"

"Because we only been together for a week," Kyra said. "If anybody else asked me to move in with them after that amount of time, I'd run for the hills, thinking they were crazy."

"I'm not anybody else."

"I know," Kyra said. "And I know you want to do the right thing. But I don't think you thought this out enough. Don't you want me to get my own place so we can, you know, see how it goes with us first."

Donovan shook his head. "You sound like my mama."

"You told her about this?"

"Yeah. She thinks I'm scared."

Kyra's eyes brightened. That was news to her. "Why did she say that?"

"'Cause I'm scared of losing you," Donovan said. "She thinks I want to hurry up and move you in and get married so that I know for sure we'll be together."

Kyra couldn't stop her tears from falling. That was the most beautiful thing she ever heard. "Is, is that true?"

Donovan wiped her cheeks, ever so tenderly. "Part of it is," he said. "But I also know that we're meant to be. I don't see the point in waiting for the inevitable. It's expensive and stressful to move into your own place. It's a waste of time and money, if you're going to end up moving in here anyway. You do want to live with me, don't you?"

Kyra nodded. She wanted that more than anything.

"Then why drag it out?" Donovan asked. "Why not do it now?"

Because we might not work. That was the only reason Kyra could think of. It was also the one answer she couldn't give him. Donovan did let fear and love interfere with his decision-making, but his heart was in the right place. Plus, for as long as she'd known him, Donovan was always right. Kyra didn't have the heart to crush his dreams, especially when she wanted the same things.

"How about we compromise," she said. "I won't move out of my aunt's house and get my own place. When I move out, I will come here with you. *But...*" she said before Donovan could get too excited. "... I don't think that should be today or even this month. Donovan, I can't think of one single thing that could come between us. But we can't go into this thinking only about us. I don't want to shuffle my kids around anymore. We got to be extra careful, because of them."

Donovan let her words sink in before he responded. He nodded. "You're right. I guess I got a little over-excited."

"I like that you're excited about us," Kyra said quickly. "That makes me feel real special." She gave him a flirty smile.

"What about tonight?" Donovan asked. "Can y'all stay here tonight?"

"Yes," Kyra said. "We can spend the night whenever you want. What happened to all of your weights and benches anyway?"

"I moved it to the garage."

"That must've been a lot of work."

"It was," Donovan said. "I had four people helping me. My back was hurting when we got through."

"I can rub your back," Kyra offered. The thought of getting Donovan topless made her giddy. Thinking about rubbing his body down with massaging oil made her nipples harden.

"Do you know anything about giving a massage?" Donovan asked.

"Nope," Kyra said. "But I bet I can rub and squeeze on you until you feel real nice."

"Is that so?"

Kyra nodded. "Definitely."

Donovan checked his watch. It was only eight-thirty. "What time do the kids go to bed?"

"Not for at least a couple of hours," Kyra said. She kissed him passionately. "You have to wait."

Donovan kissed her back. "You want me to wait for *everything*."

Kyra kissed him again. "This'll be worth it, baby. Trust me."

≈ ≈ ≈ ≈ ≈ ≈

Donovan had nearly every season of the Simpsons on DVD. Kyra knew he loved the animated show as a child, but she didn't know he was still watching it.

"Hey, don't judge me," he told her.

He popped in one of the DVD's and made chocolate chip cookies while Kyra and the kids lounged in the den. Donovan had ice cream as well. Kat and Quinell had been eating junk food all day, but they attacked the new snacks like they were starving. Kyra thought Donovan was spoiling them, but she loved seeing smiles on her children's faces. They were nearly as happy as she was.

Kat passed out first at ten-thirty. Quinell held out for another hour. Kyra turned off the television when she saw his head nodding.

"Come on," she told him. "Donovan's going to let you spend the night here. Is that cool?"

Quinell smiled, nodded and yawned at the same time. Kyra took him to the room Donovan prepared for them. Kat was already curled up on one side of the bed, snoring lightly.

"You don't mind sleeping with your sister, do you?" Kyra asked.

Quinell shook his head and lay down fully dressed. Kyra helped him out of his shoes and jeans and pulled the covers up to his chin. Quinell rolled to his side and was still smiling as he dozed off. Kyra gave him a kiss on the cheek and went to rejoin Donovan in the den. She wasn't surprised to find him yawning as well. She took a seat next to him, and Donovan put his arm around her. Kyra snuggled against his warm body.

"Long day, huh?" she asked.

"I feel like I picked y'all up at seven a.m. instead of four in the afternoon."

"I'm sorry," Kyra said. "I know they can be a handful."

"Nah, it's cool," Donovan said. "Your kids are great compared to the knuckleheads I have to deal with at school."

"Are you going to sleep?" Kyra asked.

"No. I'm going to make some coffee. Want some?"

"You don't have to drink coffee," Kyra said. "You can go to sleep if you want to."

"I haven't had you in my bedroom for a whole week," Donovan said. "I plan to enjoy tonight, for at least three more hours, before I go to sleep."

Three hours? Damn. Kyra's heart fluttered at the possibilities. "Well, in that case, I'll have some coffee, too."

≈≈≈≈≈≈≈

They ate the leftover cookies with their coffee, and then Donovan went out back to feed his dogs. He invited Kyra to tag along. Doc and Wyatt were scary, hulking creatures, especially at night. But they were friendly beasts. They surrounded Kyra and sniffed her and allowed her to pet them. Thankfully they didn't jump up and soil her clothes with their grubby paws.

Donovan didn't return to the house immediately after feeding them. He took a seat on a wicker sofa he had next to the back porch. Kyra sat with him and star gazed while she held his hand. Everything about Donovan's home was perfect. Kyra wondered if she was a fool for not taking him up on his offer to move in.

"Your dogs fit you," she said as she watched the four-legged buddies frolicking in the yard.

"Why's that?" Donovan asked.

"Because you're all big and ferocious," Kyra said. "It makes sense that you have a German shepherd and a pit bull."

"But I'm not ferocious," Donovan said.

"And neither are your dogs. They didn't bark at me or nothing."

"That's because you're with me. If you jumped the fence one night by yourself, it would be a different story."

"Same as you," Kyra said. "You're like a big, ole teddy bear. But if you have to take care of business, you wouldn't hesitate to whoop a nigga's ass."

Donovan laughed. "I haven't had a fight since high school."

"You still got it in you, though," Kyra stated. "It never goes away."

Donovan shrugged.

They sat in silence for a few seconds, and then Kyra said, "There's something I got to tell you."

"What's up?"

She swallowed. "I talked to Kat's daddy the other day."

She felt Donovan tense up. "Do you want me to kick his ass?"

Kyra smiled nervously. "No. But I am worried about something." She sat up so she could look him in the eyes. The porch light provided enough illumination to see that Donovan was already worried as well.

"What's wrong?"

"He's been calling for a couple of weeks," Kyra said. "I wouldn't call him back, and I told my aunt not to give him my cell number. She didn't, but I think she told him when to call back, so he could catch me at home."

"Are you talking about that Leonard guy?"

She nodded.

"What does he want?"

Kyra sighed. She wished she could leave her past in the past, but some things never go away. "He said he wants to see Kat. But I know it's really me he wants. He's just using Kat as an excuse."

Donovan's expression was hard to read. "What'd he tell you?"

"He said I was wrong for taking Kat to Texas, and he's gonna take me to court. He said he's going to try to get custody, but he'll be happy with visitation rights, so long as it's in Arkansas. He wants me to go back."

"Why do you think he wants to be with you?"

Kyra hesitated. She didn't want to tell Donovan the whole conversation. When she talked to him, Leonard was practically crying on the phone. He begged Kyra to come back to him. Each time she said no, Leonard brought up Kat again, threatening legal action.

"He asked me to go back with him," Kyra said. "He said I was wrong for leaving him while he was in jail. When I said *no*, that's when he started talking about suing me."

"Why did you leave him?" Donovan asked.

Kyra's stomach twisted. When she first returned to Overbrook Meadows, she told Donovan approximately 75% of her hard times story. She wanted to be completely honest with him now, but she couldn't. It would break Donovan's heart, if he knew everything.

"He ruined my life," Kyra said. "He was doing drugs and selling drugs, and the police were coming by the house all the time, them and all of Leonard's dopefiend friends. I wanted to leave him, but I felt trapped. When he went to jail, I felt like I was finally free to get away from there. That's why I came back to Texas."

Donovan swallowed her story as easily as he did the first time. Why wouldn't he? Kyra never lied to him before. "So, do we need to go to Arkansas?" he asked.

Kyra's heart grew to twice its normal size. For as long as she'd known him, Donovan never let her fight a battle alone.

"I'm not going back to Arkansas unless I get a summons," Kyra said. "Leonard's just talking noise. He's not gonna do anything. Every judge he ever saw sent him to jail. He's not going to run to them for help. And I know he can't afford a lawyer."

"But what if he really does want to see Kat?"

"Then I would do my best to work something out," Kyra said. "But he doesn't, Donovan. When I talked to him, he begged me to come back to him for five minutes before he asked about Kat. He didn't give a damn about her before he got locked up, and he doesn't give a damn about her now."

"Okay. I'm with you," Donovan said. "Whatever we got to do, just let me know."

Kyra wrapped both arms around his torso and kissed him tenderly. She wished there was a way to fully express her gratitude for everything Donovan had done for her. She could spend the rest of her life trying and still not come close.

He stood and stretched his back. "You ready to go inside?"

Kyra nodded, but she grabbed hold of him before he made it to the door. They hugged beneath the stars for what felt like hours. Neither said a word, but their touch and their tenderness spoke volumes.

≈≈≈≈≈≈

Donovan wanted to take a shower. Kyra did too, so he scrounged up another outfit for her to put on when she got out. He led her through the spare bedroom where his second bathroom was. It was a lot smaller than the main one, but there was a shower, and it was impeccably clean.

Kyra started to undress, but she changed her mind midway through. She left the bathroom wearing only a tee shirt and followed the sound of running water to Donovan's main washroom. She knocked on the door, and Donovan said, "Come in."

The shower curtain was closed. Donovan pulled it back far enough to poke his head out when Kyra entered.

"What's wrong? I forgot to leave soap in there?"

Rather than respond, Kyra pulled her tee shirt over her head. Donovan's eyes widened at the sight of her nude physique.

"Can I come in there with you?" she asked.

Donovan looked her up and down as he pulled the shower curtain back further. Water began to bounce off his body and spray on the floor. Neither of them cared. Standing fully naked, Donovan was a sight to behold. Standing fully naked *and* dripping wet put him on a whole new level of sexy. And he was easily excitable. Kyra watched as his penis responded to her body. It swelled and grew longer as she approached. Kyra stepped into the tub and pulled the curtain closed.

Donovan had his back to the water. His bathtub was large enough for him to step around Kyra and switch places with her. Now the showerhead sprayed water on the back of Kyra's neck. Her hair was soaked in a matter of seconds, but she wasn't concerned about her perm. Donovan watched the water drip over Kyra's shoulders, down her stomach and into her pubic hair. His erection reached its peak. It seemed to be pointing right at Kyra's face.

She dropped to her knees suddenly, and the water began to spray on Donovan's chest. Kyra took his manhood into her mouth with such little warning, Donovan muttered, "Oh, shit," and took a step back. Kyra couldn't take all of him in before the head pushed the back of her throat. The water was all over her now. She placed one hand on Donovan's stomach and held the base of his dick with the other. She worked her tongue as she backed out and sucked on the head for a while. She then took him in as far as she could.

"Oh." Donovan's whole body tightened. He placed a hand on her shoulder and tentatively touched her head with the other.

Kyra reached up and placed her hand over his. She pushed his fingers into her wet hair and gripped his hand tighter, urging him to do the same. When she released his hand, Donovan felt more comfortable. He clutched her hair as Kyra's head bobbed back and forth. Donovan shuddered, and she tasted the saltiness of his pre-cum. She swallowed greedily and sucked harder, wanting more.

The feel of her jaws and tongue on his meat made Donovan's legs tremble. The water was hot. Kyra's mouth was warm. Donovan looked down and lost all of his composure when he saw Kyra's lips wrapped around him, her jaws concave.

"Oh, baby, stop."

He tried to pull out, but Kyra wouldn't let him. She swatted his hands away when he tried to remove her face from his throbbing erection.

"Baby, I'm finna cum," he stressed.

Kyra heard him just fine. But Donovan was wrong in thinking that news would deter her. In fact, Kyra couldn't have been more thrilled about the prospect. The muscles between her legs were already tightening in anticipation. She was wet on the outside and just as wet on the inside. She began to moan through her nose, and that was all she wrote.

"Oh, fuck, baby!"

Donovan's dick jumped with each squirt of semen it pumped out. The pre-cum was an appetizer. This was the main course, and Kyra loved every drop of it. She swallowed when her mouth was full, and she sucked harder, making sure to get it all out. Donovan didn't think he ever had an orgasm so powerful. His toes curled so hard, Kyra heard them rubbing the bottom of the tub. She didn't back away for another thirty seconds. She looked up at him, her eyes low, her lips parted, water pouring down her face, Donovan's erection still jumping slightly in front of her nose.

"I..." He took a slow breath. "I can't wait to get inside you. I want you to cum as hard as I just did. I want you to fall asleep with me still inside you."

Kyra didn't please him in anticipation of a reward, but his comments delighted her immensely. She tongue kissed his dick again before she rose to her feet. Donovan's hands were immediately all over her. Kyra never took a *dirty* shower before. It was an experience she would never forget. She was glad that she shared it with her best friend and the love of her life.

CHAPTER EIGHTEEN
BAD MATH

The next morning Donovan had to wake everyone up at nine a.m. so he'd have time to make it to church with his mother. He was open to taking Kyra and her kids with him, but she was reluctant.

"I haven't talked to your mom since I been back," she said. "I don't want to show up at her church out of the blue."

"It's not out of the blue," Donovan said as he whipped up a quick breakfast of scrambled eggs, bacon and toast. "And it's not *her* church. It's God's house. Besides, I talk to my mom about you all the time. I told her I wanted to bring you to church with me."

"What about the fornication?" Kyra asked with a worried look in her eyes. "I don't know if I'd feel right going to church after what happened last night."

"Everyone sins," Donovan said. "I wish I could be perfect, but there are some things in the bible that I don't totally agree with."

That was news to Kyra. "Like what?"

"I don't know," Donovan said. "Jonah and the whale. Sex before marriage. Living together before marriage. Things like that."

"Wow. That's a lot," Kyra noticed.
Donovan shrugged. "Not really."
"You don't believe in Jonah and the whale?"
"It's hard to take literally."
"But you still believe in God?"
Donovan frowned. "Of course."

"How do you justify all of that," Kyra asked, "and still be at peace with the man upstairs?"

"What is this, a theological discussion?" Donovan asked. "I just asked if you wanted to go to church with me."

Kyra laughed. "I want to see your mother first, for lunch or something, before I walk into her church. I know you said everything's cool now, but I think we need some kind of icebreaker. There will be a lot of people watching us at church. It could be a little awkward."

"That's cool," Donovan said. "How about today? Me and my mom always go to lunch after church. Do you want me to pick you up?"

Kyra shook her head. Truth be told, she was afraid of Beverly Mitchell. The last time she saw her, Beverly was kicking her out of her home, accusing Kyra of corrupting her only child. But it was clear Donovan would do whatever he could to bring the two women in his life together.

"Alright," Kyra said. "What time?"

"Service usually end at twelve-thirty," Donovan said. "I'll pick you up at one. It'll be fun. I know my mom will be excited."

"I doubt that," Kyra muttered.

"As far as your question," Donovan said, "I don't try to justify my beliefs. I just pray and ask God to forgive me."

"You ask Him to forgive you for not agreeing with Him?"

Donovan snickered. "Not exactly, but, yeah, I guess so. Sometimes."

"And that works?"

Donovan put down his spatula and went to the counter where Kyra was standing. "It works because God knows me better than anyone," he said. "He knows I love Jesus, and he knows I love you, too."

Kyra grinned as she looked up at him. She knew God was pleased with Donovan. He loved his mother, went to church every Sunday, and Donovan couldn't walk by anyone in need without offering to help.

"I decided that I do want to live with you," Kyra said.

Donovan's smile was big and bright. "That's great, Kyra. When?"

"I want to wait until I get my next check," she said. "So I can buy more furniture for the kids' rooms. And I want to be able to pay some of the bills, too."

"Kyra, you don't–"

She put two fingers over his lips, silencing him. "Donovan, I'm not a deadbeat anymore. If we're going to be together, then we're going to do it *together*. You don't have to support me. I want to take care of you sometimes."

"Alright," Donovan said. "That's fine."

Kyra wouldn't get paid for another 30 days, but at least Donovan knew the exact date she would move in with him. He hugged her tightly.

They were distracted by movement in the doorway. It was Kat. She walked into the kitchen groggily and headed for her mother. She said, "Up," reaching with both hands. To their surprise, she was talking to Donovan rather than her mom.

"Oh no she didn't," Kyra said, but she was tickled pink.

"I'm just as shocked as you," Donovan replied. He bent to pick up the pint-sized princess. "*Oof*. You're getting heavy," he teased. "Are you hungry?"

Kat nodded. She held onto Donovan with one arm and pointed at the stove with her free hand. "I like eggs."

"Oh, well you're in for a treat," Donovan said. "Eggs are my specialty."

"Where are your shoes?" Kyra asked her daughter.

Kat shrugged.

"Girl." Kyra shook her head. "Let me go find–"

"Wait." Donovan reached to stop her. "Why don't you finish up with breakfast, and let me help find her shoes?" He handed her the spatula.

Kyra laughed. "Alright daddy day care. You have fun with that. And make sure Q's out of bed. I woke him up twenty minutes ago, but I haven't seen him since then."

Kat was already quite the snitch. "Q playing games. He in there." She pointed towards the den.

"What?" Kyra was not amused. "That boy knows not to wake up and go straight to no games. He didn't even ask."

She started to head that way, but Donovan said, "I'll take care of that, too. You need to hurry up with breakfast. We're hungry."

"We hungry," Kat agreed.

"And don't forget the bacon," Donovan said as he exited the kitchen.

"Bacon!" Kat tacked on.

"I don't even know where anything is!" Kyra called after him.

"Everything's in there somewhere," Donovan yelled down the hallway. "What kind of woman doesn't know her way around a kitchen?"

Kyra grinned as she pulled the refrigerator open. Donovan was doing everything he could to get her used to the idea of living with him. Kyra wanted to stick to the time frame she gave him, but it was hard to deny herself of something that felt so right.

She found the bacon in the fridge, and she found seasonings for the eggs in the first place she looked. "Talking about I don't know my way around a kitchen... I *know* my way around a kitchen," she muttered as she prepared the meal. She decided to make the best bacon and eggs Donovan had ever seen, to show him she was no lightweight.

≈≈≈≈≈≈≈

Kyra was still in a good mood when Donovan dropped her and the kids off an hour later, but it was short lived. Aunt Ruth emerged from her bedroom when she heard them enter the house. She pulled a robe over her slip and met them in the living room. Aunt Ruth looked tired and frustrated. But she looked like that all of the time, so Kyra didn't pay her any mind.

"Sorry we woke you." She ushered the kids to the bedroom, hoping to make it past their mean landlord without any trouble.

"We need to talk," Aunt Ruth said.

"Oh, okay," Kyra said. "Y'all go ahead," she told Kat and Quinell.

Kyra went and stood in front of her aunt, but Ruth walked by her and took a seat on the couch, indicating this would be one of those dreaded *sit down* kinda talks.

Dammit. Kyra hated coming home sometimes. She thought about Donovan's offer as she followed her aunt and sat on the loveseat across from her. Donovan said Kyra could move in

213

with him whenever she was ready. She kept his offer tucked away, like it was a get out of jail free card, which made it easier to deal with whatever her aunt was about to say.

"What's wrong, Auntie?"

"Where's my money, girl?"

Kyra's head cocked slowly to the side. "What are you talking about?"

"My money you supposed to pay me when you get your check," her aunt said. "You got paid on the *first*. Why you ain't paid me?"

"Today's the *second*," Kyra said. "Why you tripping about it already? It's only been *one day*."

"Yeah, and you been ducking and dodging me," Ruth said. Her eyes looked very small through her coke bottle glasses. But her mouth was big. Big and ugly, set in a sneer. She pointed a long, skinny finger at her ungrateful niece. "You knew I wanted my money yesterday. You knew I had plans for that."

Kyra couldn't believe this was really happening. Ruth had been an asshole since the day Kyra arrived with her children, but this was unreasonable. "How am I supposed to know you had plans?" she said. "You don't tell me nothing."

"You get paid on the *first*, and I want my money on the *first*," her aunt reiterated.

"Okay, whatever," Kyra said. "How much money am I supposed to owe you?"

"Fifteen hundred dollars." Aunt Ruth actually said it with a straight face.

Kyra's jaw dropped. After taxes and medical insurance for her and the kids, she only made $1,800 for a month's work at J.T. Elder. She'd be damned if this witch got 85% of it.

"How the hell do I owe you *fifteen hundred dollars*?"

"Don't be cussing at me!"

"How do I owe you fifteen hundred dollars?" Kyra snapped.

"What you mean, *how*? You been living here for two months, ain't paid no bills, barely bought some groceries. Plus I'm doing all this babysitting. You going out damned near every night with one of your man friends." Ruth waved her hand. "Girl, you got so many of them, I can't keep up no more."

Kyra's eyes burned. She felt like she might cry, but she refused to let that happen. Her face turned red as she smothered the hurt and swallowed the hateful things she wanted to say.

"The only people I've been out with since I got here is Donovan and Roland. I only saw Roland *two times*. And Donovan watched my kids one of those times."

Kyra spoke through clenched teeth. Her nostrils flared with each heartbeat. "You told me you were charging one-fifty a week for babysitting while I was at work. That comes out to six hundred dollars. As far as me going out, I only asked you to watch my kids five or six times. You said you were charging ten dollars an hour for that. That should come out to... a hundred and eighty dollars, *tops*."

"What about when you didn't come home *all night*?"

Kyra shook her head. She rubbed her hands together anxiously. Why did she think Aunt Ruth wouldn't charge for every hour she spent with Donovan? *Whatever*! Kyra didn't care. That was their first night together, and it was worth it.

"Alright, so what's that? Another hundred and fifty?"

"That's about right." Aunt Ruth nodded.

Kyra calculated quickly. The total she came up with made her stomach hurt. "Alright, so, so that's nine hundred and thirty dollars." The tears were falling now. She wiped her eyes roughly. "Why you say it was fifteen hundred?"

"The rest is your regular rent," Aunt Ruth said.

Kyra couldn't do anything but sit and stare. She was devastated, but she barely reacted. Acting a fool wouldn't do her any good. She'd been had, plain and simple. Kyra felt stupid. She felt pathetic. She felt lower than dirt. But most of all she felt stupid, stupid, stupid. How did she not see this coming?

"I'm only charging you three hundred dollars a month to live here," Aunt Ruth said. "That's a good deal. You not gon' find nowhere else to live for that."

No. The truth was Kyra wouldn't be able to find anywhere to live *period* because she'd forever be in debt to her manipulative relative. If she paid Aunt Ruth what she wanted, Kyra would be left with three hundred dollars for the rest of the month.

But there was an out.

Kyra's heart knocked as she thought of Donovan. She didn't want to move in with him under these circumstances. She wanted to go to him with her head high, her finances in order. She wanted to be independent; in a position to help him for once in her life. She appreciated everything Donovan did for her, but she was tired of always running to him for help.

But she could run, if she wanted to. Kyra fought to keep a straight face. Her mouth was itching to curve into a smile. Aunt Ruth didn't know that she had an option. She didn't know that Kyra could grab her kids, jump in her car and hit the highway *right now*, and never look back.

"You didn't tell me you were charging me rent," she said. She was just stalling at this point. She already knew what Ruth would say.

"Kyra, you can't live nowhere for free. *Nowhere*. You old enough to know that by now."

Yeah, and I'm old enough to know how to deal with a snake in the grass like you, Kyra thought.

"Alright, I'll write you a check," she said.

She must have been thinking STOP PAYMENT too hard because Aunt Ruth said, "Naw, I want cash."

Kyra still had her. "Today's Sunday. I can't get cash today."

"You can withdraw it out the ATM."

"No I can't. I just opened my account yesterday. I don't have direct deposit, and my check hasn't even cleared yet. I can't get cash till Monday."

Ruth didn't like that one bit. It showed all over her face. "Gimme a check now, Kyra, and then bring me my money on Monday. I'll give you your check back when I get my cash."

Perfect. "Okay."

Kyra went to her room. Kat and Quinell watched her silently. They heard everything, and they saw the pain and tears in Kyra's eyes. She ignored them as she dug through her purse, looking for her checkbook. She went back to the living room and sat across from her aunt. Ruth watched carefully as Kyra wrote a check for fifteen hundred dollars.

"Here."

Ruth looked at the check for what felt like a long time before she folded it and rose from her seat. She left the room without another word. Kyra returned to her room and told her children no to worry.

"We're going to live with Donovan soon."
They were both very happy to hear that.

≈ ≈ ≈ ≈ ≈ ≈

At twelve-thirty Kyra started watching the clock. Donovan would be leaving church any minute now. He wanted to pick Kyra up and take her to his mom's house for lunch. He didn't say anything about the kids going, too, but Kyra had no choice but to take them now. She didn't feel comfortable leaving them with her aunt anymore. Kyra realized she had to find a *real* babysitter or daycare for Kat by Monday morning, or she couldn't even go to work. Kyra chewed off nearly all of her thumbnail as she tried to sort things out.

When Donovan picked her up, she'd bring her kids and tell him about the fight with her aunt. She'd tell him that she was ready to move in with him. *Damn.* Kyra shook her head. She wished it didn't have to be like this, but she had no choice.

But it wasn't like she didn't want to live with Donovan. He was the man of her dreams and the love of her life. She just didn't want to go to him crawling, beat up by the world. Kyra sighed and swallowed a big slice of humble pie. She knew Donovan wouldn't care how she went to him, so she should be happy about it. This was actually a good thing, spurred on by an evil woman.

On Monday Kyra would put a stop-payment on the check she gave her aunt. Better yet, Kyra could do it today, when she got to Donovan's house. She could pull up her bank account on his computer. That way she wouldn't have to worry about Aunt Ruth trying to cash the check first thing Monday morning. Kyra grinned devilishly. That would show her! Aunt Ruth thought she was the master manipulator, but Kyra could be a slick bitch, too.

But Kyra wasn't an *evil* bitch. She'd pay her aunt for the babysitting. Nine hundred and thirty dollars was more than half her check, but Kyra agreed to pay that, and she would. Aunt Ruth would only be able to complain to the family about not getting the money she was trying to *steal* from Kyra – not the money she was rightfully owed.

Speak of the devil. Kyra looked up when her aunt appeared in her doorway. Kyra's whole family was either sitting or

217

lying on the one bed in the room. They all regarded their landlord with either suspicion or fear.

"Somebody here to see you," Ruth said.

Kyra thought she saw a smirk on her aunt's face. She checked the clock. It was 12:35. Donovan was early. And he didn't call to say he was on his way. Kyra didn't even hear the doorbell. She didn't care. The sooner she got her kids away from her aunt the better.

Ruth walked away, and Kyra told Quinell, "Put on your shoes. And help Kat get hers on."

He moved to do what she asked.

Kyra hurried to the front room with love in her heart, but it turned to sheer horror when she rounded the corner and saw who was waiting for her. Kyra was so shocked, she came to a screeching halt and brought a hand to her mouth. Her eyes were as big as quarters. She almost screamed.

Her visitor came all the way from Little Rock, Arkansas. He looked good. But to Kyra, he was the epitome of *ugly*. She saw drugs and needles and cash and dopefiends. She saw blood-shot eyes, lines of heroin on the kitchen counter and babies crying. Her babies. She saw pain and regret. And she felt it, too.

Leonard said, "Hey, baby."

Kyra didn't know her aunt was still standing there until Ruth said, "Hmph."

Kyra couldn't find the words to say anything at all.

CHAPTER NINETEEN
A MOTHER'S LOVE

At the same moment Kyra walked into her aunt's living room and came face to face with her worst fear, Donovan got behind the wheel of his pickup and told his mother about his big plans for today.

"Guess what?"

"What?" Beverly asked.

"Today you're going to see Kyra."

He backed out of his parking spot as Beverly turned and eyed him with confusion.

It was cloudy outside, but Donovan's spirits were bright. Today's church service was wonderful. The pastor spoke about forgiveness. Beverly already told Donovan she didn't have any lingering problems with Kyra, but if there was anything she still wanted to get off her chest, she could do so today. And Kyra could forgive Beverly for kicking her out of the house fifteen years ago. And Donovan could ask his mom to forgive him and Kyra for disrespecting her home with their foolhardy kiss. And after all of the forgiving, everyone would hug and live happily ever after.

"What do you mean?" Beverly asked.

"I invited her to lunch with us today," Donovan said. "I think it's about time you two see each other. Don't you want to know what she looks like now?"

"Kyra was always a pretty girl," Beverly said. "I'm sure she's beautiful."

"She is. And I told her about your good cooking. She can't wait for me to pick her up."

"What?" Beverly frowned. "Pick her up when?"

"Right now," Donovan said. He pulled his cellphone from his pocket.

"Wait, you're not taking her to my house," Beverly said. Donovan's heart sank. He thought they had gotten past that. But Beverly wasn't being mean. "I won't have time to clean up or nothing," she said. "You can't just be bringing people up in my house unannounced."

"Oh."

"And I don't have time to cook, either," Beverly stated. "You should've told me about this yesterday. What's wrong with you, boy? Don't be going around offering my dinner to people without asking me."

Donovan's smile returned.

"What's so funny?"

"I thought you were gonna say you don't want to see Kyra."

"No, I would love to see her," Beverly said. "But not at my house – not today at least."

"Can I pick her up and bring her to Golden Corral with us?"

"Sure," Beverly said. "But not in this truck. You know I don't like to be squeezed up with people in here."

"She can sit in the back."

Beverly looked at her son like he insulted womankind in general. "Donovan, don't you *ever* put a woman in the backseat of this truck! You know there's not enough room."

Donovan's F-150 had four doors, but the back two were half-size. Kat and Quinell could ride in the backseat with no problem, but it was a tight fit for an adult.

"Take me home first, and you can go get Kyra in my car," Beverly suggested. "I need to change shoes anyway."

Beverly drove a Lincoln Town Car. It was plenty big, and a luxury car to boot.

"Thanks, Mama. That'll be perfect."

≈ ≈ ≈ ≈ ≈ ≈

Except it wasn't perfect. Kyra wasn't answering her phone. Donovan called her twice in the ten minutes it took him to get to his mother's house. Undeterred, he took Beverly's car anyway. Ten minutes wasn't a long time to be out of pocket, especially when you have a small child who needs help bathing and dressing and such.

Donovan called Kyra's cell again as he rolled out of his mother's driveway. Still no answer. As a last resort, he called Aunt Ruth's house phone. She answered right away.

"Hello?"

"Uh, hi. This is Donovan. How are you?"

She grunted. "Fine."

"I don't mean to bother you," Donovan said. "But Kyra's not answering her cellphone. Is she in?"

There was a pause before Ruth said, "Which one are you?"

Donovan's brow furrowed. What kind of question was that? Luckily he reached a stop sign. The residential street was completely empty, so he remained at the stop for a minute.

"You the tall one?" Ruth asked. "It's so many of y'all, I can't keep up."

Donovan's fury was immediate, but just as quickly he doused the embers that were starting to burn his soul. Kyra told him about her aunt already. And Donovan saw it with his own eyes when he bought groceries for them a couple of months ago. Ruth was a hater. She was no doubt lying about the supposed men in Kyra's life.

Nice try, Donovan thought and smiled again. "Yes, I'm the tall one," he said. "So, is Kyra in?"

"Naw," Ruth said. "She left with her baby-daddy."

Donovan thought he was ready for this woman's acid, but that comment threw him for a complete loop. He couldn't even pretend to be okay.

"Wh, what?"

"You said you're Donovan?" the older woman asked.

A car horn sounded. Donovan checked his rearview mirror and saw that he wasn't alone on the street anymore. He made a right at the intersection and pulled over in front of a random house. He put his car in PARK and tried to slow his heartbeats.

"Yeah, I'm Donovan. When did Kyra leave?"

"About ten minutes ago. I don't wanna get all in your business, but you look like a good man," Ruth said. "Kyra told me you coach for Western Hills."

Donovan's breaths were hot and heavy. "Kyra left with Kat's father?"

"Yeah," Ruth said. "Leonard been calling her. They talk all the time. He just came down from Arkansas to see her."

Donovan's head was spinning. He didn't know what to believe anymore. He knew this woman was lying, but how much of it was a lie? Surely she wouldn't say Kyra wasn't there if she really was.

"She using you," Ruth confided, "if you wanna know what I think about it."

"I don't," Donovan said. "I just want to know where Kyra is."

"I told you she ain't here. You don't believe me? *Kyra!*" The woman barely took the phone away from her face before she screamed. *"Kyra! You in here?"* She was very loud. After a moment, she said, "See. She ain't here. She with Leonard, like I told you."

Donovan's eyes burned. What the hell was going on here? Kyra told him Leonard was trying to contact her, so Donovan believed that Kat's father might come to Overbrook Meadows. But why would Kyra leave with him? Why now? Donovan told Kyra he was going to pick her up after church, so she and Beverly could talk. Kyra wouldn't leave with some loser.

"Where the kids?" Donovan was speaking without thinking now. He was on the side of the road with nowhere to go. His mind was racing. His heart was, too.

"She left the kids here," Ruth said. "I like you, Donovan, and I feel bad about what Kyra's doing to you. I want to tell you the truth about how she's using you and why she came back here. Did Kyra tell you why she came back to Overbrook Meadows?"

Donovan swallowed roughly. He knew Aunt Ruth was full of shit, but some of it had to be true. Kyra was always vague about what happened in Little Rock. Donovan wanted to know everything, and he knew she was holding back. But he couldn't trust the woman he was talking to. He should hang up.

"You're lying."

"You don't have to believe me," Ruth said. "There's a million people in Little Rock who know what I know. Aunts, uncles, cousins, *everybody*. I can give you any phone number you want. I'm trying to help you, Donovan. You need to know what was *really* went down over there. You don't know Kyra like you think you do."

Donovan's soul was tormented. He felt like Ruth was carving chunks off his heart, slice by slice. "What are you talking about?" he breathed. He didn't want to know, but his mind would concoct all sorts of terrible scenarios until she told him. Even if Ruth gave him a bastardized version of the truth, Donovan needed to hear it. He could decide for himself what parts he wanted to believe.

"Drugs," Aunt Ruth said. "They was on drugs."

Donovan nearly sighed in relief until the word "*They*" registered. "Who? Kyra?"

"Yes, she was," Ruth said.

She sounded solemn, but Donovan could almost see her grinning, like the devil himself. His eyes filled with tears even as he barked at her. "You're lying!"

"I'm not lying!" Ruth snapped back. "I'm trying to help you, so stop telling me I'm lying! Kyra was on drugs, and Leonard was on drugs, and that's why them people came and took her kids. I know she told you they took her kids..."

Donovan's silence was answer enough. Ruth hummed into the phone. "Uhn uhn uhn..." She sounded different than before. Her smugness was unmistakable now. Donovan realized she wasn't lying, not about this, and he lost the slippery hold on his composure.

Dark shadows filled the streets as the gray clouds above blocked out the rest of the fleeting sunshine. Donovan heard a crackle of thunder. He saw a bolt of lightening streak down to the earth, miles ahead of him. His vision blurred, but it wasn't the rain.

"The CPS took Kat and Quinell from her," Ruth continued. "Kyra was getting high on heroin with that boy. She was a dopefiend, just like her mama."

Thinking about Kyra's mother broke Donovan out of the trance this evil woman had him under. Donovan tried to love his neighbors and forgive his enemies, but Kyra's mom was one person he still despised. She let drugs replace the love she once had for her children, and she ruined all of their lives, especially Kyra's. Donovan could not believe that the woman he loved was in any way similar to her despicable mother. He refused to accept that.

"I'm getting off this phone," he growled. He wiped his eyes and nose angrily. Why did he entertain Kyra's spiteful aunt in the first place? He knew Ruth wasn't right. Kyra told him so nearly every day.

"Why don't you ask Kyra?" Ruth said. She was tired of this conversation, too. Donovan's nose was so wide open, he wouldn't listen to any negative comments about his pearly white princess. "You ain't gotta believe me," Ruth said. "Ask Kyra. Ask her if she was on dope. Ask her if them people took her kids. Ask her your damned self!"

She hung up in his face. Literally. Aunt Ruth had an old school telephone.

≈≈≈≈≈≈

Donovan returned to his mother's house a few minutes later. Beverly took one look at him and knew that this was the kind of pain only a woman could cause. She sat with him in the living room while Donovan told her about the conversation with Aunt Ruth. Beverly tried to make him feel better with the same reasoning Donovan used when he was on the phone with Kyra's aunt.

"She's lying, Donovan. Why do you believe her? You told me how she was."

As he talked to the woman who knew him best, Donovan managed to get his emotions under control. His eyes were dry as he shook his head, his body slumped over, his forearms resting on his knees. He looked up at his mother.

"I don't think she was lying, Mama."

"Why do you believe that, Donovan? Sit up, baby."

He sat back on the sofa, but his body still slumped. Beverly had never seen his spirits so low.

"Because of the way she sounded," Donovan said. "She said everybody knew about it. She said I could ask Kyra herself."

"And that's what you should do," Beverly urged. She was nearly as exasperated as he was. "That lady's trying to come against you and Kyra's happiness, Donovan. I can feel it in my bones. You don't need to think nothing else bad about Kyra, until you talk to her yourself. When was the last time you called her?"

"When I was on my way over there," Donovan said. "She still not answering."

"Call her now," Beverly suggested. "She's the only person you can get the truth from."

Donovan knew that was the best advice anyone could give him. He dug his phone from his pocket. Even that movement took a lot out of him. He felt completely drained. But Donovan's face lit up when he checked the display on his cellular. He had a missed call from Kyra. And a message.

"She called," he told his mom.

"When?"

"I had it on silent, from church," Donovan said as he accessed his call log. Kyra called him two minutes after he talked to her aunt. What a fool he was! The whole time he was giving his mother this sob story, he could've been talking to Kyra.

"Did she leave a message?" Beverly asked.

Donovan didn't respond because he had the phone to his ear, already listening to his voicemail. Beverly waited. Twenty seconds later Donovan sighed and smiled. "She sounds fine. She said she was outside, and she didn't hear her phone ringing."

"She didn't say anything about her baby's father?"

Donovan shook his head. His smile wavered. He was so happy to hear that Kyra was alive and well, that he momentarily forgot about the terrible things her aunt said about her.

"I'm gonna call her."

Donovan's pulse thumped as he returned Kyra's call. His mother watched him nervously. Kyra answered after a couple of rings.

"Hey. I'm sorry I missed your call."

"I was going to pick you up," Donovan said.

"I know. Baby, I'm so sorry. Are you still coming?"

She sounded normal. Donovan held out hope that the things her heard about her were not true.

"Did you leave?" he asked. "I called your home phone. Your aunt said you left."

"What? I didn't go anywhere," Kyra said. "I was here. You talked to my aunt?"

Donovan knew Ruth was a liar! He half smiled at his mother.

"She told me Leonard came from Arkansas, and you left with him."

There was a pause. Donovan's smile slipped again.

"He did come," Kyra said. She cleared her throat. "But I didn't leave with him. I just went outside with him so we could talk, without the kids hearing us. My aunt knows I didn't leave. I don't know why she told you that."

Goose bumps sprouted on Donovan's forearms. He had a feeling Ruth was mixing lies in with the truth. But Kyra didn't tell him about Leonard at all. He had to bring it up first. The whole time he had known her, Donovan never doubted Kyra's word. But now he wondered if she was going to tell him Leonard paid her a visit. He wondered if maybe Kyra did leave with him after all.

"Wh, what's wrong?" she asked. "I was gonna tell you. But I wanted to talk about it later. I got a lot of stuff to talk to you about. I can't believe she told you I left with him." Kyra growled. "I can't stand her, Donovan. I gotta get out of here. A lot of stuff happened today. I need to talk to you in person. Me and the kids, we gotta move out."

There was so much to process. Donovan felt like his world was slowly turning upside down. He had a million questions, but one was more important than all of the rest.

"Your aunt told me you were on drugs, Kyra. She said CPS took your kids. Is that true?"

In the five seconds it took for Kyra to come to terms with the fact that her biggest secret was out, and she didn't have the opportunity to tell Donovan herself, her boyfriend's face fell apart. Beverly threw her hands over her mouth as she watched him.

Kyra wanted to scream, and she wanted to cry, and she wanted to kill her aunt. Her brain quickly decided that crying was the only one of those options that was acceptable. Her eyes twitched, and then the tears flow unabated. She wiped her nose and said, "I'm sorry, Donovan. I was gonna tell you."

Her admission broke down the last wall of defense Donovan built around Kyra. He knew she wasn't perfect, but Donovan never would've believed Kyra fell into the same pattern of drug abuse as her mother. After all they went through as children, it was unthinkable that Kyra put Kat and Quinell through the same hell.

"How could you do that?" Hot tears flowed down Donovan's face. He didn't know why, but this almost felt like a personal slap, in *his* face. He felt like everything he did to protect Kyra when they were children was all in vain. All of the help he offered Kyra since she came back was based on a lie. What else had she lied about? Donovan had no idea, and he hated that he couldn't take Kyra's word for it.

"I need to talk to you in person," Kyra cried. "I'm sorry, Donovan. I didn't lie to you, I just didn't want to talk about that. I was too embarrassed."

Her voice was laced with regret. Her breath came in shudders. Donovan knew she was hurting, but so was he. And Kyra was the one who caused it, with her lies and her half-truths and her, her *drugs*! It was hard enough to *think* it; Donovan was by no means ready to talk about it.

"I gotta go."

"Please, baby. I'm sorry!"

"Kyra you lied to me. All I ever did was try to help you. I never did anything to hurt you."

Donovan's eyes were nearly bloodshot. His mother was crying, too. She placed a hand on his shoulder and rubbed comfortingly. But there was nothing Beverly could do to make the pain go away.

"Donovan, I need you! Please don't leave me!" Kyra cried.

"I gotta go," he said.

"Donovan, please."

"Kyra, I'll call you later. I gotta go. I need to think."

"Baby, please!"

"Kyra please let me call you back!" Donovan didn't mean to shout, but his heart, mind and soul were all swirling in a whirlwind of uncertainty. But as upset as he was, he still loved Kyra too much to simply hang up in her face.

"I'm sorry!" she wailed. Kyra released a litany of sounds that weren't intelligible before ending the call herself.

≈≈≈≈≈≈

Donovan stayed with his mother for another thirty minutes. Beverly didn't offer much advice. She thought Kyra was

227

wrong for doing drugs and even more wrong for keeping it from her son, but there was no need to speak on it.

Instead she pulled Donovan into her arms when he got off the phone. He surprised her by allowing it. They were quite a sight. Donovan was nearly twice his mother's size. She could barely wrap her arms around him, but a mother's love cannot be hindered by simple physics.

Beverly rubbed Donovan's shoulder while he sobbed on hers. He only cried for a few moments before he sat up and wiped his face. Beverly went to the kitchen to get him a drink of water and a face towel.

After a while Donovan rose from the couch and went to the bathroom to straighten up. When he emerged, he looked almost normal. Except for his eyes. They were filled with so much pain, it broke Beverly's heart. She had to look away.

Donovan went to his truck and got his toolbox. He took it to his mother's bathroom and hunkered down under the sink. Beverly tried to stop him. She told him he didn't have to do that today. But Donovan insisted, saying it would only take a minute.

He took the pipes apart and rescued a diamond earring his mother lost two days ago. He put the pipes back together and washed his hands and gave her a kiss on the way out.

Beverly stood on her porch watching the road after he drove away. She finally went inside because, after a great crackle of thunder, it started to rain.

CHAPTER TWENTY
RAINY DAYS

Kyra hung up the phone. She looked around her room and saw that Kat and Quinell were both crying, nearly as hard as her. Kyra wiped her face and ran to the bathroom. She closed the door and sat on the toilet and hugged herself as she cried her eyes out, as hard and as quietly as she could.

She would've stayed in the bathroom indefinitely if it wasn't for Quinell and Katavia. They had no idea what was going on except Mama was upset and they were no longer going to live with Donovan. Kyra washed her face and exited the bathroom, red-eyed and red-nosed, but strong enough to face her children and deal with the mistakes she made. She sat on the side of the bed and reached for both of them. They were eager for her affection. They held her without words.

Kyra knew she had to confront her aunt, but at that moment she needed to be there for her children. She had to let them know that she would always be with them, no matter how badly the world treated them. If it was just the three of them, so be it. They could take on the world together, and they would be just fine. Together.

≈ ≈ ≈ ≈ ≈ ≈

When Donovan left church at twelve-thirty and spoke to his mother about having lunch with the love of his life, Kyra was standing in her aunt's living room staring at a ghost. Leonard put on twenty pounds while he was in jail, and his hair was shaved close to his scalp now. He was still attractive. He looked stylish in his baggy jeans, Polo boots and collar shirt, but Kyra reacted as if he'd risen from the dead and still had graveyard dirt clumped in his mouth.

She didn't say anything at all while Leonard looked her up and down, deciding how he would approach this delicate situation, wondering how much control he still had over Kyra. Aunt Ruth stood off to the side, watching them both. Kyra may have remained frozen for another minute, but Quinell hurried from the bedroom with Kat in tow. Kyra turned quickly and pushed them back inside the one room Aunt Ruth allowed them.

"No!" she nearly screamed. "Stay in here. I'll come get you in a minute!"

She slammed the door in Quinell's confused face. She turned back and saw Leonard watching her peculiarly. He tried to look over her shoulder, but Kyra effectively blocked his view. Her brain was going a mile a minute, but she had no idea what she should do. Aunt Ruth shook her head at the whole sorry scene, and she finally retreated to her bedroom.

"What's going on?" Leonard asked Kyra. "Why you running the kids off like that?"

Kyra approached him cautiously. She hadn't seen Leonard in more than six months. The last time they were together, Leonard was at the lowest point of his addiction. Kyra was too, even though she was a relatively new user. The police were there that night. They took Leonard to jail. Kyra remained free, but it was by no means a blessing. She spent the next three months fighting to regain custody of her children, fighting to prove to total strangers that she was not the lowlife their paperwork said she was. Leonard didn't know anything about that struggle, just as Kyra didn't know what he went through in jail.

"You can't talk to me?" he said. "You ain't got nothing to say to me?"

He sounded more hurt than upset. Kyra finally found her voice.

"What are you doing here?"

"I been calling you for weeks!" Leonard said. "What'd you expect me to do?" He was loud, but it was frustration rather than anger.

Kyra's heart knocked against her sternum. Her nervous system flooded her blood with adrenaline, which helped her make smart, quick decisions.

"Let's go outside," she said, moving in that direction. She knew her aunt was eavesdropping. And the kids were already traumatized enough. Kyra needed to get Leonard out of her life as quickly as possible. Getting him out of the house was the first step.

She opened the front door and was greeted by cloudy skies, the taste of ozone in the air. The weatherman predicted rain for later in the day, but Kyra knew it was coming a lot sooner.

In the driveway she saw a new sedan with Arkansas plates. The drive from Little Rock was five and a half hours. Kyra knew that Leonard cursed her name plenty of times along the way. If his goal was to rattle Kyra by catching her off guard, he couldn't have done a better job.

She stepped into the front yard, inviting Leonard to follow her. Inside the house Donovan called Kyra for the first time. Quinell heard the phone and saw Donovan's name on the display, but he didn't answer it. He had been forbidden to, ever since Leonard started calling the house.

Kat's parents faced each other on Aunt Ruth's lawn. Leonard stared into Kyra's eyes for a few seconds before he asked the question that had been burning in his heart for the past six months.

"Yo, baby, why you leave me?"

Kyra had been waiting just as long to give him his answer. "You the one who went to jail, Leonard."

"But you didn't try to ride it out for me or nothing, Kyra. Soon as I got locked up, that was it. You didn't take my calls. No visits. Nothing. It was like you just said *fuck him*. You forgot about me when I needed you the most."

"*You needed me*? They took my kids, Leonard." Even as she looked into the eyes of the man who caused the worst pain she would ever know, Kyra tried to keep the blame out of her voice.

"I know they did," Leonard said. "I can't tell you how many times I cried about that. I heard that you got clean and got them back. I was proud of you, even though you didn't give a damn about me."

231

"I'm sorry," Kyra said. And she meant it. "I'm sorry I wasn't there for you. But I had bigger problems for myself. I couldn't help you no more."

"I didn't ask for no help," Leonard said. He was more fair-skinned than Kyra. She watched his face redden with anger. "All I wanted was to know that you still had my back."

Kyra shook her head. "I didn't have your back no more, Leonard. I couldn't."

"Yeah, I found out for myself," he said. "You had your cousins telling me you didn't want to be with me no more. But you couldn't do it yourself?"

Kyra lowered her eyes. She regretted the way she handled their breakup, which was nothing more than full abandonment. But no one understood the power Leonard had over her. Kyra had to lose everything to finally find the strength to break free. She feared that if she talked to Leonard, even from jail, he would've convinced her to believe in him again.

"What do you want now?" Kyra asked. She didn't feel weak at all anymore. The worst Leonard could do was sue her for visitation rights for Kat. And even that was no longer a frightening scenario. Not with Donovan by her side.

"I want you to come back to me."

Kyra shook her head. "That's never going to happen."

"Why not? I still love you, Kyra. And I know you love me, too. I see it in your eyes."

Kyra frowned and blinked away whatever misleading messages her eyes were giving off. "Leonard, getting back with you is the absolute last thing I would ever do. I'd turn my kids in to CPS myself before I do some mess like that."

He flinched. "Kyra, this ain't you, baby. Why you talking to me like that?"

"This is me now," she said. "This is the me *you* made, Leonard. And stop calling me baby."

"Come with me," Leonard said. He took her hand. "I got this rental. Let's go somewhere and talk."

Kyra jerked her hand away. "I'm not going anywhere with you. We talking now, and you ain't said nothing."

"I got a room," Leonard said. "Come with me. We need to, we need to talk things thing out, Kyra. You all mad. You need to calm down. Relax a little. Get you a little taste, so you can think about what I'm saying..."

"A little taste?"

"What?"

"I heard what you said." Kyra had her hands on her hips now, the last of her compassion gone.

"I didn't say nothing."

"Whatever, man. Are you high right now? You still shooting up?"

"No! Why you gon' say some shit like that?"

"Let me see your arms."

"What?"

"Let me see your arms, if you not getting high."

"Man, this some ol' bullshit," Leonard said. "I love you, Kyra. I never did nothing but love you. I treated you the best I could, better than I treated anybody!"

Kyra rolled her eyes. She took note of how Leonard still wouldn't show her his arms as he embarked on a tirade about how much he loved her and how wrong she did him.

Kyra listened because she wanted to know how long he'd be there before he mentioned Kat. She would've cut his rant off, however, if she knew Aunt Ruth was on the phone with Donovan at that very moment, divulging her ugliest secrets.

By the end of his speech, Leonard was crying. Kyra was pissed because she gave him this much of her time. She knew Donovan had called her by now. She hoped he would round the corner in his truck, so she could show him the loser who was threatening to take her to court.

"What does all this have to do with Kat?" she asked.

"Yeah. And I want my baby, too!" Leonard said. "Where she at? Let me see her?"

"Get out my face," Kyra said, shaking her head.

"You can't stop me from seeing my daughter!"

"Call the police and show them the papers that says today is your visitation day. I'll wait on you. I'll be right here."

"I'ma sue your ass. You can't take my daughter out of state."

"What's your daughter's middle name?" Kyra asked.

Leonard didn't even try to guess.

After five seconds, Kyra told him, "Leonard, if you get cleaned up, I'll do whatever I can to allow you to be in Kat's life, even if it means I have to move back to Little Rock."

"I am clean. You don't know what you talking about."

"Boy, you just tried to give me *a taste* three minutes ago. You full of shit, and you know it. I don't wanna be with you no more, and you know you don't give a damn about Kat. So why don't you just leave me alone? I don't want child support from you or nothing. I just want you gone."

He sneered at her before spitting his worst venom. "You chose to get on that dope, Kyra. You remember that shit?"

Kyra shook his comments off easily. She knew who she was then, and she knew who she was now. "You're right. And when I was high, they wouldn't let me have my kids. I got clean, and they gave them back to me. You gotta do the same thing, Leonard. You can start by showing me your arms right now."

He looked like he wanted to punch her. Instead he said, "Man, fuck you. I ain't gotta show you shit."

Kyra shook her head and walked away with a grin. "I guess I'll see you in court then."

Her spirits were high when she returned to her room. It upset Kyra to see that she missed two calls from Donovan. But she was excited about the news she had for him: Leonard was most likely out of their lives forever, and she was ready to move out of her aunt's house.

Donovan didn't answer when she called him back, so Kyra left him a message. He returned her call, and that's when Kyra's life was turned upside down a second time.

≈≈≈≈≈≈

Now she sat afraid and dejected on her bed, trying to comfort her children when she was dreadfully in need of comfort herself. Donovan knew about her drug use, and he knew that she lost her children to the system. The worst part was Donovan had to hear about it from Aunt Ruth.

Kyra thought she handled her first confrontation of the day very well. Leonard was gone. She was pretty sure he was still on drugs, but most importantly Leonard was gone. Kyra's next confrontation would be a lot worse because afterwards she

234

wouldn't have anywhere to live. So be it. Because if Aunt Ruth thought she could run her mouth like that and not get a mouthful in return, she had another thing coming.

Kat and Quinell finally stopped crying. Kyra got off the bed, and Kat reached for her. Kyra forced a smile and told her, "Mama will be right back. I have to go talk to your Aunt Ruth." She told Quinell, "If things get loud, just stay calm and look after your sister. We'll probably be leaving here as soon as I get back."

Quinell's eyes brightened. "We're going to live with Donovan?"

Kyra's whole face cracked as she shook her head. She pulled it together right away, but Quinell saw it. "No, but we'll find somewhere to go. No matter what, we'll always have each other, right?"

Quinell nodded.

Kyra rubbed the top of his head and hugged both of her children at once. She then turned and left the room. She closed the door behind herself and allowed all of her anger to rise to the surface as she marched to her aunt's room. Kyra didn't go to church as much as she should, and she was far less saved than Donovan.

The only thing she promised herself *not* to do was put her hands on Aunt Ruth. And even that was flexible, depending on how the witch responded.

≈ ≈ ≈ ≈ ≈ ≈

"What the hell you tell Donovan all that shit for?"

"What?" Aunt Ruth hopped out of bed with a speed and agility that belied her age. She met Kyra head on in the doorway. "Don't you be coming up in my room with all that noise!"

Ruth didn't have time to throw a robe over her nightgown, and Kyra saw much more of her skin than she ever wanted to. Aunt Ruth's chest was sunken. Her breasts hung like the old women in the African tribal videos from the 1930's. Without her glasses, Ruth looked ten years younger. But she was still hideous, as far as Kyra was concerned; ugly inside and on the outside.

"Why did you tell him that?" Kyra nearly screamed.

"He called *my* phone!" her aunt screamed back. "I can say whatever the fuck I want on my goddamned phone. You must've forgot whose house this is."

"It don't matter whose house it is! You still didn't have no business telling my personal business."

"What personal business?" Ruth said. "That you was a dopefiend? That them people had to come take your kids? Everybody know that. It ain't no fucking secret, Kyra. You need to quit lying to these folks, is what you need to do."

Even Aunt Ruth's breath was stale. Kyra couldn't think of one single thing she liked about this woman.

"You don't even know what you're talking about," she said. "And it didn't have nothing to do with you anyway!"

"It got everything to do with me," Ruth countered. "You down here right now because of what you was doing in Little Rock."

"I changed," Kyra cried. "I'm not like that no more. And you know it!"

"Then why you scared to tell the truth?"

"Tell the truth to who?"

"Donovan for one," Ruth said. "That boy didn't know nothing about it. You call yourself being all in love or whatever. Why can't you tell him the truth?"

"It's not your business!" Kyra shouted. She didn't understand why her aunt couldn't grasp that.

"He called *my* phone," Ruth repeated. "I didn't call him. He called me!"

"He didn't ask you about none of that shit you told him!"

"Well, *I* think he need to know about it," Ruth stated. "How about that? I told him 'cause I think he need to know."

"*But why*?" Kyra bawled.

"Because you using people, Kyra. You using people, and it ain't right, just like you doing to me. You didn't wanna pay me my money when you got paid. You fucked off your food stamps. I told you them people would give you some money just to live here, but you didn't wanna do that either. Everything I tried to get you to do, you wouldn't do nothing! And then you got this man and the other one coming over here, taking you out to fancy places."

"So? What about it?"

236

"They wouldn't have done nothing for you if they knew the truth!" Ruth said. "If you wasn't gon' tell 'em, then I had to be the one to do it. You can try that sneaky shit somewhere else, 'cause you sure as hell ain't doing it here!"

Ruth was in her face, chin up, top lip curled in a sneer. She looked like she could defend herself if Kyra took a swing. But the more Kyra studied her face and listened to the words coming out of her mouth, the more she realized it wasn't worth it. This confrontation was a waste of time.

The world had not been kind to Aunt Ruth. She had three marriages that ended in divorce. The one thing she had to show for it all, her son Michael, hadn't called the house since Kyra had been there. Aunt Ruth was bitter and lonely, and she was sick and tired of being bitter and lonely. She tried to ruin Kyra's life because misery loves company.

Kyra knew that the longer she stayed there, the more she would lose to the curse that had been placed on Ruth's household. Kyra felt like she'd been running all her life. Now it was time to put her Nikes on again.

"You ain't even worth it," she said and abruptly left the room.

Aunt Ruth followed her down the hallway.

"What you mean by that?"

Kyra ignored her. She went to her room and locked eyes with Kat and Quinell who were sitting on the bed where she left them. She tried to give them an encouraging smile, but her eyes were wet and sorrowful. Kyra dropped to her knees and dragged both of her brother's suitcases from under the bed. She threw them on top of the mattress and told Quinell, "Get all of your clothes. Put them in that one."

Quinell hopped off of the bed and ran to his dresser. He yanked it open and scooped up the contents of the first drawer.

"What are you doing?"

Aunt Ruth was standing in the doorway. Kyra disregarded her as she gathered Kat's toys and Q's school supplies.

"I ain't say you had to leave," Ruth said. "I'm not putting you out, Kyra."

No one responded. Kat sat on the bed with her eyes on her aunt.

"Get all your shoes," Kyra told her. She had to snap her fingers in Kat's face to get her attention. "Get all your shoes," Kyra said. "Get Quinell's, too. All the shoes you can find. Put them in this bag." She gave her daughter an empty trash bag. The toddler crawled off the bed and got to work.

"Where you gon' go?" Ruth asked. "You ain't got nowhere to go, Kyra."

Kyra didn't respond, but she heard everything. The fact that Ruth's assumption was correct made her Kyra's tears flow even harder. Where was she going? The women's shelter? Back to Little Rock? It was hard to believe that thirty minutes ago Kyra had a man who loved her and wanted her to move in. She was sure Donovan still loved her, but they weren't on speaking terms. She knew he would no longer welcome her with open arms.

Kyra and her kids continued to pack hastily while Aunt Ruth hovered in the doorway saying things that didn't matter at all, like, "I'll call him back and tell him it wasn't true," and "I'll give you your check back, and you can pay me just a thousand," and "I won't charge you for rent, if you stay, Kyra. I'll only charge you for babysitting – as long as you keep getting groceries."

In a last desperate move, Aunt Ruth revealed her dark heart and a possible motive for what she did: "I said I'll give your check back, Kyra. You don't have to leave. Just pay me five hundred dollars a month – and get groceries.

"Where are you gonna go, girl? I'm not kicking you out. I told you I would help you. I told you that before you came down here. I told you I would take care of you. You don't need nobody's help but *mine*. Don't worry about that boy. Just stay here with me, and let me help with those kids..."

Kyra finally understood that her aunt was crazy as well as lonely. She invited Kyra to live with her under the guise of helping her get back on her feet. But Ruth hated every bit of independence Kyra developed. And she hated everyone in Kyra's life who offered to help her. She wanted to run Donovan off so Kyra would be totally dependent on her aunt, but only an insane person would think that could actually work.

Kyra told her, "Excuse me," when she took the first load out to the car. It was pouring rain by then. The sky was fierce with thunder and lightning. Kyra was completely drenched five seconds after she walked outside. She threw the suitcase in the trunk and returned to the house for the other one.

Aunt Ruth glared at her. Kyra was shivering. Rain water mixed with tears dripped off her face. Her sneakers squeaked with each step. Quinell wanted to go with her when she took the second load, but she told him, "No. It's raining. Stay in here."

After two more trips, Kyra had all of her belongings stuffed in the trunk and the back seat of her car. She returned to the house for her children, who were as eager to get away from Auth Ruth as she was.

"Put your jackets on," Kyra told them.

She was nearly out of breath. She spoke in shudders, constantly sniffling and wiping her nose with the back of her hand. The white of her eyes was complete pink. Thankfully, her children had never been so well-behaved.

When everyone was ready to go, Kyra checked their bedroom one last time before she picked up Kat and pulled the hood of her jacket over her head. Quinell grabbed the last of his toys and stuffed them in his pockets before following her.

Aunt Ruth waited in the living room with a black robe wrapped around her body, looking like death itself. All she needed was a sickle.

"Where are you going, Kyra? It's raining out there. You can't take them babies out in that rain. You need to come sit down, and let's talk this out. I got your check right here. You don't have to pay me, if that's why you leaving."

Kyra didn't understand how someone could be so fundamentally stupid. After everything Ruth did to her since she moved in, she had the nerve to think she could make it all go away with money.

Kyra wanted to tell her to go to hell. She wanted to tell Aunt Ruth that she was an ugly, old hag who was going to die alone, that she'd wish for death a hundred times before God pinched the wick on her pitiful existence. But what was the point? Putting Aunt Ruth in her place wouldn't heal Kyra's broken heart. It wouldn't make Donovan forgive her for lying to him.

Kyra and her family exited the house and hurried to her car. Kyra felt the rain soaking all the way down to her underwear as she leaned in the back and fastened Kat's car seat. When she finally got behind the wheel, Kyra turned the ignition and was not surprised that her car wouldn't start. That was the devil trying to take away her last bit of sanity.

Kyra closed her eyes and said a quick prayer. She knew she'd keep her family in the car until it stopped raining before she'd return to her aunt's house. They could set out on foot when the rain cleared up.

Kyra opened her eyes and turned the key again.

This time the Escort started right up.

≈≈≈≈≈≈

Donovan was deeply depressed when he left his mother's house. The drive home was a lonesome one. It was hard to believe that his life changed so drastically, so suddenly.

Last night he was with Kyra and her children. This morning they made plans to have lunch with his mother. Three hours later Donovan talked to Aunt Ruth, and the clouds blocked out the sun. Now Donovan's disposition was just as gloomy as the skies above Overbrook Meadows.

He didn't know where life would lead him or what was to become of his relationship with Kyra. He thought he'd have time to consider his next move, but when he rounded the corner onto his street, Donovan saw a familiar car parked in his driveway. There was a knot in his stomach as he pulled in behind Kyra's Escort and put his truck in park.

It looked like the sky was dumping rain from buckets. Through his windshield, Donovan could see Kyra watching him in her rearview mirror. Her eyes were dry but grief-stricken. For the first time since she returned to Overbrook Meadows, Kyra looked completely lost and vulnerable. Donovan hadn't seen that look in her eyes in more than fifteen years.

He turned his truck off and sat for a few seconds. He watched Kyra in her rearview mirror until the drops of rain on his windshield made it impossible to see. He opened his door and stepped out into the downpour. After a moment, Kyra did the same. Donovan walked slowly towards her, oblivious to the coolness of the thousands of raindrops headed in his direction. His expression was hard and indecipherable. Kyra's eyes were large and apologetic, filled with hurt. They met at her bumper.

Kyra looked up at him. Her mouth moved. Sounds came out, but they weren't words. She wanted to tell him how sorry she was, for using drugs and for not telling him about it. She wanted to tell Donovan that he was her everything, and she didn't know if she could live without him. She wanted to tell him that he didn't have to take her back, but she needed somewhere to go, just for a couple of hours, so she could dry off and get her bearings and decide what her family's next move was.

She wanted to say these things, but Donovan only heard a long, desperate moan that was drenched with so much grief and regret, merely listening to it caused damage to his psyche. It broke his heart, much worse than learning her secrets did.

He reached for her. She didn't respond. Donovan stepped to her and wrapped both of his arms around her. Kyra stiffened, for a moment, and then she went completely limp, as if she'd been carrying the world's burdens for too long, and she had no strength left. Donovan held her tighter. Kyra buried her face in his chest and sobbed uncontrollably.

It was hard to say how long they remained this way. They were not deterred by the constant rain, the rumbling thunder or even the four eyeballs watching them anxiously from Kyra's Escort.

They held each other like they did when Donovan was twelve and Kyra was eleven, and they got caught in the rain as they walked home from school one day. All of the other kids ran for cover when the thunder clouds ripped open. But that was also picture day, and Kyra wore pumps that were slippery on the sidewalk. Rather than fend for himself, Donovan walked with her the whole way, holding her hand so Kyra wouldn't slip and fall. It was one of her most endearing memories.

When she was strong enough to stand on her own, Donovan released Kyra. Without a word, he walked to the Escort and opened the back door. He bent to reach inside while Kyra stood stoically in the driveway. Her throat caught when Donovan emerged from the vehicle with Kat in his arms. The toddler held on to him tightly as Donovan reached back inside the car and grabbed one of Kyra's suitcases with his free hand.

He looked Kyra in the eyes and told her, "Come on," and then he turned and walked to the house.

Kyra didn't move. She was too stunned. Quinell finally exited the vehicle. He went to his mother and took her hand. Kyra didn't look down at him, but she did follow when he led her to Donovan's front door.

By the time they got inside, Donovan was in the kitchen. He held Kat in one arm while he searched his pantry for marshmallows. He already had four packs of microwavable cocoa on the counter.

CHAPTER TWENTY-ONE
THE FINAL CHAPTER
THE REALEST EVER

They didn't talk about what happened at all that first day. Kyra's kids were as stressed out as she was. Donovan saw the fright and uncertainty in their eyes. As a teacher he knew that what they needed most was love, structure and a sense of normalcy. It would have freaked Kat and Q out even more if Donovan and Kyra disappeared and had a long talk, so they barely left the children's sight.

Everyone changed out of their wet clothes, and then they had cocoa with marshmallows in the kitchen. Donovan made ham sandwiches for lunch. Afterwards he went to the den and played video games with Quinell while Kyra and Kat napped and watched television in the living room. Donovan took them to CiCi's Pizza for dinner. When they got home, he suggested they play a family game. Quinell picked Chutes and Ladders.

The board game was as lame as Donovan remembered, but Kat and Q liked it. They were in good moods when Donovan sent them to bed at ten o'clock. Kyra wasn't in a good mood, but she hid her emotions well throughout the day. She finally broke down when she crawled into bed with Donovan at eleven-thirty. He held her while she cried, and he wouldn't let her talk about anything that happened that day.

"We don't have to talk about it tonight," he told her. "Just go to sleep, baby. I know you're tired."

Eventually Kyra did fall asleep, though her mind was filled with worries. Donovan took her in tonight, but he wouldn't discuss what their situation was. Kyra didn't know if he'd put her out in the morning or ask her to stay forever. To make matters worse, Kyra forgot to log on to her banking account and request a stop-payment for the check she gave her aunt. She knew that she might have as little as three hundred dollars to her name come sun up, but somehow she was able to sleep.

≈ ≈ ≈ ≈ ≈ ≈

The next day Donovan called-in to work and suggested Kyra do the same. She did as he asked. Donovan's word had always been law for her. Donovan made a few more phone calls during breakfast, and then they took Q to school. When he got out of the truck, Quinell asked his mother, "Are we going back to Mr. Mitchell's house when I get out?"

Kyra lowered her gaze. She and Donovan still hadn't discussed it, and she didn't want to put her foot in her mouth.

Donovan leaned forward and told the boy, "Of course you are. Where else would you go?"

Q smiled and nearly skipped into the building.

Kyra continued to keep her eyes averted as Donovan pulled away from the school. She was so ashamed of herself, she feared she would never be able to look Donovan in the eyes again.

≈ ≈ ≈ ≈ ≈ ≈

Two of the calls Donovan made that morning were to daycare facilities. The first one was on Seminary, not far from Quinell's school. Donovan took Kyra to meet the staff and check out their services. After a brief tour, Donovan and Kyra left the building, and he asked what she thought about the place.

Kyra toted Kat on her hip. She was quite perplexed about everything Donovan was doing. "Think about what?"

"About this daycare," he said. "Is this somewhere you'd feel comfortable leaving Kat?"

"Oh, um, they're kinda expensive."

"You're not going to find a licensed daycare that will take care of a two year old for less than one-fifty a week," Donovan stated.

244

"But I only make two thousand a month," Kyra said. "That's almost half my money."

"If you know someone who babysits from their home, you can try that," Donovan said. "But real daycares are reliable. A babysitter might turn you away if she stayed out at the club too late the night before. Plus daycares have healthy snacks and educational activities."

"But what am I gonna do about finding somewhere to stay?" Kyra asked. "I can't live off fourteen hundred a month."

"I thought you were staying with me."

Kyra's heart shuddered. "We haven't talked about anything yet."

"I told Q he was coming to my house after school," Donovan said.

"But you haven't said anything to me."

"I just said, '*I thought you were staying with me.*'"

Kyra couldn't get a read on him. She could tell he was still upset, but he was trying his best not to show it. He was having a hard time looking her in the eyes, which made Kyra feel even more self-conscious.

"Donovan, you know what I mean. We haven't *talked*, about what happened, about what my aunt told you."

"Let's get Kat situated first," he said. "Do you like this daycare, or do you want to see the one closer to your job?"

Kyra didn't want to do anything until they talked, but she knew she wasn't going to get her way. "I wanna see the other one."

"Alright. Let's go."

≈ ≈ ≈ ≈ ≈ ≈

Donovan took her to the Child and Family Solutions daycare near J.T. Elder, and Kyra quickly fell in love. The center looked like a small school, complete with a playground in the back and two former teachers running it.

Donovan said the main question Kyra should ask herself is whether or not she felt comfortable leaving her daughter there every morning. She said yes. They went to the front office and filled out paperwork. Kyra felt like she was signing her life away, especially since she and Donovan hadn't talked about what

245

happened, but she knew he wouldn't let her do anything she'd later regret.

"Are we keeping her today?" the co-owner, a woman named Mrs. Hampton, asked after Kyra was done with her paperwork and her first payment had been processed.

Kyra said, "No."

But Donovan said, "Yes."

Mrs. Hampton grinned. "You young couples... Do you need a minute to think about?"

"No," Kyra said. She had no idea what Donovan had in mind, but he was always three steps ahead of her. "We're leaving her today."

"Great," Mrs. Hampton said. She got up and led them out of the office. "Right this way. I think they're doing arts and crafts now..."

When they got back to his truck, Kyra asked Donovan, "Why didn't you want me to keep her today? I'm not working."

"You will be," Donovan said. "We have to get a bed for Kat. And I'm not setting up another bedroom without your help."

"But Donovan..." Kyra had a strange mix of emotions. On one hand she was excited that he still wanted to be with her. But she was also worried because she hadn't told him what happened. "Aren't we going to talk about any of this?"

"Yes," Donovan said. "We can talk right now." Rather than start his truck, Donovan turned in his seat and looked at Kyra. He sighed. "What do you want to tell me?"

Kyra's eyes widened. She couldn't believe she was the one begging for this conversation. This was a terrible idea! "I, I don't know..."

"Start with Leonard," Donovan said. "What happened yesterday?"

That was an easy one. Kyra told Donovan about Leonard's unexpected visit. She told him how Leonard refused to show her his arms and how he cursed her out before he left.

"Is he still going to take you to court?" Donovan asked when she was done.

Kyra shook her head. "No. I don't think so."

"What if he does?"

"I don't know." Kyra shrugged. "What do you think I should do?"

"You'd have to get a lawyer," Donovan said. "If Leonard's as bad as you say he is, you'll probably win the case. But if he gets clean, and he *really* wants to be with his daughter, you can't and shouldn't fight that."

"I won't," Kyra said. "But he doesn't care about her."

"Time will tell. What about your aunt? Why is she so mad at you?"

Kyra told him about the argument over her paycheck and how much she was supposed to pay for rent and baby-sitting. She also told him about the things Aunt Ruth said when they were packing up to leave her house.

"She wanted me to be dependent on her," Kyra concluded. "But she treated me like crap the whole time I was there. It doesn't make sense."

"Stuff like that happens all the time," Donovan said. "You'd be surprised how many parents abuse their kids, but they'd go crazy if someone took their babies away."

Kyra's chest tightened. She knew what was coming next.

"CPS took your kids from you, in Little Rock?"

Kyra nodded. She sniffled and started crying before she even began the story.

Everything she told Donovan about her and Leonard's relationship was true with one glaring exception. Towards the end, Kyra was not only complacent about Leonard's drug use, but she was also fascinated by it. Nearly everyone in the hood had it bad, but Leonard had an escape. It was cheap and it was long-lasting. And after watching him get high for a year, Kyra didn't see any negative side effects.

But Kyra didn't think she would've used drugs if not for the death of her grandmother. When she first moved to Arkansas, her granny was the one person who kept her sane when all Kyra wanted was Donovan; her best and only friend. Kyra slipped into a bout of depression after her grandmother's funeral, and Leonard's form of escape became more and more appealing to her. Kyra couldn't blame anyone for what happened next, because she made a conscious decision to get high

Leonard was all for it when she asked to snort some of his powder one day. It looked like brown sugar, and Kyra thought the high was just as sweet. She compared it to the marijuana she smoked from time to time, except heroin was fifty times more powerful. It didn't make her hungry or giggly or paranoid or hyper. All Kyra wanted to do with her heroin high was sit down somewhere and enjoy it and not think about all of the things life had taken from her.

She started snorting a pill every day after work. She didn't realize she was hooked until she tried to go without it one night, and she got an upset stomach. Kyra's bones hurt like she had arthritis. When she gave in and snorted her daily pill, all of the pain went away. She never got her fix with a needle, but Kyra was as addicted as any other junkie.

The raid came three months after Kyra snorted her first line. By then Leonard was a full-blown addict, and he started to make dopefiend mistakes. Not only did he sell crack to an undercover police officer, but Leonard made the drug deal at their home (an ultimate no-no for any dealer).

An hour later the police kicked in the door waving guns and an arrest warrant. They took everybody downtown. Kyra hadn't committed any crimes, but she was as high as a kite, and the police refused to return her children to her. When they told her, Kyra lost her mind. She cried and screamed to the point that she had to be taken to the hospital and treated for anxiety.

A social worker gave her a card when she was released from the E.R. Kyra's brother picked her up and took her to his home. Kyra could barely walk. She staggered into Duke's house looking lost and wild. No one could comfort her. To make matters worse, Kyra's body craved the very drug that cost her everything. She barely got out of bed for the first few days of her withdrawal. Kyra cried and shivered and vomited and sweated the heroin out of her system.

She didn't think about Leonard at all, not in those early days. The only thing on Kyra's mind was where her babies were. Who was feeding and tucking them in at night? How did she let this happen? How did she become her mother? And who the hell had her babies? Would she ever see them again? Would she ever be able to look in the mirror without hating the woman staring back at her?

It took more than two months for Kyra to convince the social workers that she was not an irresponsible dope head. Kyra learned a lot about herself and her decision-making during that time. When the CPS returned Q and Katavia and closed the case,

Kyra ran as fast and as far away as she could. She ran from Leonard, she ran from the social workers, and she ran from every friend and family member who knew what happened. All she wanted was a fresh start.

"If I could go back in time, I probably still wouldn't tell you what happened," Kyra said to Donovan as they sat in his truck in the daycare's parking lot. "It's too embarrassing. I feel like the biggest fool ever."

"If you didn't learn anything from it, then you'd still be a fool," Donovan said. Kyra was crying, but at least she got it out of her system. "But I know you did learn from it, and you have changed," he said. "I understand why you didn't tell me, and I'm not mad at you anymore. I love you, Kyra. I always have, and I always will."

Donovan's forgiveness meant the world to her. Kyra scooted over so she could hug him. Donovan held onto her for as long as she wanted. After awhile Kyra's tears subsided, and her breathing returned to normal.

She said, "Thanks for listening."

"You have to let your aunt cash that check you gave her," Donovan said.

Kyra wasn't surprised by that, but she asked him, "Why?"

"Because she did give you somewhere to live for two months. Plus you already gave her the check."

"I was gonna put a stop-payment on it."

Donovan shook his head. "You can't do people wrong just because they did you wrong. Let her cash the check. If she doesn't deserve it, God will deal with her."

"I'll only have three hundred dollars left," Kyra complained.

"I know. That's why I'm taking you to the welfare office to get some food stamps," Donovan said. He laughed when Kyra gave him a look. "I'm just kidding."

"But what are we gonna do?" Kyra asked. "Seriously."

"I guess I'll have to carry you this month," Donovan said. "You can carry me next month, to make up for it."

Kyra knew she should be happy, but she also felt apprehensive. No one ever had her back like this before.

"Donovan, I can't keep setting myself up to owe you money. I don't like it. I wanna show you that I can take care of myself."

"Kyra, I'm not doing this for you. I'm doing it for *us*. I told you that. Why do you feel the need to prove something to me?"

"Because you always been there for me," she said. "I just want to show you, for once, that I can stand on my own two feet."

"I understand what you're saying," Donovan said. "But you're not in a position to take care of me financially. Not right now, anyway. You got three hundred dollars, and you just promised that money to the daycare. If you want to prove something to me, you can do it by going to work every day, taking care of the kids and paying your daycare bill."

"That's not enough."

"What do you want to do, make my mortgage payment?"

He chuckled, but right away Kyra said, "Yes. That would be great. How much is it?"

"A thousand dollars."

"Okay. I'll pay that."

"Only if you let me pay for daycare," Donovan said.

Kyra realized they were essentially swapping bills, but paying for Donovan's home sounded a lot better than paying for Kat's babysitters. "Okay," she said. "That's fine."

"You're silly," Donovan told her, but he was in a good mood for the first time that day.

"I'm in love with you," Kyra told him. "I don't think you'll ever know how much I love you."

Donovan's smile disappeared as he looked into her eyes. "I assure you, you don't love me as much as I love you."

"Yes I do. Ten times more."

"Nope. Not possible."

"I'll prove it."

"I would love to see that."

"You'll see," Kyra said, though she had no idea what she could do to show her eternal devotion to this man.

She kissed him, for starters. Donovan was very receptive. He slipped his tongue inside her mouth, and Kyra's whole body grew warm.

They were still making-out three minutes later when Donovan remembered they were parked in front of the daycare. They drove away laughing.

They didn't know it at the time, but as fate would have it, Kyra never laid eyes on Leonard again. Two months after he returned to Little Rock, Leonard got caught up with a desperate crew of addicts. He tagged along for a burglary that went bad when the homeowner showed up, and somebody started shooting. Leonard was sentenced to life without the possibility of parole for his role in the burglary-turned-homicide.

≈ ≈ ≈ ≈ ≈ ≈

Donovan took Kyra to a discount furniture store where he purchased a twin-size bed for Katavia. He wanted to get a couple of dressers to help fill out Kat's new room, but they finally reached his spending limit.

"That's good," Kyra told him.

"Good that I can't afford to furnish her room?" Donovan was confused.

"Yes. I mean no," Kyra said. "It's good because I want to buy stuff for her room when I get paid next month. I really want to help."

Donovan knew how much that meant to her, so he didn't argue this time.

Kat's bed required assembly. They loaded it in the back of Donovan's truck and headed home. When they got there, Donovan was surprised by how eager Kyra was to get to work. She helped him clear out the extra bedroom, and she helped tote Kat's mattress, box spring and other materials into the house. It was hard work, but Kyra was cheerful. This was her first project at Donovan's house. It made her feel like she belonged there, which was a feeling she'd been searching for her whole life.

The room looked rather bare when they got done. There was nothing in it but a bed, a file cabinet and a few boxes of papers Donovan didn't know what to do with. Donovan thought they had a lot of work left to do before it would look like a *girl's* room. But this would be the first room Kat ever had to herself, so Kyra thought it looked great. Plus she and Donovan worked well together. They laughed and flirted and kissed whenever they got within kissing distance.

They took showers (separately, to Kyra's dismay), and met in the kitchen afterwards for lunch. Donovan started to make a DiGiorno pizza. But Kyra wanted to make tuna fish sandwiches, so she'd have a snack for the kids when they got home. Donovan sat at the kitchen table and watched as Kyra prepared the meal. Occasionally she'd ask where something was, but for the most part she already knew her way around the kitchen.

Donovan stood abruptly and left the room. When he returned to his seat, Kyra noticed his mood was different. Something in his eyes gave her goose bumps.

"What's wrong?" Kyra was at the sink cooling her hardboiled eggs. She looked back at Donovan and saw him place something on the table. "What's that?"

"Why don't you come over here and see what it is?" he suggested.

Curious, Kyra dried her hands and walked to the table. Her eyes widened when she saw that Donovan had placed a condom on top of it. The hairs stood on the back of her neck.

Donovan stood and approached her slowly. "I warned you."

"About, about what?" Kyra's eyes darted from the condom to her man. Donovan wore a tee shirt with long, basketball shorts. The bulge of his erection was a lot more visible than it would've been in jeans.

"About you and the kitchen and that refrigerator," Donovan said. "And you had the nerve to wear that dress. I think you're taunting me."

Kyra didn't think her dress was sexy. It was loose fitting with floral prints. "What's wrong with my dress?"

"Easy access," Donovan said. He pulled his tee-shirt over his head as he closed the distance between them.

Kyra gasped. Donovan got a light workout while putting Kat's bed together. His muscles were primed. His skin was smooth and chocolaty. The swelling in his shorts looked huge.

"Are you serious?"

Rather than respond, Donovan placed both hands on her waist and walked her backwards. Kyra's blood was already racing. She shuddered when her back came in contact with the refrigerator. Donovan pressed his body against hers. He kissed and sucked her bottom lip. Kyra felt his erection on her stomach. Donovan's hands slid down to her hips. He gripped her flesh and grinded between her thighs.

"Oh." Kyra felt a tightening and a sudden slickness between her legs.

Donovan's tongue invaded her mouth. His hands slid up and down her frame. He reached under her dress.

"Uh."

His hand between her legs sent a jolt all the way up Kyra's spine and down to her toes. Donovan looked her in the eyes as he rubbed her labia through her panties. His breaths were slow and heavy. He kissed her again as his fingers slipped past her underwear, and the longest one disappeared inside Kyra.

"Oh!"

She was about to cum. This was ludicrous. He barely touched her! Kyra's head was spinning. Her breath came in hitches.

"Baby what, what are you doing to me?"

Those words came from Donovan, which shocked the hell out of Kyra because she thought he was reading her mind.

He let go of her for a second so he could take his shorts off. He was completely naked now. In the kitchen! Kyra leaned against the refrigerator and tried to control her breathing as Donovan retrieved his condom and slowly put it on. He watched her eyes as he rolled it towards the base of his penis. Kyra couldn't get enough of that. Watching Donovan put condoms on was so damned sexy.

He stepped to her again with a serious expression. Kyra was nearly panting. Donovan reached under her dress and pulled her panties down her legs. Kyra lifted each foot so he could get them past her ankles. Donovan pulled her dress up to her waist and kissed her again. Kyra's legs were trembling. Her throat caught when she felt herself being lifted into the air. Donovan didn't grimace at all. Kyra felt weightless in his arms.

She wrapped her legs around his waist, and Donovan leaned her spine against the cool refrigerator. He held her aloft with just one hand on her ass while he positioned himself for insertion. He then moved his hand to her other butt cheek. His grip was tight. Kyra felt his fat head pushing at her wet entrance.

Donovan asked if she was ready, and he slowly lowered her onto his erection when she nodded.

"*Ahh. Donovan.*"

He pushed all the way in on the first stroke. Kyra threw both of her arms around his neck, but she didn't have to support herself at all. Donovan pressed his body closer to hers until Kyra's back was nearly flat against the refrigerator. And then he went to work.

"*Oh, Donovan!*"

He pumped his hips slowly. Each plunge was deeper than the one before. Kyra closed her eyes as the pleasure radiated through her whole body. She felt like she was floating on his penis. Donovan kissed her passionately. He stroked hard and slow. Kyra felt him all the way in her belly.

He seemed to be digging deeper than ever before, probably because the refrigerator didn't have any give like a springy mattress. There was no escape. There was just Donovan and his dick and Kyra's relatively small body that was completely under his control at that moment.

Unexpectedly Kyra found herself airborne again.

"*Uh!*"

She tightened her grip around Donovan's neck. He took a step back so that Kyra had to depend fully on him for support. She still had her legs wrapped around his waist. Donovan used his powerful arms to move her up and down on his dick until Kyra picked up the groove and began to grind on her own. The position was so exotic, she felt her climax building within seconds.

"*Oh, Donovan! Uh. Baby! Oh, Donovan!*"

Up and down she went. Each time Donovan pushed all the way in, until their pubic hairs meshed.

"*Baby! Oh, baby! Oh! Ah! Ah!*"

Kyra's slick walls gripped his penis like a fist when she came. Donovan grunted and pushed her against the refrigerator again. Kyra's legs trembled as she coated his penis with her orgasm, and she lost her scissor grip around his waist. Donovan grabbed one of her thighs and spread it open wider. He pumped his hips faster and harder.

SCURR!

Kyra didn't know what that sound was. The kitchen was spinning. Her first orgasm rolled into a second one without a pause. Donovan was beating it up. Kyra heard their thighs clapping, she heard her own satisfied moans, and then she heard the strange sound again.

SCURR!

This time she felt the refrigerator move, and she realized Donovan plowing so hard he was literally sliding the heavy appliance on the kitchen floor.

Whap! Whap! Whap!

His hips were moving as fast as a locomotive. His expression could've passed for angry. Donovan buried his face in the crook of Kyra's neck and started moaning and talking to her at the same time.

"Baby, it feels so good. *Oh, Kyra! Oh, Kyra! Oh, shit, Kyra!*"

He slammed in one last time when he came. Kyra screamed with pleasure. She felt his manhood jumping inside her. Her walls squeezed and milked the cum out of him. Donovan's release lasted forever. Every little move he made titillated Kyra and made her cry out again.

Finally Donovan lifted her off the fridge and carried her to the living room. He gently placed her on the sofa, and Kyra rolled to her side. She closed her eyes, still in the midst of a delicious orgasm. She felt so good, she almost sucked her thumb as she drifted off to sleep.

≈ ≈ ≈ ≈ ≈ ≈

Donovan awakened her a couple of hours later.

"Do you want me to pick up the kids?"

Kyra sat up and slowly regained her bearings. She squinted at the wall clock. She still had time to get Kat and Quinell, but she'd have to leave the house in twenty minutes.

"No, I'll get them. I want to stop by Walmart to get a comforter for Kat's bed." She yawned. "Man, I was knocked out."

"I know," Donovan said. He knelt on the side of the couch and kissed her on the lips. "You were sleep for so long, I had to finish up your tuna."

"I'm sorry," Kyra said. Memories of their kitchen romance put a smile on her face.

"I also had time to go get this," Donovan said.

He held up a black ring box, and the fog in Kyra's head cleared up in the blink of an eye. She jumped to her feet so quickly, she nearly lost her balance.

"Whoa," Donovan said. He chuckled. "Listen, this ring has been in my family for generations. This is the engagement ring my grandfather gave my grandmother. It got passed down to my father when my grandmother died, and he passed it down to me. I wanted to get you a new one, but my mom says I should give you this."

He was still down on one knee. He opened the box as he spoke, revealing the most beautiful diamond ring Kyra had ever seen. The rock wasn't huge or necessarily flashy, but it was perfect for her. The fact that Donovan's mother wanted the heirloom to go to Kyra completely blew her mind. Kyra knew that she would cherish the ring for the rest of her life.

She squealed and flushed and burst into tears as Donovan proposed.

"Kyra, you know I love you more than any woman I've ever known. You're my best friend, and you're the love of my life. I know we were meant to be together forever, and I know that the love we share is real. It's the realest ever. Will you marry me?"

Kyra couldn't speak, but she nodded feverishly. She didn't think her life could ever be better than it was at that moment. Donovan reached for her trembling hand and slid the ring on her finger. He stood, and Kyra threw her arms around him. She hugged him as tightly as she could. Donovan wrapped both arms around her and spun around the room. When he put her down, Kyra peppered his face with kisses.

"Oh, and there's something I have to tell you," Donovan said. "My mom always wanted to give me away at my wedding. I know a dad is supposed to do that for his daughter, but Mama's pretty adamant about it, and I told her it was okay."

Kyra didn't care about any of that. They could get married at a three-ring circus for all she cared, so long as she was Donovan's lawfully wedded wife at the end of the ceremony.

"I love you so much!"

"I love you, too," Donovan said. "Are you sure you don't want me to pick up the kids?"

"No," Kyra said. She checked the clock again as she wiped the tears from her eyes. "I really need to get some stuff from

Walmart. And I want to tell them the good news!" She held out her hand and stared at her ring. She couldn't stop smiling at it.

"Make sure you put on some panties before you leave," Donovan suggested.

Kyra blushed. Her eyes darted to the kitchen. "I don't think I can ever go in there again without thinking about what we did," she confided.

"That's good," Donovan said with a grin. "I want you to remember. Because the next time we're alone in the house, we're doing it again."

Kyra swallowed. "In the kitchen?"

Donovan nodded. "Or in the garage. Or the other bathroom. The den..."

Kyra's inhaled deeply. "Okay."

Donovan moistened his lips. "Stop looking at me like that, or I'll take you in there right now."

Kyra checked the clock again. *Damn.* "Sorry, I gotta go." She headed to the bathroom for a quickie shower.

"That's cool. See you later, scary," Donovan called down the hallway.

"I'm not scary," Kyra replied, although she was walking a little bowlegged from the work he put in earlier. She wondered if the refrigerator was still pushed back against the wall. Her smile was ear to ear.

THE END

BY KEITH THOMAS WALKER

ABOUT THE AUTHOR

Keith Thomas Walker, known as the Master of Romantic Suspense and Urban Fiction, is the author of eleven novels, including *Fixin' Tyrone*, *Jewell and the Dapper Dan* and *Dripping Chocolate*. Keith enjoys reading, poetry and music of all genres. Originally from Fort Worth, Keith is a graduate of Texas Wesleyan University. He currently works in administration at one of Texas' largest hospitals. Visit him at www.keithwalkerbooks.com.